Abi Maxwell is the author of an acclaimed story collection, LAKE PEOPLE, and her fiction has also appeared in McSweeney's. She studied writing at the University of Montana and now lives in New Hampshire, where she grew up, with her husband and son.

'Maxwell's landscape is not modern culture but traditional folklore . . . secrets are kept, secrets are told . . . beautifully precise' Jane Smiley, *Harpers*

'A provocative and absorbing coming-of-age novel' *Woman & Home*

'Maxwell's prose brilliantly conveys their adolescent angst and survival instincts' *Lady*

'There's a plain-spoken quality to Maxwell's writing that suggests comparisons to Marilynne Robinson and Alice Munro' *Minneapolis Star Tribune*

'Abi Maxwell has written a lush and luminous gem of a novel: heart-breaking in some moments, heartwarming in others, and always rich with wonder and surprise. *The Den* is a book with depth and mystery and soul' Chris Bohjalian, bestselling author of *The Flight Attendant*

'Tantalizing . . . Maxwell has written a deeply satisfying, haunting work of literary fiction. Driven by characters who are uniformly engaging and beautifully realized, it is not to be missed' *Booklist* (Starred)

ALSO BY ABI MAXWELL

Lake People

The Den

ABI MAXWELL

TINDER
PRESS

First published by Alfred A. Knopf, Penguin Random House LLC

First published in Great Britain in 2019 by Tinder Press
An imprint of HEADLINE PUBLISHING GROUP

First published in paperback in 2020 by Tinder Press
An imprint of HEADLINE PUBLISHING GROUP

1

Cataloguing in Publication Data is available from the British Library

ISBN 978 1 4722 6329 2

Typeset in 11.75/15.25pt Adobe Garamond Pro by Jouve (UK), Milton Keynes

Printed and bound in Great Britain by Clays Ltd, Elcograf S.p.A.

HEADLINE PUBLISHING GROUP
An Hachette UK Company
Carmelite House
50 Victoria Embankment
London EC4Y 0DZ

www.tinderpress.co.uk
www.headline.co.uk
www.hachette.co.uk

'We must not always talk in the market-place
of what happens to us in the forest.'

— NATHANIEL HAWTHORNE, *The Scarlet Letter*

PART ONE

———

Jane

I

LATE JUNE, an afternoon some twenty years ago. The fact that my sister could disappear not even a speck in my consciousness yet. The sun was high and shining, and Henrietta and I were just about to see Kaus, the one who started all of this, for the very first time. We had some money – I don't know how, we weren't babysitting yet – and because it was summer we had the time. Our father worked and our mother shut herself off in her studio on the third floor, so there was no one to stop us from going to the little store to buy candy. The owner kept a rack of smut right there in the open, and for this reason our father had prohibited us from entering, but no matter. This was the summer my sister had turned fifteen, started wearing an underwire bra, blow-drying her hair, and saying easily, 'La, de, da,' to every command our parents gave.

Anyway, we didn't look at the smut. Just bought our candy – loads of it – then walked on. I had thought we were headed home, but when we reached the abandoned mill my sister didn't lead us back over the bridge but instead a little farther along. She strutted a few paces ahead of me as we went, and both of us stuffed our mouths. I can still remember the strange coating all that sugar gave my tongue.

Eventually we reached Church Street, which was not a street I had walked before. It ran along the river, and the far side of the road was crowded with a thick line of trailers. I knew I ought not to stare, but just the same I could not stop myself from taking in long, aching glances of life over there. We lived in an old farmhouse on a virtually empty road, so this hubbub seemed a dream. Women were out in their lawn chairs with cigarettes and portable phones and magazines; babies were in plastic pools; and everyone, from my view, was loud and happy. The sun was at our backs, and before us stood the trestle, which was yet another place we were not supposed to go. That abandoned railroad bridge rises roughly forty feet above the river, and it continues to be the spot where all the bad kids congregate to smoke and spit and jump into the water all summer long. The bridge's iron trusses run beneath the tracks, and on that day with my sister their X's seemed to gleam like the most tantalizing of warnings. The reflection of the trees – pines, mostly, and maples – danced upon the water, and I wanted desperately to join with them in that cool, fresh place. And so I was shocked, and disappointed, when I looked ahead and saw that as Henrietta walked she let all her candy wrappers fall in her wake, then blow over the bank, toward the river.

'Litterbug,' I scolded her. She didn't respond, so I repeated myself, and when she still didn't respond I just kept at it. Not yelling, because I didn't want to be heard by the neighborhood, but hissing. Loud enough, surely, for Henrietta to hear over the river. Still, she went right on ignoring me. I knew

4

that if I really cared I could have just picked her trash up for her and dealt with the injustice of it later. But I was getting angry. We both had thin hair, mine mousy and nondescript and Henrietta's, back then, a dark, shining brown that somehow hid the thinness. Her hair was long, too, so when I could bear her haughty strut no longer I reached forward and tugged. When my sister spun around that hair flew up and circled her pointed face and remained, a momentary defeat of gravity. I had a flash just then of my Henrietta transforming into a wild, yellow-eyed animal.

She didn't say a word. Just grabbed my bare arm and pulled me toward her. She kept holding on to me, and her nails began to dig into my skin. I wanted to call out, but I understood this as her vicious command to shut up. We had come to a red two-story house that didn't quite fit in. It wasn't a trailer, there was that, but there was also something uncanny about the place. Where all other yards on the street were small and crowded with people, this one was oddly spacious and vacant. The curtains were drawn and the windows closed. I would have thought that the house itself was empty, had Henrietta not waited there so expectantly. But there we stood, together in the loudest of silences, until a teenage boy emerged from the house and stood on the front step, bathing in the sun's rays.

Kaus. According to Henrietta, this was the first time she'd ever seen him, though she too must have been a liar. *Kaus.* Over and over again I would repeat his name, just to feel its sounds emerge from the back of my throat and cross the length of my tongue. *Kaus* – a soft, pillowed name, or a sharp and biting one?

He stood there gazing toward the river while we stood

5

there gazing at him, and then he shifted and withdrew a cigarette from a pack in the pocket of his cutoff jean shorts with
a motion so fluid it was preternatural. Despite the breeze that
skimmed up off the river, he lit it the first time he tried, and
then that boy walked our way. He didn't speak to us, and we
didn't speak to him. Still, his intention was clear. Kaus cut
across the street to walk right by Henrietta, and as he passed
her he turned his head and blew a long, gentle stream of
smoke her way. And my sister, she cocked her head and
opened her thin lips and drew it right in.

We didn't make it to the trestle that day; my sister just
turned me around and led me back home. That night, when I
took my bath, I saw that she had left five little welts on my
upper arm. A sign, I later decided, of the beginning of the end.

Our house was half a mile up the hill from town. The way our
parents told the story, they had gone for a drive through the
countryside when they were young and in love, and had
passed our house for the very first time. Or barn, really,
because the barn was the thing. It was the largest in the entire
county, and it was the whole reason we had ever ended up on
this land in the first place. On that drive our father had pulled
over and walked right onto the property without worrying
over whether or not anyone lived there (no one did), and he
ran his hands over the barn's shingles as though they were the
skin of a lover. *Hand-hewn beams,* he said when he slid open
the door, and, *Christ! That one sill extends nearly seventy feet!*

Our mother, once brave enough, tiptoed to the house and
peered in the windows. 'That godforsaken wallpaper,' she

would say when our father told the story. At the time, Henrietta was in her belly, taking hold of life, though my mother didn't know it yet. They went home to their apartment in the little city to the south, and our father lay on their mattress on the floor and dreamed aloud, and our mother, because she just wanted sleep, said something like, 'For Christ's sake, Charley, then do it,' without thinking he ever would. A week later they owned the place – the down payment made with the bit of inheritance they had received from our father's parents. The floors were dirt and the stairs, our mother claimed, were planks weaker than her own hands, but it was cheap and, as our father said, it was theirs.

By the time Henrietta and I came along, there were barn cats and chickens, and once in a while two pigs or a meat cow, and always there were Shania and Dolly, those strong black mares with coats and gallops sleek as oil. Our father claimed he'd had those mares forever.

Our father did not make much money – he was a cook, and eventually the head cook at the hospital – but with that house and barn he had his dream, and I suppose that is why he seemed compelled to sacrifice all else in order to give our mother her dream, too. He supported her choice to stay at home while we went to school, despite the fact that in addition to working it was also he who cooked, cleaned, and performed nearly all other household tasks.

But our mother was an artist – a painter, though she rarely ever sold a piece – and a woman who, I am sure, never fully wanted children. This fact kept her at a remove, and at night, when dinner was through and the dishes were done, she would open the family heirloom box of real silver, remove the velvet caddy that held the dinnerware, and reach into the bottom, beneath the velvet sheath of grapefruit spoons. There she would find one of her thin joints. She would swipe a wooden match across the top of the woodstove, take a few puffs, and then our mother would transform into a woman so distant, and so fully within herself, that Henrietta and I – spying from the top of the staircase – would be stunned and overcome with a disconcerting mix of desperation to be seen by her and to disappear and become her.

'Sylvia,' our father would sometimes say, and each time I heard that – her first name – a little swell of fear would rise up in me. *Sylvia,* a name so singular, so volatile. Not our mother but a woman who, at any moment, could leave this little life of ours.

Henrietta, though, the fact that she – her whole self, spirit and body and all – could leave our life, that had never occurred to me, not yet. I was twelve years old that summer of Kaus and always told my sister everything I had to tell. I would have told her anything at all. And I knew my sister, through and through I did. She had perpetually tanned skin and short toes. Her thumbs arched gloriously backward, and she was double-jointed in her fingers, so that she could bend the top portion of each finger downward while keeping the rest of it perfectly straight. At night she stuck her chewed gum to her headboard, and she could sniff a thin rope up through her left nostril and pull it out through her right one. She could do a backbend and

8

three perfect cartwheels in a row and even a front handspring. She dreamed about boys, not 'smut dreams,' as she called them, but just peaceful little dreams in which she and a boy would drift along in a rowboat or walk hand in hand. She also dreamed about riding horses, and in nightmares she dreamed that a giant wave crashed over her. But that summer, after I saw that boy, I had the strange sensation of beginning to realize something that I had always known. My sister – there was a layer to her, invisible but palpable as her skin itself, that would not ever be opened to me.

The day after I saw him for the very first time, my sister dragged me along with her to town once again. Typically I would have gone without hesitation, but on that day I'd happened to be immersed in a new book: *Flowers in the Attic* by V. C. Andrews. Reading, I'd understood even back then, was my particular gift. The one thing I could invariably do better than my brave sister. I was fast, but there was also a deep, peculiar understanding I received by letting my eyes rest hazily upon a page. I turned pages virtually by the second, and just as I had a strange sense that my mother would flee, I also felt this gift would, and so each night I stowed my book beneath my pillow, where no one could get at it. I read undiscerningly – mysteries, romances, horrors, anything. I felt it my duty in life. But uncharacteristically, my father had taken note of that particular book and said I could not read it, that it was beyond my age. My mother had heard him and said, 'Jesus, Charley,' and that had been that – I had kept on. I'd stayed up half the night with that book, feeling that I'd better finish it before my parents came to their senses and tore it from my hands. I wasn't finished when Henrietta showed up at my door to drag me into town, and I would have just as soon kept on reading. But Henrietta told me to go with her, and so I went.

She vomited before we left the house. This, of course, was early in the mess, so I hadn't quite caught on yet – maybe I didn't want to. I said, 'Don't you want to lie down?' or something of that nature, and then, eventually, when she shuffled me out the front door, 'Well, I better not catch it.'

'Can't catch hotness, sister,' she said, and tossed her hair back.

I followed her as she strutted down the center of our road like she owned it, her newfound maturity made even more brazen overnight. When a car rolled toward us, Henrietta didn't even move out of the way. It was Mr Cutler, our only neighbor, whose house lay up the hill, just barely out of sight. We had always known him, at least vaguely, but he was a strange, overeager man whom we did our best to avoid. He must have been in his fifties, yet despite his age, when he caught us on the road he would always ask us what was new and cool. 'Are these jeans cool?' he would say. 'What music are the kids listening to these days, anyway?'

Today he leaned out the window of his yellow sports car and said to Henrietta, 'You have yourself a boyfriend yet?' The question alone surprised me, but when she responded simply that she did, my jaw dropped.

Mr Cutler let a smile spread over his clean-shaven face, and then he eased his car down the hill and out of sight. My sister continued walking. I scurried after her, calling, 'That boy's your boyfriend?' and, 'The one from the red house?' and, 'How do you know he's your boyfriend?' plus a handful more varieties of the same question, none of which she would answer. She just waltzed ahead of me while I followed like a dog, over the bridge and into town.

I never did figure out what exactly made Henrietta go to that little store on a daily basis in the early days of that summer. On that first day after Kaus, though, rather than going straight in as we always had, my sister just leaned against the building and bent one leg up so that her foot rested flatly against the brick. She tilted her head back, very exhausted, very adult, and she said, 'God, I could kill for a cigarette.'

I don't know that I said anything to that. I don't know that I could overcome my shock in order to do so.

She said, 'God, what?' and, 'Don't look at me like that,' and then, as insurance against my tattling, she marched right into that store and spent five whole dollars on five hundred Sour Patch Kids for me.

In the previous school year, I had entered the upper middle school, a building shared with the high school, and there I had come to understand that my sister was not popular. *Henry-shmeta,* they called her, and *Hairy-etta,* and the worst, born from nothing I knew of, *Bloody-hairy-letta.* My sister. Thin and wispy, made of wind. When she was mocked, she would steadfastly look the accuser in the eye. It was a powerful, deadening look, one she had learned from our mother, and cruel though it was, it only increased my awe of her. I was bewitched by my sister, loved her to a dangerous degree.

———

That sticky afternoon, I followed Henrietta away from the store. I stuffed penny candy into my mouth by the handful and I rattled on about those children in the attic, all the horrors of the novel I was devouring. I was aware as we walked that she didn't listen to a word I said, but it didn't stop me. That story was so good. I could have gone on retelling it forever, but suddenly my sister swung around and swatted me. Once again, for the second time in my life, we had walked down Church Street, and now we had approached that red house. I shut up. My sister looked upward, put her hands on her hips, and said, 'I knew it.'

I must have asked what she knew, but she paid me no mind. She just went on. She said, 'He's not home. That jackoff.'

'Who?' I asked, though of course I knew.

'His bedroom window would have been open.'

Bedroom window. I latched right on to that. His bedroom.

'Anyway, his stupid grandmother's home,' she said. She began to chew at the left corner of her mouth, which sent her pursed lips to the opposite side. It was a habit our mother frequently told her to quit, saying it made her look like a horse. Sometimes Henrietta chewed so hard she would bleed. Now, though, she stopped right away to announce: 'The bitch.' Then my sister turned smartly on her heels and soared down the road toward the trestle. I chased after her. The sun glared before us, and in its blinding light I could make out only the shadowed forms up on the tracks above the water, and their occasional, ghostly leaps downward. I could hear their hollers and splashes, but so far as I could tell, even when we reached the base of that massive bridge, our own presence remained unnoticed by the jumpers.

The trail to the trestle had been carved up an eroding bank beneath the bridge where the tracks crossed over the road. My sister scurried right up it like a single-minded bug. I followed her haphazardly, increasingly aware with every step that I was once again headed somewhere I was not supposed to go.

There had been at least one teen death there. I never knew anything about how it had happened, and I'd never been even remotely sensitive to the fact that an actual boy had been lost to an actual family. I'd simply let his death open in my mind like the fiction I read: troubling, compelling, capable only of creating the sort of emotion I could enter or exit at will. It would have been dramatic, his life and subsequent death. A pregnant girlfriend? A murder? A half-hearted fall, not entirely on purpose. A terrible, hungry mystery.

By the time I had made my way to the top of the path, I was covered in dry silt. My sister had already crested the hill. I peered over the edge to watch her walk onto the tracks, but just as I gathered the nerve to continue after her, she threw her chin back over her shoulder and glared at me. I under-stood. I squatted back down, then inched my way over to the safety of an old pine. Tucked behind it, I spied. The voices were too distant to discern, so I took in all the details. Graffiti on the iron sides of the bridge: *Mike loves Amanda* and *Tammy loves Rob* and *Tammy is a whore* and *PEACE*. Litter, too – old Pepsi cans, empty bags of Fritos, empty and stomped packs of cigarettes. Four girls, not including my sister, and three boys. The boys held hands and launched themselves over the edge. I heard their splashes, and soon I heard their voices become ever clearer. It took a moment for me to realize that their route back up the bank would cross right by me. Quickly I slid around to the far side of the pine as their scrawny, sun-darkened bodies climbed that path and returned to the trestle. If they saw me hovering there, they didn't let on.

And then came Kaus. Where the other boys had scrambled, and grabbed for limbs or roots, and lost their footing more than once, Kaus seemed to simply glide up that bank. When he spotted me behind the tree he gave a wink, and then he held his pointer finger in front of his mouth and blew. *Shhh.*

Kaus, glistening. One time I would hear him speak his ancestral language, but it wouldn't be for me. It would be for Henrietta, who'd begged and begged. They'd been naked, stretched out on the old afghans she'd spread on the floor of the barn. First he whispered in her ear and then he put his hands under his resting head and just kept on talking. It didn't occur to me then that his words carried any meaning. I'd been on my tiptoes, hidden outside the barn, spying, and this speech of his was the most magical thing I had ever heard.

Of course, in our town, we had never heard any other language but English, save for the French and Spanish learned in high school. Until his family moved in that summer, I don't know that we'd ever even seen anyone from another country walk our streets. Which surely contributed to the oncoming trouble.

Emboldened by his kind gesture, when he was back on the trestle I scampered higher up the bank to watch. Once again there was no mistaking his direction or purpose. Straight to my sister that boy walked. When he reached her he grabbed her hips and pulled her forward, toward his own body. My sister curved her back, their middles pressed together momentarily, and then, smooth as dancers, those two folded open to stand side by side. Kaus tucked one of his hands into the backside of her shorts, and in this way they walked down the tracks, away from the others. Everyone kept watch. Besides the shock, I remember being aware that this scene was the best thing I had ever witnessed, better even than a book.

When my sister and Kaus stopped walking, they sealed their bodies back together, but this time they both faced the river, with his front pressed against her back. He reached his hands around her waist, right down into her shorts. Henrietta, from what I could tell, kept her vision fixed on the water below, and Kaus kept his own face buried in her neck. Then, suddenly, my sister's head burst back. The kids on the trestle laughed and clapped. In response my sister, without a trace of preamble, stepped forward, right off that bridge.

And still the show wasn't over. I panicked with her down there in the water, but she came up soon enough. I had moved completely out of my hiding place by now, and I ran right over to meet her as she approached, but she neither scolded me nor stopped to speak with me. She just blew a kiss on her way past, then walked right back up into that crowd. This time Kaus had a cigarette lit, and when my sister approached him he held it to her lips. She drew in deeply and somehow, despite all that had just occurred, this was as sexy an act as I'd ever seen.

I don't know that I ever even finished *Flowers in the Attic,* or any other book that summer. All I know is that even more alluring than anything I could read was Henrietta, her unfolding. That summer she transformed out of my sister and into a girl – a woman, really – whom I scarcely recognized. She'd been the only girl to jump off the trestle that day, and when she fell her arms had been stretched out like wings. On our walk home she showed me what this meant. The underside of her arms, their light, nearly translucent skin, had already turned a terrible, yellowish shade of purple.

'Dad is going to kill you,' I said.

'He won't know.'

'What are you going to do, wear long sleeves all summer?'

She did. It became her signature style. The next morning she walked downstairs wearing a long-sleeved flannel that she'd cut off just below her bra, so that a long, thin expanse of belly was exposed. At some point that summer, there was a baby in there. The start of a baby, I mean. That infinitesimal cell that would have grown into one.

The very next morning, I woke early from a fitful, anxious sleep. The knowledge of my sister's love affair tormented me. I ran across the hall and knocked on her bedroom door. When she didn't answer I turned the knob, but it would not open. I turned it again, and I rattled it, and finally I realized that my sister had locked her door. So far as I knew, she had never done this before.

'Henrietta?' I called. I knocked and knocked, and when she still would not answer I began to imagine what she might have done: snuck out the window, or maybe even snuck her boyfriend in. Eventually, I pounded at the door and yelled her name.

'Damn you,' she finally yelled back. I froze and waited for

her footsteps across the creaky wood floor. But all that came was more scolding: She was sleeping, she said, and if I didn't leave her alone I would be dead meat. I left her door. I went downstairs, sat on the couch, and turned on the TV but really just watched the clock. My sister slept and slept and slept. It was afternoon when she finally emerged. I had made sandwiches – making lunch, during our summer days, was something Henrietta had long ago come to rely on me for. Without me she would have lived on plain saltines and once in a while a spread of fluff. But now she refused my offering of an egg-salad sandwich.

'Smells like ass,' she said. She threw open the fridge door and just stood in front of it.

'Waster,' I snapped. 'You're wasting electricity.' It was what our parents would have said.

'God,' she said. 'There's nothing to drink in this house.'

We were a family of milk and water and orange juice. Was it a can of soda she was after? Or alcohol? She slammed the fridge and walked out. Out of the kitchen, out of the house, out of the driveway. Gone until evening. And when she returned, my parents said not a word.

For weeks it continued in this way. Emerging late, disappearing, and thoroughly done with me. Once, early on, I followed her, but just as she crossed the little bridge into town she turned around and spotted me. It was enough. I went home. My desire, at least in the beginning, to stay on Henrietta's good side won out over my curiosity.

Still, I was sick with worry. She was getting rapidly thinner.

She'd started vomiting each day before she left the house, and in this new, vanishing body her legs stuck out like broomsticks from the wide breadth of her shorts, and her arms seemed so weak they might as well have been crafted from the broomsticks' brush counterparts. My question, called from outside the closed bathroom door, 'What are you doing in there?' and her flippant response – 'Just pulling the trigger, god' – had become practically our only interaction.

And so, while my sister was out, I began to scour her room for clues. For years she had written in a journal, and though I had always been hopelessly nosy, I'd also always understood this particular activity as her private affair, and a sacred one. I had never so much as glanced at those pages. Yet now I flipped relentlessly through them, searching for his name. What I found, though, was both shocking and unsatisfying: page after page of my sister's journals was dedicated solely to our father's horses, to their conditions. All this time, I discovered, Henrietta had been keeping copious notes about the temperature in the barn, and whether or not there had been rain or snow or wind, and the horses' perceived comfort, and their measurements, and their diet. I had never known my sister to do anything so careful and routine, and I was mystified. Yet nowhere in that room was one single trace of Kaus and her secret life with him.

But I did not have the courage to go out searching for her, not yet. So, to occupy my mind, I began to write imaginary stories of their love affair. It was my first attempt at fiction. The names I always kept the same – Henrietta and Kaus – and I always included that trestle in the story. I would write their meeting, their compulsive need to be together, and ultimately, every time, their eventual ruin. This was no happy love story; no matter what I intended, Kaus would break Henrietta's heart over and over again.

I scared myself with those stories I wrote. They became so real to me. If I imagined Henrietta thrown into the river by her lover, I would spend the entire day terrified not only that it must be true, but that my thinking it had made it so. And in this terrible way, the heavy, endless summer days passed ever forward with me at their center, alone. Only occasionally would my mother emerge, and then only to grab something to eat. She never took the time to prepare whatever it was – she just grabbed a block of cheese or the jar of peanut butter and then retreated back upstairs without a word. Sometimes, on days when her work must have been going along poorly, I could hear her pacing overhead. I could hear her hit a wall sometimes, or throw what I assumed was a paintbrush across the room. Yet she would not give up for the day until dinner-time, so for the first time in my life I was left entirely to my own imagination. Finally, it took me over. I became so certain that my sister was in terrible trouble that I marched right into town to search for her.

This would have been mid-July. The tiger lilies were out in full force. Their fiery heads lined the roadsides, burning a path to my sister. They led to town first. Up and down Main Street I walked, without sign of her. I ducked into the little store, but even then I understood this simply as preparation; she wouldn't be there, not now that she had him. Finally I gathered my courage and I marched myself down to Church Street. Determined, I climbed up the bank and onto the tres-tle. I stood at the start of the bridge, right in the center of the tracks, but even so, I kept my arms stretched out for balance.

I was aware of being unwelcome, but that did not matter to me; as that particular afternoon stretched on it seemed ever more dire that I find my sister, that I save her.

'Henrietta?' I called pathetically to the teenagers on the bridge.

They all looked at me, laughed and smiled and shook their heads, and then they went back to spitting and jumping off the bridge, and Henrietta, I understood they were saying in these careless movements, had moved on. Henrietta was now *that* kind of girl.

Of course she was. I ran off the bridge and straight to the red house where he lived. I pounded on the door. I hadn't thought of what to ask, but it turned out I didn't need to ask anything. It must have been Kaus's grandmother who answered. Her cheeks were like soft, full balloons.

'No,' she said when she opened the door. 'No, no, no.' Just a little puff of a word. I wandered home, sick for my sister to return.

Finally, I resorted to tattling on Henrietta, though of course my parents already knew that she was perpetually absent. Still, my speaking up made my father do the same. He told her she could not traipse around all day. My mother, though, she sighed and said, 'Let her have her freedoms, Charley.' This had been after dinner, after Henrietta and I had gone upstairs and then been called back down. After our mother had smoked a bit of her little joint, too.

'Then she has to take Jane with her. Henrietta, when you go out in the day you have to take Jane with you.'

'La, de, da,' Henrietta said.

And our mother, 'For Christ's sake, Charley.'

During that period, there were just two shining moments when my sister spoke about Kaus. Once was when I found her on the living room floor, our father's oversized atlas spread open before her. 'Luang Prabang,' she said easily as she ran her pointer finger over the dim orange border of the place he had come from. 'Muong Beng,' she said. But when I crouched down next to her and asked her what she knew about that place, she cackled, slammed the atlas shut, and said, 'It's shaped like a limp dick, that's what.'

The only other time was when my mother, sister, and I happened to be in the kitchen together. It was then that my sister said dreamily, 'I'd do anything for Kaus.'

We were eating the red pistachios that our father loathed and drinking a rare treat of lemonade made so thick with sugar that we could feel the grains on our tongues.

'Don't you let your father hear that,' our mother said sharply, and then, without washing the red dye from her hands, she returned to the safety of her third-floor studio, leaving us girls, once again, to fend for ourselves.

II

OUR FATHER was a storyteller, and when we were children his favorite of all stories was 'The Den.' It was based on the old foundation in our own woods, just through the field and over the stone wall. Once upon a time, our father would say, that foundation had been a small home for a family of five: mother, father, three sons. The parents were immigrants from Scotland, come over to work at the mill, and the three boys had been born here, on their unfinished floorboards. Poor and good, the whole lot of them. From there, the details of the story changed according to our father's mood – one day the five of them walked to town; one day they went for a snow-shoe; one day they spent the whole afternoon inside, making a grand dinner for their father, because it was his birthday, and he loved nothing more than beef stew followed by a chocolate cake with sugar glaze, et cetera, et cetera. Eventually, no mat-ter what other details he'd included or abandoned, our father would come upon the date: January 19, 1852. *Cold Friday*. The day when the temperature dropped to an impossible 31 degrees below in a matter of hours and the mercury froze in its gauge and a violent, piercing wind blew across the field and through the woods, breaking the family's windows in. The mother and three boys huddled in a bed in the middle of the room while their father ran through the woods and across the field to the house that would become, in some one hundred years, our own home.

Back then, our house belonged to Mr Josiah Bartlett, who on that night shepherded the cold father inside, then left to suit up and drive his own sleigh into the storm to save his neighbors in the woods. It was a short distance, and because his horses and sleigh were strong and well built, Mr Bartlett made it quickly through the blinding snow and wind, but he knew before even dismounting that no family remained. Despite the ungodly storm, an eerie calm had spread around the house, enclosing it. When Mr Bartlett climbed down from his sleigh, his footsteps seemed to echo. Snow blew at his sides yet somehow did not cross his field of vision, which led directly through the broken windows to the fireplace. There, before the glowing remains of the fire, sat five coyotes, steam rising off their hunched shoulders. They turned their heads to him in unison and Mr Bartlett met their hungry gaze for one moment, and then the snow and wind overtook him. He crawled the few paces back to his sleigh, using his hands as a guide. Once mounted, he ran those horses home as fast as he ever had. After that, not one member of that Scottish family was ever seen again, not even the father, who should have been waiting safely in Mr Bartlett's parlor.

Our mother, whenever she heard our father tell Henrietta and me this story, would remark that coyotes hadn't even lived this far east back then. Sometimes our father would ignore this comment, and sometimes he would say, 'But Sylvia, how do you really *know*?'

I sided with him. It didn't ruin the story. In fact, the idea that according to science coyotes hadn't yet existed here made it even better to me, even more mysterious. About the family's actual fate, our father was always vague, leaving us to our own interpretations. I always imagined that family to have transformed out of their own bodies and into those of the wild dogs. Yet no matter what each of us thought, the story itself was still a part of our landscape, our very own fairy tale. During snowstorms, my sister and I would pretend to hear howls. In all seasons we would go out to the foundation – The Den, as our father had named it – and spend hours inside its four crumbled walls. We'd start a fire in what remained of the fireplace. We'd play house, Henrietta the mother and I one of the children. We particularly loved fall out there, when the wind felt like a flood of ghosts sweeping through the woods, carrying leaves on its collective back. When we really did hear the howling at night, our father wouldn't say anything reasonable about the danger the chickens or whatever other animals we had at the time might be in. He would just look at us conspiratorially and say, 'Is it a coyote? Or is it that family's voice?'

I was always certain it was both, and I was certain – though I never said as much – that it was a good thing, what had happened to that family, because if it hadn't then we never would have even known about them, and we certainly wouldn't be able to hear them calling out at night more than a century later.

———

By the summer of Kaus, we had more or less outgrown our father's storytelling, but despite all else we at least continued to have family dinner together nearly every night. It was at one of these meals that, just as my father reached with the tongs for a second ear of corn, we heard what we at first thought was a dog's bark, but then transformed into a long, clear howl. When that howl ended another began, and soon it was as though we were surrounded right there in our own house. We hadn't heard those animals for so long, and I believe we had all assumed that they no longer existed on our land. Now, as the calls went on, our father remarked that the coyotes must have returned to The Den, and, like old times, he began to tell the story. He didn't spare one single detail, and he even added names for the Scottish family, which he had never done before: Thomas and Elspeth Ross, Colin, Evan, and Jeremiah. Hearing them felt like a revelation, like those people had suddenly come to life. I looked to my sister. She had gone white. Which I suppose could have been from all the vomiting, but actually, I don't think it had that sort of negative effect on her, at least not yet. In fact, during that period, despite her thinness, I remember Henrietta as a more sanguine being than ever before. My father concluded his story by repeating that the coyotes had returned, and as he said it I realized just where my suddenly colorless sister must have been hiding with Kaus.

The truth is I never did figure out exactly why she turned so white, though; my sister was not afraid of those animals. She was not afraid of the wilderness, not any part of it. So had it been a fear that she would be caught? That with the story our father was teasing her? But if so, why then did she promptly return to The Den? Because I was right, of course. The very next day I stalked through the woods, and when I heard their voices I skittered to the small, rounded gully that lay just east of the foundation. Our father had said that gully had once been the village's dumping pit. There were rusted metal drums and large springs down there, and even a ruined antique car. I had spent many childhood hours sitting near that car, imagining its story. Now, though, with Henrietta and Kaus in The Den, I stayed at the top edge of the gully and peered out. I could see them clearly. Though I didn't quite believe that my sister would go so far as to have sex, I did half expect to find her doing just that. Yet what I witnessed was the dreamy if adolescent sort of conversation I came to equate with real, true love: *Do you believe in fate? Love at first sight? Is your mood always determined by the weather? Is your personality determined from birth?* I listened, and lingered in that foundation long after they had left, believing, for the moment, that all three of us were involved in a gentle and thrilling affair.

Yet of course no such calm, dreamy fate was possible. It was that Saturday night that I woke to the creak of the stairs, which I had done many times that summer, as my obsession with my sister had heightened my senses and lightened my sleep. This time, though, the creak was not imagined. I sat up and listened as my sister very clearly tiptoed her way down. At least to my knowledge, she had never gone out at night before, so I could not help myself. I followed the moment I heard the door close. She went to the barn. (Because it was more comfortable there? Because she believed there would be coyotes in The Den at night?) She slid the northern door open and entered, and then she slid the door shut, though not quite all the way. Our barn had separate lofts over the east and west wings. There was only one staircase, which led to the western loft, and to get to the eastern loft you had to crawl on a ladder that lay across the open space, some ten or so feet above the barn floor. No one ever went to that side of the barn, and all that was stored up there were useless doors and windows left over, so far as I knew, from the people who had lived in the house a century ago. The moon was full, and because she'd neglected to close the door all the way, I could see her clearly. She went up those stairs, crawled across the ladder, and threw a heap of blankets down. When, eventually, she returned to the ground floor, she unfolded the blankets. Candles, matches, and cigarettes were hidden within.

When I heard footsteps on the grass I knew it would be Kaus. I skittered to the far side of the door, but there is no way that I was out of sight. He had to have seen me. And yet he was undeterred.

I don't know whether or not that was my sister's first time. I'm fairly certain it was. Kaus walked in and she bent over lightly to pick up a wool afghan. She shook it outward, and the blanket caught air and fell like a parachute to the ground. She lay the second blanket atop the first. Kaus went to the far edge of this makeshift bed, and she crossed over to him. Nothing clumsy about these movements, either. It was all performed seamlessly as a dance. Henrietta began, with his shirt. She balanced on her tiptoes to pull the T-shirt over his head, and then she moved on to his jeans. The crack of the zipper split through the night. Kaus, all this time, stood absolutely still. Oddly, all the animals of the barn were still, too.

But once he was naked a horse let out a long sigh, and Henrietta pointed to the floor. He moved to lie down, and then, slowly, she removed her own clothes. Once naked, she simply stood there, skinny, pale, her small breasts cradled in the light of the moon that poured in through the wedge between the sliding door and the wall. In time the light seemed to ease her down atop him.

I should have been shocked, maybe even disgusted, because this was sex and I was only twelve. But those two – my sister, in particular – looked so sure, so unafraid, that I was simply stunned, and left with nothing but the blaze of the act itself.

The very next morning, my sister rose much earlier than usual. It was a Sunday, which my father had off, and when Henrietta arrived in the kitchen he announced that he wanted to do something *as a family.* Our mother refused.

'Charley,' she said. 'Charley, you know I am deep into this painting.'

My father, in response, said that he would just take his girls. But Henrietta also refused his offer, and retreated back to her room. Torn between the opportunity to observe my sister after her night in the barn and the gift of having a day alone with my father, I just sat there, unmoving. But to my surprise, my father abandoned me. He said he would go fish alone, and left the house within minutes.

I went upstairs. Henrietta's door was locked, and she wouldn't respond to my knocks and calls. I assumed she was sleeping again, but an hour later she arrived through the front door, leaving me baffled, yet I had no chance to ask questions, for suddenly, at long last, Henrietta came to me with her troubles. It was the breakthrough I had waited all summer for. Apparently Kaus wasn't home – she had been to his house. Also not at the trestle, and not in the woods. None of their usual meeting spots. She told me all this, then grabbed my arm and dragged me into the living room, where she said, 'Be quiet, we're watching a movie.' The movie, as always, was the one video we owned – the story of a boy and girl who get abandoned by shipwreck and eventually come of age alone together on a deserted island. There's one scene that Henrietta, in the past, would rewind and replay over and over again. In it, the boy and girl make love for the first time. It happens in the water, in a tropic, pristine pool beneath a waterfall. Slowly, as they make love, the pool fills with blood. To us, it was a dirty, gripping, and delicious scene, but that day Henrietta turned the TV off the moment the scene began. She slammed down the remote, picked up the phone and dialed, then slammed the phone back down without talking, and then repeated this action two more times before she said, 'I'm going to kill him. The slut. I am going to fucking kill him.'

This went on for a few days, and though she was losing her mind, I have to admit that these days were my happiest. She was suffering but she was mine, I had her back. Or at least a version of her. She had begun to scheme, her eyes alight with a sickening pleasure. 'I could tie him up,' she said, so focused. 'Push him off the trestle and make him drown. I could trick him, he's so desperate. Get him all tied up like I'm really going to give it to him, and then I could just push him off. He'd float away,' she said dreamily, 'and be gone.'

'I could shoot him,' she said. 'Dad has an old hunting gun

somewhere. I could just shoot him. But that would be way too much to clean up.'

Soon, though, her ideas for murdering her lover transformed into simple plans to ruin him. At first I thought this was a positive development. And then I realized that these new visions of ruin could actually take place.

'No one will believe him,' she would say. 'He's a liar who sells drugs, for Christ's sake.'

'Drugs?' I ventured.

'Just weed. God, Jane.'

So it was that we began to keep a list of misdeeds we could commit and blame him for. We could break the school windows, or even our own; we could spray-paint a stranger's car; we could steal our parents' money or liquor. Nothing too terrible, though she did once suggest harming herself, which gave me a scare. She said I could strangle her just enough to leave bruises on her neck, or I could whip her back. When she was too tired, I wrote the ideas down for her. She kept the list folded up in her jewelry box, beneath the spinning ballerina that rose when the lid lifted, and she told me I could get it and add to it any time I wanted.

'Even if it's the middle of the night. If you have a good idea, don't waste it, Jane.'

This – my sister rallied alongside me – was heaven. And then there was a phone call. Kaus, of course. Just like that, she was gone from me again.

This time was different, though. Previously, my parents had scarcely taken notice of Henrietta's whereabouts. Now, within a week of her reunion with Kaus, fights among my mother, father, and sister began. I was told to stay in my room, and for the first time in my life my parents kept watch to make sure I wasn't spying from the top of the stairs. During these fights my mother took on a loud, biting voice I had never known her to own. I could hear her through the heating vent in my bedroom, though I couldn't make out the words. All I know for sure is that early one morning the fights were through and my mother and Henrietta were gone. They stayed away overnight, and when, the following afternoon, they pulled back in, my mother got out of the old truck and walked around to the passenger side. I had gone out to the driveway by now, but I knew to keep my distance. I could see that Henrietta was slumped against the truck door. Our thin mother opened that door slowly, and like a rag doll my sister fell lifeless into her arms. She got situated with her feet on the ground, though, and with their arms wrapped over each other's shoulders they walked to the house and up the stairs. The night before, I had watched as my father changed the sheets on my sister's bed – something we girls had done ourselves for ages. Now I understood why he had. Henrietta was eased into those crisp sheets, and there she stayed for almost a week. Rather than painting, my mother brought soup, water, damp washcloths, and medicine to Henrietta. She sat with her on the bed and quietly ran a hand through her daughter's oily hair.

Surely, I thought, surely such wreckage would signal the end of Kaus. Surely, once she stood back up, my pale sister would be mine once more.

'Sylvia,' our father said not two weeks later, as we all sat together at the dinner table once again. 'Sylvia, I'm not about to chain the horses up.'

We were eating a bland spaghetti I had prepared. It was because of a novel I had read at the very start of summer, a happy little mystery set in Italy. It had been filled with thick tomatoes, rich cheese, and long, melting pasta, and I had been transported, and when the book was through I'd announced that I wanted to cook. My father had taken a list and bought supplies for me to prepare dinner once a week, and the routine had stuck, and so had the recipe, which, on this night, had come out poorly. So there we sat, eating our tasteless meal, made even more dismal with the mood, and all of us aware that our father had already lost the battle – that always, our father lost the battle with our mother.

'One night only,' she said.

Our father asked how she herself would like to be chained up for one night only.

The problem – as our parents understood it – was that somehow, after countless years, the horses had suddenly become smarter and figured out how to free themselves from the barn. In the past they had freed themselves from their stalls, but they had never escaped entirely. Now our father told us that Mr Cutler had called to complain three times in one week, saying politely that Shania and Dolly were ruining his gardens, and today he had literally nailed a note to our front door. Our mother read it aloud to all of us: *Though I aim to be eternally pleasant, I am afraid that if those damn horses eat one more rose I will be forced to do something very, very unpleasant.*

Perhaps it was the strangeness of the note, its uncertain tone, that kept our parents from focusing on a problem that surely they could have otherwise figured out. And why didn't I help them along? Just a few hours ago I had been to the barn, where I had rifled through the lovers' supplies, believing – wrongly, I realized at the dinner table – that they were through. I had opened the blankets and touched the candles and had even found their cigarettes. Now, I could have screamed to realize that Henrietta was back in the barn at night. I should have, but I simply looked at her, willing her to understand that I understood. Yet she just sat there blankly. There was no more discussion about chaining them up. My mother left the table, and without a word our father finished his dinner. When he was through he didn't put his fork down but just released hold of it. It hit his empty plate and clanked. When he left the room he shut the dining room door – a door shut only in winter, to preserve heat at night. Henrietta and I sat alone at the table, listening as in the kitchen our father pulled on his boots and went out to the barn to chain his horses up.

That night, just after dusk, while my parents sat together in the living room, I walked across the hall to my sister's room, expecting to try – and fail – to get her story out of her. I was only vaguely surprised to find she wasn't there. I stood in her open doorway for a moment, then walked across the wood floor and stood alone in the center of her room. I turned in a slow, full circle a few times, absorbing her absence. I thought of telling my parents. Instead, I walked downstairs and out the door, entirely unnoticed, just as she must have gone. I crossed the yard to the barn and slid the door open so slowly, clenching my teeth at every creak and sigh of the old building. I tiptoed in, yet quickly discovered that she was not there, either. I went up the barn stairs, across the ladder, and inspected her secret belongings for the second time that day. Untouched since I'd last touched them, from what I could tell. I picked the bundle up and dropped it down over the ledge, to the first floor, and then returned down there. I went to the horse stalls and said hello to those poor, chained horses. I remember that I patted and kissed their snouts and talked to them in a way I never had before. 'Where's Henrietta?' I asked them. 'Why is she always leaving?' After that, I went to her things. I spread out the blanket as though I were my sister. I sat on it, then lay back and dreamed of being her. Then I sat up again and opened that pack of cigarettes. It was the first time I had ever smoked. It took a long time to light, but once I figured it out I inhaled and coughed and doubled over, feeling dizzy and sick. I spit on it to put it out and then I threw it to the corner, and when my head stopped spinning I bundled all her things back up again but didn't even bother returning them to her hiding spot upstairs. It was my signal to her, or, if my father came to the barn first, my outing of her. I went to bed.

It was only an hour or so later that I woke up. This time, it wasn't to any creak of the old house but to the smell of smoke. I knew in an instant what I had done. I ran down the stairs. I don't know if my panic woke my parents or if they too had smelled it. Anyway, they were close behind me as I ran. The front door was open, so I didn't have to stop and squeeze the

iron latch – only fly through the screen. There stood Henrietta, on the porch, facing the house and not the fire. She still
wore a cutoff shirt, and her torso gleamed in the light of the
flames. She also had a wad of green gum in her mouth. Usually her gum was pink, so this color struck me. It glowed
nuclear there in the night.

'What are you doing out?' my mother demanded, as though
that were the problem. As though we could be so lucky.

We could hear the horses' screams; that was the worst of it.
When the middle beam buckled and the entire structure went
down our father sank to his knees. He had yelled for someone
to do something, to stop, he had even yelled for God, but now
he was finished. My mother had run inside to call the fire
department and Henrietta and I had stayed on the porch. I'd
been keeping my eyes on my father, but when he went to his
knees I looked up, but not to the barn. My vision landed on the
stone wall just at the edge of the field. There, in the light of the
fire, I watched as a figure leapt over the rocks, into the woods.

By the time the firemen arrived, there wasn't anything to be
saved. Still, they worked for hours spraying the flames, and
within a day the cleanup crew and dumpsters showed up. I
stayed in my room, where hour after hour I replayed the
events in my mind. Somewhere between 9:00 and 10:00 p.m.
I had put out a cigarette. But how well had I put it out? And
when I'd thrown it, how close to the hay had it landed? By
11:00 the entire barn had been engulfed.

'How do barn fires start?' I'd tiptoed to my mother's studio
to ask more than once.

'Sparks.' She'd shrug every time, and not even look up at me. But I had wanted details, wanted to know exactly how long it was possible for a spark to smolder before it caught. I was looking for someone to say that one to two hours was way too long from cigarette to fire. I knew my father would have told me the answer, which is exactly why I didn't ask him. Instead, I focused on the next piece in the story: The barn buckles and a figure crosses over the stone wall at the edge of our field, into our woods. I watched that figure over and over again in my mind. I was guilty, I knew I was. I also knew that my sister had been standing right there, that if I were looking for a chance at innocence, she would be my obvious choice. But I would not make that my sister's story. So, as I drifted in and out of sleep each night, I held that figure close. With its existence, it seemed to me that there was one tiny seed of hope that I had not caused the fire.

When the police officer came to our house, our father cursed at having thrown out that threatening note from Mr Cutler.

'Jesus Christ,' our mother said. 'This isn't some witch hunt.'

'He threatened us,' our father told the officer, but then I watched his entire demeanor shift. He let out a loud breath and slumped into a chair at the kitchen table. 'I'm sorry,' he said. 'Forget I said that.'

The officer nodded. He was old and overweight and he had an almost constant boyish smile. He gave us his card, asked us to call with any information, and left. Soon after, we heard that Mr Cutler had indeed been questioned, and that it had led to nothing. 'Did you know he has a daughter?' I heard our father ask our mother. 'That never occurred to me. Lives in Florida. She and her family were visiting that whole week.'

Our mother just shrugged and wandered to the living room. She had never suspected Mr Cutler of anything, and anyway, she wasn't interested in assigning blame. From her perspective, barns burned down all the time and – surely because of Henrietta – we were better off not finding out exactly why ours had.

I like to think of the trajectory of our family's lives as deter- mined by Henrietta's actions, but the truth has to be that after the fire we could have gone on in our new way: each of us in our own place, silent, contained. The truth is that it was I who, one night at the dinner table, could no longer bear the silence I had caused, nor the tight, angry face of our father. It was I who mumbled, with no other reason than to call our little family back, 'I saw a coyote.'

'What did you say?' my father asked.

It was like a bolt of lightning. I knew what I had said, but suddenly my mind lit up and I knew what I had seen, too. Kaus. His fluid leap over the stone wall. Just then I was sure. I could be innocent. I said his name. 'Kaus,' I said. 'At the fire. Running away.'

I couldn't have looked up at Henrietta after that, I know I couldn't have. Still I can see the look she shot me. I can feel it, the way it held my being. So cold, so exquisitely cold and pitiless.

———

37

After that, it all happened so quickly. He was blamed, and until he was sent away, Henrietta was forbidden from speaking to him, and my parents kept a careful watch on her to ensure that she wouldn't. Only once was I asked for my story, and even though by that point my surety had begun to fade, I still told it. A few weeks later, I overheard my parents saying that Kaus had been sent to YDC, that mythical child prison we had heard rumors of at school.

Our parents fought over the punishment, our mother demanding that he was up against too much, that he had been marked as guilty from the start, that he couldn't be asked to make his way in our small, white town.

'His family doesn't speak English, Charley,' she said.

But our father was insistent. 'You do not burn down a barn,' he told her. 'You do not burn down a goddamn barn.'

'A cigarette, Charley,' our mother said. 'It's not as if he burned the barn down on purpose.'

A cigarette. Though I'd known this all along, this was the first time I had actually heard it. I went to my room, my head pounding. I closed my eyes and watched as over and over again a coyote, and not Kaus, crested that stone wall. I opened them and drew my sister to mind. My sister. What had she been doing out on that night, anyway? I closed my eyes again, and magically that figure leaping over the stone wall transformed once more to the form of that teenage boy who had loved her, who had stolen her, who for all I knew could have killed her.

Anyway, someone had to do something to keep that boy away from my sister. And god knows my parents wouldn't have.

III

IN THE days when Henrietta and I would play house in The Den, we especially liked to pretend to be the people who used to live there, and act out how they might have spent their time. Mostly it was in chores. Henrietta would stand at the crumbling fireplace and pretend to stir a pot of stew; she would place an imaginary loaf of bread on a stone to bake in the fire's warmth; she would wield a stick for a broom and sweep about the house, listing orders for me: Bring the flour, bring the sugar, go outside to wash and hang the laundry. It's nighttime, go to bed. That part, I think, was my favorite. I would lie down on the pine needles and Henrietta would tuck me in and give my head a quick kiss. I would close my eyes, gulp in that sharp, earthy smell, and then I really would picture the people I imagined had lived in that house. I would see their slow walks to the well to fill buckets with drinking water and their naked bodies bathing modestly in the stream. I would see the snow and cold, the candlelight. I loved that they had lived in our woods rather than near the road; it allowed me to imagine that they were people whose bodies had practically grown up from the soil itself. I saw them bedding down in the moss on hot afternoons, and then making the long trek to the nearby lake to fish for dinner.

Because of the coyote story our father had told us, our game of house always had momentum, and perhaps that is why we were so drawn to it. We were cooking, we were cleaning, we were sleeping, and danger perpetually lurked. 'Keep an eye out,' Henrietta would tell me dutifully before I passed over the threshold. 'I think I saw one! I think I saw one!' I would yell, rushing back into the square foundation, slamming and locking the imagined door behind me. But then I would go to the imagined window and peer out, or I would unlock the door again. I would tempt the mythical animal to come and get us, desperate to find out what lay on the other side of that destruction. In the realm of possibilities, death did not exist to me. Rather, I wondered if we, too, would become coyotes. Or perhaps we would just spin in the belly of the animal until an unsuspecting hunter came along and cut him open to set us free? Once I asked Henrietta's opinion, and her response had been to quit playing and walk home. I understood, sort of. My sister was practical. Our game in the woods felt like the only place and time she would enter with me into that fantastical world that I so loved. I wasn't to push it too far.

Once, while digging around on the outskirts of the foundation – doing my chore of gardening, as Henrietta had instructed – I found a bent, rusted shovel with no handle left. It was the first artifact I had ever found out there, and as I held it in my hands I felt time shrink. Of course I lived in a house that was just as old as that foundation, probably older;

every day, I shut doors and climbed stairs that others before me had shut and climbed. Also, our house was filled with antiques and I understood that some time ago they had not been relics but tools. Yet none of that had quite the effect that holding that shovel had. Perhaps it was because I had been the one to actually unearth the tool. My hands in the dirt, I had been pretending to be the child of that home, and when those hands found the metal it was as though I actually became, for a moment, that very child.

Over the years, we found a few other things out there. A chunk of off-white broken ceramic, an hourglass-shaped bottle with a chip at the rim. We placed all the artifacts inside the house, in the section near the fireplace that we had designated the kitchen. Throughout Henrietta's love affair with Kaus, those artifacts had remained. Before the barn burned, I would wonder if she told him about what that place had been to us, or if she – at least privately, without Kaus knowing – was, in a sense, continuing our game of house, this time with a husband.

After the barn burned and Henrietta went nowhere but to her room, The Den became my retreat. I would lie out there and watch the leaves rustle overhead. Soon school began and the wind shifted, became sharper. Our mother shifted, too; she began to make us pancakes or eggs or even just fill our bowls with cereal in the morning, and after school she would meet us in the kitchen with a snack – apples and cheese, crackers spread thick with peanut butter. I would eat; Henrietta wouldn't. She would go to her room. My mother would stay with me, asking questions that I felt were her obligatory effort to pull her family back together; she never commented on my responses, but just returned to her studio the moment I finished speaking. I would wander outside. Often I would leave through the rarely used front door and loop around the far side of the house toward the woods, thus avoiding the former site of the barn.

Sometimes, though, I would be overcome by another mood entirely, and I would go right to that site. As with The Den, only granite remained, but there had been a cellar in the barn, which meant that now our land housed a gaping black hole. I would stare down into it and wonder over the fate of the horses' bones, hoping they had been tilled back into the soil and not thrown out with the metal and plastic that had gone into the dumpsters. I had no religious upbringing, had never even been to church, but at some point I began to pray while I stood there. *Please,* I would say. Please what, and to whom? I wasn't quite sure. Still, *Please, please, please.* Also, *I am so sorry.*

'Good news!' my father said one evening in early September when I wandered in from the edge of the barn's pit, dazed. The table was set and my mother and sister were already in the kitchen. We looked at him, waiting. His statement felt so improbable.

'New neighbors!' he said. He told us that Mr Cutler was moving out, going to Florida, and that a new family had bought the place already. The father, an orthopedist named Dr Hennessey, had recently begun a job at the hospital where my father worked, and he was staying in the small motel in town while his wife and twin daughters stayed on in Boston, waiting for the house to be ready.

'I never saw a sign up,' my mother snapped. 'Was Mr Cutler's place even for sale?'

'Christ, Sylvia,' our father said. 'Obviously it was for sale.' My mother glared at him, but I understood his tone. For years our parents had wished that a family with children for us to play with had lived nearby, rather than our strange neighbor. But now my mother refused to join in the excitement. She wanted to know why this new family wouldn't buy a fancy house on the wealthy street in town, as all the doctors did.

'Thirty acres,' our father said. 'And for cheap.'

Our mother scoffed. City people moving in on her turf, she meant. It was a hatred central to her character, and it was exasperated by the fact that the very next week, after Mr Cutler had vacated, worker trucks and machinery began to drive up and down our road.

'That house was in fine shape,' our mother would say. 'If they wanted a new house they should have bought a new house.'

But I was intrigued. I began to cross from The Den through the woods to the edge of the road to monitor the progress. I couldn't tell exactly what the workers were doing, other than painting, because most of the work took place inside. Still, looking at the outside of that house was enough. The new paint job seemed to bring out its elaborate features, and it was as though I had never seen it before. It was just the kind of place I liked, with scalloped shingles, high gables, and dripping gingerbread trim that reminded me of those gothic tales

I so loved. I would huddle behind the stone wall and stare at the attic window, dreaming up the sorts of mysteries that might lurk there.

Finally, one afternoon I watched as the moving trucks pulled in and began to unload. That very night, our father told us that the Hennessey family would arrive on Saturday, and that the following week, Henrietta and I would begin a new job. Apparently, the Hennesseys wanted to go on a date every Friday, and they needed a sitter.

'Nine-year-old twins,' our father said. 'It will be a blast!'

'No,' our mother told him. She said it was too much. It was her new role. In addition to helping us before and after school, she would stay with us on the weekends and ask us the sort of questions I'd always imagined a typical mother might ask – did we have enough clean clothes for the week, was there anything she might iron, was there something special we wanted from the grocery store. Often, when my sister sat at the table, my mother would stand behind her and lift her long hair up and let it fall down lightly, piece by piece. She was protective, now, of her girls – at least of Henrietta – and she didn't want us to babysit, especially not at a stranger's house.

'They're not strangers,' our father argued. In a way, I suppose he was right. Our father and the doctor had formed a friendship, inspired, so far as I could tell, by the proximity of our houses to each other. They would eat lunch together at work, and they'd even once gone out for a beer, something we had never known our father to do. Now he looked at our mother and he pleaded. 'Let them earn some money,' he said. 'It's right up the road.' And then he nodded upstairs, toward the room where Henrietta spent so much time, and he said, 'It's good for them, Sylvia. Gets them out of the house.'

Our first night babysitting, I dressed carefully and put my hair up, trying to appear as mature as possible. Henrietta, however, wore her typical outfit: ripped jeans, an old, over-sized flannel shirt – this one, thankfully, not cut off – and the cheap sandals that she refused to retire despite the fact that her feet must have been freezing in them. Twenty minutes before we were due at the Hennesseys' I said goodbye to my parents and then I waited at the door, calling and calling for my sister to hurry up, yet she just slouched around, scuffing her feet and looking at her fingernails, carelessly applying lip gloss and twirling her hair. Finally my father told her to get going before she lost her first job.

We walked silently up the hill. It was late September by then. The crisp air reminded me of just how long it had been since I had walked beside my sister. Now I racked my mind for something to say to her but could think of nothing. We walked in silence until ahead of us in the dim light we saw the doctor appear on the road near his new house. Then Henrietta said, 'Jesus God.'

I knew what she meant. Because Dr Hennessey was a father, I suppose I had expected him to look more or less like our own father – a bit run-down, a bit heavy in the middle, and harboring the mildest of eyes. But this doctor was young and he was gorgeous.

'Henrietta,' he said as we approached. 'And you must be Jane.'

'Dr Hennessey,' my sister said easily.

'Jack,' he said. 'Call me Jack.' He shook our hands, and I remember noticing that his skin was impossibly soft. His look, too. He had a singular way of looking intently at each one of us when we spoke, as though our words were little treasures he had waited for.

'I was just checking out the lamp when I saw you coming up the hill,' he said now, and pointed. It was an old-fashioned streetlamp, which they'd installed at the edge of their drive. A streetlamp on a country road – right away I thought of how my mother would mock it.

Henrietta, however, must not have had the same thought. She said, 'Wow, Jack, that is so cool.' *Jack.* Even though he had just told us to call him that, her use of the name still seemed so bold.

'Can't get the thing to work,' he said. 'Anyway. Show yourselves to the door. Les is waiting for you.' He pointed toward the porch, and Henrietta walked ahead of me, her constant, newfound slouch suddenly gone. It was she who rang the doorbell, and when Les answered, my sister immediately extended her own hand to shake. 'I'm Henrietta,' she announced, as though she were the happiest person in the world. 'And this is my sister, Jane. Welcome to the neighborhood!'

The twins were seven, not nine, and they did not listen to their mother. The front door opened onto the stairway, and as Les ushered us in she called up for her girls, but they did not respond. Next she rushed us through the front room and into the kitchen. She went to the new, gleaming granite countertop and began to fuss about, straightening the small stack of mail, wiping down an already clean counter, and stopping now and then to yell again for her girls. Finally she stopped and looked at us and said, 'It's that damn attic, they're obsessed.' Then she went right back to rushing about, and as she did so she listed orders for us: 'Spaghetti for dinner. You girls do know how to boil pasta, right? Only one soda and one dessert each. No eating outside of the kitchen. Lock the doors after we've left, okay?'

Henrietta hovered near her as she spoke, but I stood in the doorway between the two rooms, staring at Les. I suppose that she had already disappointed me. Upon seeing the doctor, I had immediately imagined the sort of woman he would be married to. She would be tall and thin – of course she would be, I was still so young, so brainwashed – and her hair would be slightly tousled and she would float about rooms while she perpetually held a glass of wine in her long fingers. But here was Les, *Les,* no taller than I was, with short but overgrown hair, no makeup, and jeans and a sweatshirt that looked appropriate for mowing the lawn.

'Of course,' my sister said now and then as Les spoke. 'Right . . . Absolutely.'

Eventually Les walked past me, to the closet by the front door. She removed her coat, and just then the doctor walked in. 'Ashley!' he called. 'Amber! Get down here!' This time they marched down immediately. They were identical, dressed in matching spandex-and-sequin dance costumes, with high, swinging ponytails that were just the color of the fallen yellowed pine needles.

'Ready?' Dr Hennessey asked his wife. With her, his tone

seemed different, at least from my view. Sharper. But what did I know? She reminded us once more to lock the doors and then she put her coat on, kissed the girls, and walked out.

Later that night, when babysitting was through and Dr Hennessey dropped us back home – for our mother had insisted that we were not to walk down the road by ourselves, not that late at night – we would find our mother on the couch, alone, and because Henrietta would disappear upstairs, to the privacy of her own room, I would be given a rare, delicious moment of time with her. 'It was spectacular,' I would tell my mother, and explain all the individually packaged snacks, a totally foreign commodity in our own home. I would tell her about the second refrigerator in the pantry that was devoted entirely to canned and bottled drinks and she would say 'Sounds like a waste' and 'Sounds like a hassle to me' and, simply, 'Well then,' all so clearly unimpressed. And though I still felt utterly taken with the life that I had just witnessed, I would decide right there on the couch with my mother that such an existence was not what I was after. Instead, I knew right then, I would become a woman like my mother: distant, unengaged, artful, and decidedly un-rich.

That night, as soon as the parents left, I plopped down on the old-fashioned spotless white couch in the front room, but before I could even lean back Ashley scolded me, saying it was meant for adults only. I jumped up, ashamed, but my sister strutted right over. She said, 'Well, how lucky that *I* am an adult.' She spread her arms easily, then fell back onto the couch's low arm. She put her feet up on the cushions – shoes still on – and leaned over toward the glass coffee table. That table was empty, save for a fountain pen in a marble holder. My sister grabbed the pen and held it to her lips, pretending it was a cigarette. The girls folded over with laughter, and from that moment on they loved Henrietta, and not me.

Anyway, babysitting that night was uneventful, or relatively so. Right away the girls led us to the second floor, where a rope hung from the center of the hallway. Together they tugged on it, and down came a folding staircase. We followed them up and Ashley pulled the light on. The attic was long and wide and just as I had imagined it would look. The ceiling was sharply slanted, and we had to duck and even crawl near the edges. The falling sun streamed in through the window I had spent so many afternoons staring at. There was another window just like it at the eastern end of the attic, with a table and chair right next to it. That, a broom, a small boom box, and a black camp chest of costumes made up the entire contents of the space.

'This is how you tell us apart,' Ashley said as she stood in the center of the attic, the sun bathing her face. She tugged on her left earlobe, showing us her scar. She said that she had once torn her own earring out, and now, *for life,* she had a slice right through the flesh that split the pocket of fat in two. She then grabbed Amber and pointed to a red splotch on her neck. 'And this is her mark,' she said.

'You mean her hickey?' Henrietta asked.

I froze, shocked and disappointed by my sister, but the twins just kept on, undeterred. One of them said, 'Our mother said our house is probably haunted, so we're trying to call the spirits.'

'Have you seen any ghosts?' I asked unabashedly.

The girls didn't answer. They just said, 'Want to see our spirit dance?' and then they turned the music on. Suddenly they were leaping slowly around the attic to strange, ethereal music, towing long scarves from the costume box in their wake.

My sister stood up and turned the music off. 'Lame,' she announced. 'Spirits don't even exist, but if they did that is not how you would call them.'

The girls wanted to know how else to do it.

'Later,' my sister said firmly. 'Right now I want to see the rest of your house,' and with that she went down the stairs. The girls looked once at me and then ran right after her. I walked across the attic, to the window that looked out toward our woods. I closed my eyes and breathed in deeply, then heard a noise. I opened my eyes and turned around quickly. Surely the noise had come from below me, but suddenly I felt just as the twins did: The house was probably haunted, and if we wanted to call the spirits, the attic would be the place to do it.

The Hennessey home, to us, was totally lavish. The girls each had their own pink-carpeted room with a canopy bed, and a small, low, cubbylike passage had been installed in the wall between the two rooms, with a little square door that opened into each. The girls showed us how they could pass things to each other through the cubby, and could even squeeze themselves through. The only instruction our mother had given us, aside from not walking home alone at night, was to not go into the parents' bedroom. 'Common decency,' she had said, but during our tour the girls led us right in there, and we did not stop them. The room had a king-size bed stacked high with matching throw pillows, and, the girls showed us, a sliding door at the far side that led out to a balcony.

'The widow's walk,' Ashley said. 'It's the best part, besides the attic.'

'But there's no ocean,' I said. 'Widow's walks are so you can see ships.'

'Whatever.' Ashley shrugged. 'It's a widow's walk.'

'It's great,' my sister said, awestruck. I looked at her. She was staring out at the expanse of untouched woods below, which was just barely visible in the remaining light. The placement of the Hennesseys' house was high up on the hill, and it made the view much larger than we could see from our own home. My sister's statement was so plain and true, so unlike the self she'd become, and it became a little glimmer of hope for me. Somehow, it said that she cared, though about what I was not sure.

In the kitchen, my sister threw a piece of spaghetti at the ceiling to test whether or not it was done.

'Holy crap, my mom will kill you!' Ashley said.

'First rule of babysitting,' Henrietta told her. 'Do not tell your parents.'

We sat on the stools at the kitchen island to eat. My sister let the girls have two cans of soda each, and after dinner gave them two heaping bowls of ice cream.

'Repeat after me,' she said as she scooped. 'Do not tell your parents.'

'Do not tell your parents,' they repeated together.

'Swear it,' Henrietta said. She leaned forward and crossed herself. It was a motion I had never before seen her make. Her hands floated in front of her face and her voice became cryptic as she said, 'Swear it on your virgin bodies.'

I don't know if the girls were shocked by that word, *virgin,* or by Henrietta's manner – likely both. Anyway, they were silenced, as was I. My sister looked hard at them, then pulled the bowls of ice cream toward herself and guarded them with her arms. 'I'm waiting,' she threatened.

'We swear,' the twins said, and one after the other they crossed themselves.

That night, after the girls were in bed, my sister led me back through Les and the doctor's bedroom, to the balcony. There, she leaned back, put her feet up, lit a cigarette, and said, 'I still smoke. Keep your mouth shut about it.'

'I will,' I said, careful to sound indifferent, but inside I was thrilled. No matter what I had done, my sister had brought me back into her fold.

Henrietta continued to talk as she smoked. She said she had decided that she wanted to become a therapist, and that she liked getting her period because it made her feel powerful. She asked me no questions as she went on, and did not even leave room for me to speak. She just talked and smoked, and then she stubbed her cigarette out on the bottom of her shoe and threw it over the banister, into their pristine lawn. Then she stood up, slid open the balcony door, and announced, 'These people are rich as stink.'

That night it became clear that our mother's decision to not let us walk home was certainly not the safest. 'D-R-U-N-K,' Henrietta would say proudly to me of Dr Hennessey after he dropped us off. 'Drunk as a skunk.'

When we climbed into the car that night he said, 'Cold as Canada out there. You girls ever been to Canada, eh?'

We told him we had not. Next he asked if we had ever fishtailed. 'Speed up, slam the brakes on. Need snow. Or rain, maybe. The car slides. Fishtails,' he explained.

'Yes,' Henrietta said. 'I've done that.'

'When?' I demanded.

'I do have a private life,' she announced.

Jack gave a hearty laugh to that, then said, 'What do you girls like to do, anyway?' We were coasting slowly down the hill, his foot resting heavily on the brake, making the minute's drive last so much longer.

'I like to ride horses,' Henrietta said.

'God, doesn't that sound good.' He said that our father had told him about our barn. 'A tragedy,' he said heavily, and waited a beat before telling us that he'd gone to college in the West and had once taken a horse-packing trip into the wilderness there. Henrietta responded by telling him that she preferred western to English riding, and that what she really wanted to do was become a barrel racer.

In the backseat, I seethed. I felt I could see clearly what was happening. Whether or not she still loved Kaus, my sister had already developed a crush on the doctor. It wasn't my practice to speak up to her, but in the darkness of the backseat I felt emboldened. I said, 'Dad's horses weren't even for riding. It's not like you're a rider, Henrietta.'

She twisted her body around to look at me. The dashboard lights were bright enough to make her face just barely visible. It had gone to ice, but for the doctor's benefit her voice remained upbeat, almost singsongy. 'My god, Jane,' she said. 'How can you know so little?'

Jack pulled into our driveway, handed Henrietta a twenty-dollar bill, and said good night.

'Thank you for the ride,' she said easily to him. And then, to my utter shock, 'I love your car. I love driving a stick shift, if you know what I mean.'

'You can't drive!' I barked, but my sister said nothing, just scoffed. We got out and went to the porch. He waited while we opened the door, and then he pulled back out, but he headed toward town rather than his own house.

'Bone doctor,' my sister said flippantly. '*Boner* doctor, more like.'

'Henrietta!'

'Figures he wouldn't go home,' she said. 'Did you see how high she hikes her pants up? Rule number one of a healthy relationship: He's got to want to fuck you. God, even I know that.'

After that first night babysitting, I stopped going out to The Den. I just hung around home, in the living room or at the

54

kitchen table, waiting for Henrietta to come be with me. At night I could scarcely sleep for the nightmares. I dreamed of the fire, of the horses, and of a bottomless pit filled at the edges with Kaus's eyes. They held me while I fell, beckoning me to rise back up with the truth but waiting to attack me when I did. I was sick with what I had done, but never, I was aware, so sick as I must have made Kaus. Still, that thought did not stop me. I told myself that I had given everything in order to keep my sister. I wasn't about to lose her again.

But like usual, she scarcely even spoke to me. That whole week, she didn't say a word until it was time to babysit, and then only 'Hurry up.'

This time Dr Hennessey opened the door and ushered us in. Neither Les nor the girls were in sight, so Henrietta and I stood in the kitchen, talking with Jack while he drank a tumbler of whiskey on ice. Henrietta asked him questions – how he'd chosen to be a bone doctor, what he liked about it, what the grossest injury he'd ever fixed had been. I stood there and wondered what my parents might say if they could see this version of Henrietta and not the silent, heartbroken one. The doctor gave hearty answers to all of her questions, and when he began to speak about a broken femur, Henrietta went right up next to him.

'Show me exactly where it is,' she implored him.

'It's not like you don't know,' I said from across the room. 'You just studied this.'

'I don't test well,' my sister said, as though that explained anything, and she lifted her thigh for Jack to touch.

Jack cleared his throat, put his tumbler down, and pointed to her leg. Would he have actually touched it? Just then we heard Les come down the stairs. She entered the kitchen swiftly, eyed his bottle of whiskey, then said, 'Can you girls come tomorrow, too?'

'Absolutely,' my newly agreeable sister said.

'Four o'clock,' Les said, and then she began to give us our instructions for the night – spaghetti for dinner again, one soda, one dessert each. Henrietta listened to Les and gave occasional assurances that all would go as planned, but I swore that as they spoke, some other plane of language existed between my sister and the doctor. Now and then he looked at her and his eyes, I noticed, seemed to hold something in, just barely. Something beneath the surface that danced to get out.

'Our house is definitely haunted,' the girls told us once their parents had gone. They said that during the night, Amber's porcelain cat had flown off her dresser and smashed into pieces in the middle of her room. They said we had to go back up to the attic and try to call the spirits again.

'Where are your parents going, anyway?' Henrietta asked.

Amber shrugged. She said, 'They're trying to put the love back in.'

'God,' Ashley said, 'shut up! That's private!'

'Is not,' Amber said.

My sister wanted to know whether or not it was true, but the girls just wanted to go to the attic.

'Take them up,' Henrietta ordered me.

'What about you?' they asked.

She absently told them to chill out, and then she went to the pantry fridge, got herself a can of soda, told us that she

THE DEN

would be up in a minute, and in this way my sister left her
role as lead babysitter just as quickly as she had found it, and
my evenings in the attic with the twins began. That night, I
taught them to play Bloody Mary, though we used the attic
window in place of a mirror. We would spin before it, and I
promised the girls that if done correctly, a floating figure
would appear in the glass. We played *light as a feather, stiff as
a board,* and we also chanted random, made-up strings of
words. I even ran and danced with the girls to that strange
music, towing a scarf in my wake.

Now and then we would call down from the attic for Henrietta, but for the most part she didn't appear. Almost always,
we could hear the murmur of the television below us, and
when we eventually went downstairs for dinner we would
find her on the couch, a mess of snacks and wrappers spread
around her. The twins would tell her what we had done, what
they claimed to have seen. Sometimes they would put on a
dance show for her. She would pretend to be interested, but
only for a moment. Very quickly her eyes would jump back to
the television. She would be involved only when it came time
to tell them to go to bed, and despite becoming a total disap-
pointment to them, they would still listen to her. After they
were asleep, my sister would wander back and forth between
the television and the balcony. The first few times, I followed
her out there, but she told me to give her some privacy. Still,
every single babysitting night, the minute the parents pulled
back in, I felt I could actually see my Henrietta slip right back
down into herself, just as sly and vital as she had ever been.

Weeks passed in this way. The leaves all glowed, but their
show this year failed to astonish me. It was their fall that

I waited for; I wanted the trees to be bare and the world to be cold, as I was. I wanted the landscape to open up, the view to widen, as though that change would somehow erase what had come before.

But the leaves hung on. It was mid-October before the first – the maples – let go, and when they did it seemed to be in one great sweep. Henrietta and I got off the bus and shuffled through them. Before going inside, we went to the mailbox, as was our habit. I opened the box, withdrew the pile, and gasped to see a letter for her on top. There was just enough time for my mind to photograph it before my sister grabbed it from me and ran inside.

'What's she up to?' our mother asked when I entered the house. I shrugged. Why didn't I tattle? There had been no return address, but of course I knew who that letter was from. Who else would write to her? And with a dull pencil, and such a scribble? I ate my snack and told my mother nothing, then went up. There, I stood outside Henrietta's bedroom, listening for any sound. Over and over again, I lifted my hand up to knock on her door but decided better of it. So far as I knew, this was her first contact with Kaus since before the fire, and it seemed to me that it could contain anything, including the very worst: my guilt.

That Friday we returned to the Hennesseys' and found that they had lined their porch with eight jack-o'-lanterns, two for every step. They'd also hung three plastic skeletons from the rafters. We rang the bell and waited while behind us those bones clanked dully in the wind. Halloween was in two weeks, and for the first time in our lives we had no plans to dress up. Finally, Les opened the door and drew us into the living room, where they'd draped fake spiderwebbing from the ceiling of the living room all the way to the floor.

'I *love* your decorations,' Henrietta said to her, but later, once the twins were in bed, she mounted the stairs to head to the balcony but stopped and looked at me. 'How can you sit there?' she asked. 'It's too creepy.' I shrugged and she went up a few more stairs, then stopped again. 'God,' she said. 'Are you coming or what?'

I jumped up and followed after her. It did not seem like chance that she should invite me just days after that letter. Outside, I saw that she had made herself a little corner on the balcony – a lighter, a drink, a blanket. Clearly she had been coming out all night while I'd been in the attic with the twins. As we sat there together, I waited for my sister to open up. But to my surprise, Henrietta said nothing of the letter. Instead she said, 'What do you think the Hennesseys are doing all night, anyway?'

'Dinner and a movie?' I ventured. When I spoke, I could see a little puff of my breath in the light cast from Les and the doctor's bedroom.

'Anyway,' she said. 'They're definitely not parking, that's for sure.' She wrapped the blanket around her shoulders, drew her feet up into her chair, and continued to go on about them. She said the doctor missed being young, and that's why he'd moved to the country. She said he was bored with his life, his family.

As I listened to Henrietta, it dawned on me that I had never heard the doctor offer the information that she now purported to have. Still, I did not get the feeling that she was exactly lying. I did my best to keep my voice natural as I said, 'How do you know all this?'

'We talk,' she said smugly, and suddenly I became disgusted with my sister in a way I had never been before. Somehow, despite my first estimation of Les, I had decided that she was wonderful. I liked her curt manner, the way she seemed so in charge. I liked that she looked plain, that she did not live up to my mother's stereotype of a city woman. Between her and her gorgeous husband, I had decided that I chose her, and thus, I thought, her family.

With all my courage I snapped, 'What about Kaus?'

'What about Kaus?' Henrietta snapped back at me. 'God, Jane, why don't you tell me?'

I froze, did not even let my breath out. I did not know what she meant, what she knew. I had even feigned sickness one day that week to stay home from school and search her room for that letter – is that what she was getting at? The search had been fruitless and now I sat there terrified, listening to the wash of leaves below. Finally she said, 'Why don't you go find something else to do? Go call your ghosts or something?'

My face burned. I rushed from the balcony before she could see me cry, and after that I was not invited to go up there with her again.

The Hennesseys began to stay out later and later. Most of the time, I would fall asleep on their couch and wake only when Henrietta shook me, saying it was time to go. As always, the doctor would drive us down the hill, but after a few weeks into our job the ride had become more or less silent. Still, Henrietta always had the front seat, and even in my sleepy haze I felt some wall that blocked me off from them.

But on the night that I had dared ask her about Kaus, our nightly routine suddenly changed. The doctor drove us home, handed my sister our money, and we got out. We went to the porch, and just as I opened the door Henrietta ordered me to not follow her, and then she turned and ran back down to the doctor's car. She opened the passenger door, climbed in, shut the door after her, and stayed in there for roughly five minutes. It was a cloudy night, but our parents had left the porch light on, and the doctor had turned his car and headlights off. This meant that I could see their shapes in the darkness, just barely. I could see her shape move ever closer to his. I held my breath as I watched their shadows merge into one.

'What?' she demanded of me when she came back up the porch steps. 'Open the damn door already,' she said, then pushed past me to do it herself.

Halloween came and went. The twins became the first trick-or-treaters we'd ever had, and our father delighted in it. They came dressed as fortune-tellers and he asked them each to read his palm, then presented them with entire candy bars. Then November arrived, and that's when my sister disappeared for the first time. I remember the way it struck me that she should go then. I loved that month, had waited for it. I loved the early darkness, the open woods, the way stone walls were suddenly revealed like streams along the roadsides. But one day I got on the school bus and could not find Henrietta there. On the ride, I convinced myself that she must have gone home sick, but when I walked into the kitchen my mother said, 'Where's your sister?'

At that point, we had no notion of how real, and permanent, that question would become. Very calmly, my mother called the school, but found out nothing. 'Damn her,' she said when she put the phone down, and I wasn't sure if she meant my sister or the secretary. She told me to get in the car, and we drove down the hill, toward the hospital. I stared out the window, certain I could catch my sister in one of her old, familiar places, like that little store or – if we would only drive by it – the trestle, a cigarette held to her lips and some new boy draped at her side. My mother parked the car and told me to hurry up. My father's job meant that we could get free meals, and we had done so many times in the past, but at that point I hadn't been there in perhaps a year. Still, we knew the hospital well, and rushed down the halls, through the cafeteria, and into the kitchen, where we found my father in his chef hat and pants. He smiled to see us there.

'Henrietta didn't come home from school,' my mother told him quickly.

He asked what she meant. As they spoke to each other I turned, walked through the kitchen and back into the cafeteria. I grabbed a plastic cup and headed to the soda fountain, then to a table. Just as I moved to sit down, in walked my haughty sister. I jumped up.

'What are you doing?' I asked.

She smiled and asked me the same question.

'We thought you died,' I said dramatically.

'Jesus,' she said. 'I just came for a snack.' She shrugged and I looked past her, down the hall. Dr Hennessey. He was headed away from me and dressed in baby-blue scrubs and a blue cap, like all the other doctors, but I knew those broad shoulders, that slow saunter. I knew without a doubt that it was him.

'I'm not an idiot,' I hissed at her.

'What are you even talking about?' she said loudly.

'The doctor,' I said. '*Jack*. Henrietta, what are you doing with him?'

'You mean the *boner doctor*?' she said. 'What do you think I'm doing with him?' she asked suggestively. I stared into her eyes and she stared right back, and to my surprise it was she who broke first. She said, 'Not my fault everyone wants me.'

I could see that our parents had spotted her with me by now and were headed to our table. 'He's like forty,' I snapped quickly at her. 'He has a family.' And then, for the very first time in my life, I gave my sister a real, burning insult. 'You're acting like a slut,' I whispered.

She said nothing. Just stood up from the table as though she was entirely unaffected and walked to our parents, hugged them, then casually told them that she had been bored of the old routine of coming home on the bus to do nothing all afternoon and had decided to change things up. They reprimanded her, saying she had worried them, that she wasn't allowed to just make decisions like that without permission, and that was it. My mother, Henrietta, and I rode home in silence.

After that, it felt like my duty to return to the self I had become in the summer and follow my sister, figure out what she was up to. It was certainly something. Twice the school called home to say that she had not shown up. Once, I woke up with a start just as the front door slammed. Henrietta, coming in late. I hurried across my room to look out the window, and there I saw it: a small, black car headed slowly up the hill. Dr Hennessey's, I knew.

At their house, after the girls were asleep, I began to creep up the stairs and down the hall to spy on my sister. Usually I just watched her sit out on the balcony and smoke. One time, though, I entered the bedroom to find their closet door opened and my sister on the floor, crawling toward the back.

'Why are you in there?' I asked, but she didn't respond. She took her time crawling out, then she looked at me, shrugged, shut their closet door, and went out to smoke. But later that night, she shook me awake. I sat up quickly, thinking it meant it was time to go, but right away I saw that Henrietta had a black leather briefcase on her lap. It must have been oiled recently, because I still remember that camphor smell – just the same as our father would rub into his leather work boots.

'Jane,' Henrietta said. 'How do I open this?'

'What is that?' I asked.

'Come on,' she said. 'You're always reading those spy novels. How do you open a briefcase?'

'What are you doing?'

'Aren't you supposed to be smart? There's a combination. What are all the possibilities?'

'Permutations?'

'Duh,' she said. 'Like what exactly are they?'

'You should put that back,' I said. I don't totally know

why. I was intrigued, certainly, and snooping was in no way beneath me. Also, this was the first time my sister had actually come to me since that day in the hospital. Still, something about that briefcase scared me. The room seemed to pulsate around it. At any moment, I felt, the doctor would walk in and catch us.

'There's some secret in there,' Henrietta said. 'People don't hide briefcases unless there's some secret. I bet it's why they're fighting,' she said.

'Did the doctor tell you that?'

She gave me a curious look then, one I could not identify. She tilted her head and scrunched her nose, and in one way, she seemed to be saying what she always said to me: You're an idiot. But in another, it was like she was asking me how I knew that. And in yet another, she was considering this idea, that maybe the doctor would tell her. I never knew what she really meant. I said, 'Fine, there are too many possibilities. If you don't know the code you can't do it.'

'Unless you break it,' she said, and walked back up the stairs, the briefcase hanging from her hand, hitting her leg with every step she took.

After that night, my sister began to join us in the attic, and of course her presence commanded all the attention of the girls. She told them she knew how to call spirits, and that it had to do with codes. 'When's your mother's birthday?' she asked. 'Your father's?' Also, 'Any lucky numbers in the family?' She would gather the information and then she would go through a show of holding hands with the girls and chanting the numbers. 'Did you feel that?' she would say. 'I totally felt a spirit brush my shoulder.'

Finally one cold Friday she thought to ask the question directly. She said, 'Does your family have any combinations for anything?' It was only late afternoon, but the sun had already set. Out the window, the birch trees glowed against the gray world.

'For our security system,' Amber said. '7768.'

'Amber!' Ashley said. 'That's secret!'

But my sister assured them both it was okay, and then her eyes shone as she told them that she had a new idea. She said that in order to communicate with the ghosts, we had to have a Ouija board, and since the twins did not, she would just run home and get ours.

'You can't go home,' I said. 'We're babysitting.'

'How old are you?' she said. 'Five? Wait here. Ten minutes. Fifteen, tops.'

I often think about that. Of how I sat with those twins up in the attic, wondering if I should tell them it was a sham. I think of my foolish decision that it would be a worse trespass to leave those girls alone than to follow my sister, to stop her from her certain crime. We all heard the front door slam shut, but only I got up to look out the window. If it weren't for that streetlamp they had installed, I never would have seen her. But there my sister ran, up the driveway and across the road, into the woods, the briefcase held tightly to her chest.

Thirty minutes passed before she was back. The twins wanted to know where the Ouija board was, and she told them she hadn't been able to find it. She talked them into going downstairs to watch a movie, but while it played she paced the kitchen, chewing on her lips and squeezing her hands into fists. When the girls went to bed, I asked her what she had done. I told her I had seen her. I told her she could be arrested.

'What is wrong with you?' she asked me, and she returned to her pacing.

'Les!' she said when the Hennesseys came back. 'Jack!' She told them we didn't need a ride home tonight. She said the moon was almost full, the walk took only one minute, and we needed some fresh air.

'It's supposed to rain,' Les said. 'Freezing rain, actually.'

But my sister insisted. She said she had watched the weather; it wouldn't start until close to midnight. Finally Les said, 'You're sure your mother won't mind?' and Henrietta assured her that she would not. She pointed out that we could practically see our house from theirs, anyway. Jack was in the kitchen, and I remember that he didn't even look up when we said goodbye.

I think I knew, when we left that house, that it would be for the final time. There was a part of me that did not want to follow my sister, did not want to be associated with what she had done. But there was that ever-present, deeper stream in me that felt compelled to do all she said.

'Jesus, hurry up,' she snapped at me as we crossed the driveway. I turned to head toward home but she asked me what the hell I was doing. A raw winter chill had set in. We had coats but no hats or mittens. I knew where she wanted me to go, but I asked her anyway. She didn't answer. She just crossed the road and entered the woods. As I stepped over the stone wall to follow her I thought of the hours I had spent in that very spot as the Hennessey house had been worked on, staring up at the attic, sure that some secret lay within. It had never occurred to me that Henrietta could actually steal that secret. I hurried through the bare woods behind her. The birches glowed, and to this day their sight in dark November reminds me of that night. I could have stopped her.

In The Den, Henrietta reached into the chimney and withdrew the small metal box that our father had used on boyhood canoe trips. I hadn't known she had it. She opened it up, removed pitch wood and matches, and in one try lit a fire that she must have arranged ahead of time.

'I didn't know you kept that box in the chimney,' I said.

'Well,' she said. 'You don't know everything, now, do you.' She took a flashlight from the box and went to the corner – our childhood kitchen – and brushed away leaves until the briefcase and her huge duffel bag were revealed.

'What are you doing?' I asked.

'We need to figure this out,' she said without looking up. She took a deep breath and twisted the numbers into place. Slowly she opened the briefcase and stared down at a stack of uncut hundred-dollar bills as deep as the case itself.

'Put that away,' I snapped, terrified.

'I didn't think the code would work,' she said absently. It was as though she were speaking to the woods, the air, anything. 'Did they make it? Are they Boston mobsters? Is this why they moved to our lame town?'

'Henrietta, don't touch that,' I said.

'I thought it would be some paperwork,' she said. 'I thought

I would just get some dirt on them.' She ran a hand over the top sheet of money.

'Put that away,' I snapped again, but she wouldn't move. I said her name but she wouldn't look up. I said it again and again. Finally she slammed the briefcase shut and whipped around at me.

'Forget it,' she said, her voice now returned to itself. 'You're so juvenile.'

She had never called me that before, but it struck me as exactly the right word. I was cold and scared and my entire body was shaking, my teeth literally chattering, but still I tried to win her back. I said, 'That's the way they make money. You can buy it that way at the mint. I read about it.'

'Just forget it,' she said, as though it was nothing. 'I don't know why I even bothered showing you.' She turned away and covered the case and her bag with leaves again. I heard her take another deep breath. I tried to do the same, but it had no effect. She kept breathing loudly, though, purpose-fully. Were those few moments the ones in which she devised the plan for her future? She couldn't have had the plan when we left the Hennessey house; if she had, why would she have brought me to the woods with her? Henrietta took one final loud breath, and then she turned and walked slowly toward me. She brought her face so close to mine that our noses nearly touched. Before she even opened her mouth I knew an attack was coming, and I knew it would work. Her words, when they came out, were only a whisper. She said, 'Mind your own damn business, Jane.' Her breath spread across my skin. I took a step back but she stepped with me, this time coming somehow closer. 'If you have ever cared one bit about me then you had really better mind your own damn business.'

I did.

'Did Jack bring you home?' my father asked when I walked in. 'I didn't see his headlights. Where's Henrietta?' He stopped then, and looked at me. 'Jane,' he said. 'Jane, you're freezing.'

'She's outside,' I said. 'We walked. She wanted to walk.'

'Jane,' he demanded.

'It's fine,' I said, my anger at her suddenly somehow larger than my fear. 'We're fine.'

'Jane,' he said again, but I just told him I was going to warm up, and then I stomped my way to my room. I heard him open the door below and go out on the porch, where he must have looked around quickly for my sister. A moment later he came upstairs. Despite changing into sweatpants and a sweatshirt and crawling beneath my blanket, my body still shook. My father noticed and asked me what was going on. I sat up and shrugged and he asked me again where my sister was.

'I don't know,' I said. 'Maybe she has a new boyfriend.'

'Stop it,' he said.

'Okay,' I said, and I lay back down. I'm not sure what my father did at that point. He left my room, but from there did he wake my mother up to get her advice? Did he go back outside? Did he call the Hennesseys? I covered myself up entirely, even my face, and I closed my eyes, and very quickly I vanished into a heavy sleep. The howl of a coyote woke me up. I know that seems impossible, and yet there that howl remains, climbing steeply as the steepest of mountains. I read once that a coyote's howl looks on paper like the shape of its own upturned, yearning mouth. It is true. Over and over again I hear that sound, I draw that sound. I know that sound on that night better than any other, and yet how could it have possibly been there? Why have I never asked my father if he heard it, too?

I sat up and realized that the rain had begun, its sound reverberating against our roof. Right away, I thought of Henrietta out there in the cold, wet night. I ran to her room and saw her door opened, her bed empty. Downstairs, I found my father pacing the kitchen, the floor creaking beneath his weight. It was nearly one o'clock in the morning – more than two hours since I'd come home. I don't know why he hadn't woken me earlier to demand more information. Now he didn't need to ask any questions. I simply told him what I knew – part of what I knew. That she had been in The Den, that she liked to sit out there and have a fire.

'For Christ's sake,' he said, and he pulled his boots on. 'What does she think she's doing?' he asked. He took the flashlight that we kept plugged in to the kitchen wall. I followed him to the door. He said, 'Don't wake your mother.' I turned the back porch light on and watched my father run across the field toward the woods, his head tucked downward beneath his hood. When he disappeared I kept watching, imagining all possible horrible outcomes. *What if my sister really was gone?* I asked myself. What would I do? Where would I go? It was a kind of game, a cruel one that, in just a moment, when my father reemerged from the woods with no Henrietta, would come to life and grab my heart between its hands and press it flat.

'Sylvia!' my father called the moment he came in the door. He pulled his boots off as he ran toward the stairs. I followed.

My mother was already sitting up. She wore a white flannel nightgown with red reindeer embroidered across the chest. When she saw us she flung the covers off her legs and she said, 'Where is she?'

Eventually, I drifted off on the couch. My parents had already called the Hennesseys and then the police. I think that when I lay there in the dark, I still expected my sister to walk in. But when dawn arrived through the window and I opened my eyes the room looked somehow different. Sisterless.

I got up. It was six a.m. My parents were in the kitchen, my mother standing before the woodstove and my father pacing back and forth in front of the low bureau that we used for a kitchen island. The world had begun to mourn with us; the temperature kept dropping and the cold rain turned to sleet and ice that fell so hard and so steadily that its sound became a reliable lament. In my mind I rehearsed the ways in which I could speak up, the outcomes it could lead to, and over and over again I decided to follow my sister's instructions: *Mind your own damn business, Jane.* She would return, I told myself. Or the police would find her. But if I spoke up, she would never again return to me.

By nightfall of that first full day of her absence, the temperature had dropped, the rain had frozen, and the wind had picked up. Still, our father shepherded us out to the car and drove the ghostly streets into town, to the police station, where he demanded help.

'These things happen all the time, sir,' they told us.

'When?' my father asked. 'When exactly do they happen?'

The officers responded that they were up against a wall, and indicated the storm.

'She's fifteen years old,' my father told them slowly, in a near-growl, his lips tight and his teeth barely opening for the words. 'Aren't you required to search for a fifteen-year-old?'

Apparently not. It turned out that though there were state laws to dictate the search for a missing person, local police departments had no obligation to follow such laws. Meaning that the search for my sister was left entirely to the discretion of the town's police chief. And why, exactly, would he go into the cold, icy November storm to waste his time searching for Henrietta? Henrietta Olson, who just months ago had been sleeping with the teenage drug dealer who burned down her family's barn?

'She's not exactly a rule-follower, if I remember right,' the police officer said before we left. 'She's probably just off with a friend.'

My father stood up and kicked the chair he had been sitting in. He held the door open for us to leave the station, and then he slammed it shut. Back home, he tore through the phone book, calling the parents of every student he could find in our entire school, asking after his daughter. He went to that little red house and found Kaus's grandmother, who shook her head and asked him to leave. He didn't go to work, and instead drove up and down the frozen, treacherous streets of our town, searching for his daughter. Our mother, during this time, sat at the kitchen table wrapped in a blanket, the fire in the woodstove roaring behind her. She held the portable telephone in her hand and an empty expression in her eyes that struck me as hauntingly similar to what Henrietta's had been since summer.

'My god, I'm sorry,' the doctor came to our door to say.

'No,' our father said. 'It's not your fault.'

'If there's anything I can do,' he began. I stood on the threshold to the kitchen as he spoke. He caught my eye, and I felt that he was passing something to me in his look. He said, 'Maybe she's all right. Maybe she knows exactly what she's doing.'

I almost spoke just then. I definitely said my sentence in my mind, and I think I began to say it aloud. *So you know she has your money.* But my mother cut in. She said, 'I just don't understand it, Jack. I don't understand what the hell you were thinking.' Meaning, of course, that the doctor was supposed to have seen us safely home.

Finally, the police showed up to inform us that they would search our property. But it was already Monday. Henrietta had disappeared on Friday. The wind and freezing rain had not stopped since then, and a few power lines in town had even fallen. School had been canceled. I stood in the window and watched as those officers slid their way out across the frozen field, over the stone wall, and into the woods. There, branches cocooned with ice bowed down to block their path and eclipse all possibility of a quick search. But would they have done a better job had the weather been sunny and warm? They lasted, halfheartedly and tentatively, for two short, cold mornings, surely thinking as they walked of their own warm homes.

While they searched, they also finally ran her most recent school picture – tenth grade, taken just weeks before she disappeared – in all the state's papers. Yet on the very day the photo was published, Henrietta's letter turned up. It was I who found it. I'd been in that old foundation, and it occurred to me to do what, shockingly, I had not yet thought to do: reach inside the chimney, just as Henrietta had done, to an interior gap in the brick. Her box. And inside, her letter.

I'm gone, I will be back, I am safe.

With that, the police were done.

IV

IN THE early days after Henrietta was gone, I was able to fool my mind into imagining her in some new, shiny life. It didn't make me happy, but at least it kept the image of a lifeless body at bay. Yet as the weeks passed and my sadness deepened, I could not imagine a new life for her, because I could scarcely call her form to mind. I could not even conjure her voice. At night I would beg some nameless god to send me dreams about her, but the rare times that they did arrive I would wake up drenched in a cold sweat, and as I came to my confusion would return to hopelessness.

I didn't go to the Hennesseys', did not even pass through the woods to spy on them from the far side of the road. I did not dare. Even if I had misinterpreted Dr Hennessey's look, and his strange remark that maybe Henrietta knew just what she was doing, still they had to have known that my sister had stolen their briefcase, and their silence had the effect of silencing me. I kept my distance, terrified that one day they would come to me, demanding information that I did not have.

Though my parents failed to speak with me about Henrietta's

absence, my father would come to my room now and then with
one book or another – all an attempt, I understood, to put some
life back into me. None of it worked. I didn't read a thing, not
until my father entered my room one dreary day with an old
book of his that he must have bought at an antiques store. My
father loved history, particularly local history, and the built-in
shelves that lined the walls of our living room were filled with
his beautifully bound yet disintegrating books. The one he now
carried was bound in old, flaking leather. *The History of Middlewood, Volume I.* He sat down on my bed with it in his lap and
carefully opened it to the table of contents and then flipped
forward about a quarter of the way into the book, handed the
volume to me, and left the room.

I looked down. Chapter Twelve: 'Incidences and Odd
Occurrences.' It took only a moment to see why he had given
it to me. My father had called the story 'The Den,' but in this
book it was called 'Cold Friday,' and it was no story. I ran my
finger over their names as though to test my vision: Thomas
and Elspeth Ross, Colin, Evan, and Jeremiah. There was the
story my father had given us our entire lives, real, true, in
print. There was my father's exact language: *Mercury had
begun to plunge. Violence of the day.* I read it all aloud like an
incantation. *Five wild, hungry dogs, their backs hunched, their
mouths dripping, their eyes at once cold and bloodshot.* And this:
No trace of the Ross family remains.

The story itself was only two paragraphs. I read it again
and again, and then I read the others in that chapter. There
was one of wolves sucking the blood from the neck of seven
sheep; another of a witch casting a spell upon oxen; one of a
body rising from the nearby lake at the boom of celebratory

fireworks. I read it all and then I closed the book, ran my hand over the disintegrating cover, and saw the author's name: Josiah T. Bartlett. The very same man I had just read about. The one who had lived in our house, the one who had gone to rescue that family in the storm only to find coyotes in their place.

It didn't matter that science claimed coyotes couldn't have existed out here back then. With that history book, I felt I had the proof. Now a family that had existed purely for the sake of disappearing had become real in the most terrible of ways; but also, the possibility that a person could morph out of their own form and into another suddenly became indisputable to me.

I pulled back my curtain to look out the window to the woods. Immediately my sister appeared in a rewrite of that story. It was like a miracle. I looked out and I knew that Henrietta roamed somewhere deep in our woods, unrecognizable yet eternal.

Night after night, I pored over the words in that thick book. When pages began to fall out I taped them back against their binding. I had a desk in my room, and I kept the book and nothing else on it. I always kept it open to that story, believing, in some small, impossible way, that this would invite more details to come in. I searched that story as though I was ravenous and that was my only food. I had decided that it held all the clues. It did not escape me that like that family, Henrietta had also disappeared on a Friday. I thought of that night with my sister and I willed it to have been colder. Had my fingers been frozen? Had I gotten frostbite but not recognized it? Mercury sank to 31 below, the book said, so as winter descended I looked up to the sky and prayed for a temperature so low to fall upon us on a Friday night. That, I believed, could offer some portal into the world my sister had entered.

At a certain point, my parents began to fight. Surely, beneath their words lay the loss of my sister. But as winter fell heavily upon us and it became clear that our house needed a new roof, their fights, ostensibly, were about money. My father said my mother ought to work; my mother said my father ought to not try to destroy what remained of her spirit. Soon the fight became over what my mother called my father's romantic attachment to our ruined farm.

'A ranch house in town would practically cost less than a new roof,' my mother said.

And my father: 'Oh, practically. For Christ's sake, Sylvia.'

And one time – only once, so far as I know – 'What about when she comes back, Sylvia? Just how, exactly, will our daughter find us?'

The arguments went on and my desire to eavesdrop waned. Noise in our house traveled easily through the poorly insulated walls and the floor vents, so I spent more and more time in the woods, in The Den. There I lay upon the frozen, snow-covered ground that had last held my sister, and I watched the branches of the trees overhead. I listened for any movement, for the hammer of a woodpecker or the scurry of a rabbit. 'Henrietta?' I would ask tentatively. 'Henrietta, is it you?' Sometimes, when I closed my eyes out there in the cold, I could watch my sister move back out of her new, alternately ghostly or animal form, and appear before me. Yet even then she would never linger. In this vision she would look sharply at me, then reach for some seam in our universe, tear it open, and slip right back through.

It was early January when I finally heard a voice out there. 'Go.' Soft, windlike. I rose quickly and spun around to see who was behind me. Darkness was draped like a black but transparent sheet. Snow dusted the jagged pines and the long, soft arms of the maples above me. Something skittered and ran over the snow. I followed, calling her name as I went.

And so began my focused search. 'Henrietta?' I said as I stalked through the woods. 'Henrietta?' as I fell knee-deep in the snow, freezing, tired, and hungry.

A small creek ran at the base of a gully in our woods and then cut across the lower section of our field. Above the creek stood our old well house. There were many times, after that first evening, that I lay out there in The Den and heard a voice and saw a quick, fleeting being and then ran breathlessly through the woods, chasing it. Soon all chases ended up at that well. This, I decided, held some significance. I scoured all the books I could find for any mention of wells. Eventually I felt I understood: That well was a portal through which I could find my sister – not the solid, blood-circulating version I had lost, but my sister all the same. I began to hang my head inside the well's rotting frame. I had become unafraid of darkness, of spiders, of gravity, of anything. I needed only to discover a way to travel down to the base of that well, at which point I was sure I would lose my body and drift upward, into the arms of Henrietta. With this end in mind I filled that deep chamber with my voice and its echo, and I kept an eye out for signs that my calls had worked, that some being from the other side had heard me.

Of course there was never any sign. My search ended before dawn one morning when I woke in my bed with my parents at my side. They told me that the night before, I'd been found in the snow on the side of the road, just at the edge of the woods, passed out, freezing. A young man driving a snowplow had spotted me. I'd been wearing sneakers rather than boots, and this, they said, is what saved me; in his headlights he'd seen the glow of their reflective strips.

'You could have died,' my father said. I understood. I stopped going to the woods. I stopped reading our town's history. At the library I checked out cookbooks. I read my father's books about building. I read my math textbook. I listened to the drip overhead, in my mother's studio – the roof had yet to be replaced, or even patched – and I kept a tight hold on my mind. I did not think of what could be; I did not think of what my sister might have become, or whether or not she would come back. I allowed myself no imagination. I passed nearly four years in this way.

Once, two years after she had vanished, the French teacher from school showed up at our door saying she'd seen a girl out in Montana who looked just like Henrietta. 'She knew that town,' the teacher said. 'I told her all about it.' She wiped at her nose with a crumpled tissue as she spoke. 'I always told her how wonderful it was out there,' she said. This teacher had a son who lived there, who'd gone to college and stayed. She said she'd been visiting him. That this particular sighting had occurred at the county fair.

' "Henrietta!" I called,' the teacher told us. ' "Henrietta, I know it's you!" ' But this girl, this supposed version of my sister, she'd simply shrugged, then run off to board the Ferris wheel. Then, from the highest point in the sky, she'd yelled back down to the teacher.

La, de, da, the teacher claimed the girl had yelled.

'Fucking liar,' our mother said once the teacher had left. 'Fucking woman has always been a drama queen.'

Our father wasn't so devoid of hope, though. He left his job, packed his bags, and went to Montana. He spent two months out there, wandering the streets, while at home my mother and I sank alone. Finally he came home only to return the very next week. He stayed for another month, and when he once more made his way back – this time in an old truck he'd bought out there instead of by plane – my mother sent him straight to a therapist. After that, our father spent the greater part of one year sleeping and taking antidepressants, and I practiced erasing that French teacher's story from my mind.

In my final year of high school I made a close friend. I have long since lost touch with her, but back then she broke me free a little bit. She had moved to our town from New York City and she liked to steal my mother's marijuana and she liked to gaze at the sky. Once, as we leaned together against the granite in the sunken hole that used to be the barn and smoked one of my mother's joints and watched the dark and beautiful clouds, I realized that so far as this friend knew, I had never even had a sister.

On my birthday she gave me a copy of her favorite novel,

and because I loved her I read it. It was a story of a small town, a sad young man and his sad young siblings, an impossibly obese mother. It was fantastical, ever so slightly it was. I read it three times. Since the end of my family, she was the first person to view me innocently. To love me in that way. But of course she knew nothing of the real me.

'Apply to college,' she used to tell me. 'Don't you want to leave this town?'

And didn't I? Instead, I graduated high school with straight A's and then went home. My only friend went to college in Colorado, and I never responded to her letters, and eventually her parents moved once more. I was busy enough while she was still home, but once she was gone my father started to take notice of me sitting blank-faced on the couch. He began to ask me questions – what did I plan to do, what did I want to be. My mother joined in, and together they put their collective foot down: Get a job or enroll in the community college in the next town over. I signed up.

Before I chose my classes, I had to meet with the professor who would be my adviser. So far as I know, she had been chosen at random, but it was the kind of chance choice that makes me wonder about the organization of the universe. She was slight and gentle, and when we spoke she offered me mint tea with milk warmed in her office microwave. Her shelves were filled with old novels and volumes of poetry bound some one hundred years earlier, and they were lined up perfectly, and alphabetized, not one title – so far as I could see – out of place. She asked me what I liked and I shrugged. She asked me if I wanted to study math or science or English or maybe a foreign language. I shrugged again. She asked me why I had decided to go to college – all of these questions given so kindly, with no pressure, I felt, for a response. I felt so good in that sun-filled office, so comforted. That smell of old books and sweet milk and cool air welled around me, and suddenly I found myself looking up at her, pointing to her desk, and saying with every ounce of untainted heart that I had left, 'I love that book.' It was a small, green, hardback copy of *The Scarlet Letter* that was so old it did not even have a copyright date. She handed the book to me and asked why I loved it. I thought of those mystic woods. I looked up at her and I said simply, 'Hester survives.'

She gave her copy to me, and I still have it today. So it was that I began to study English literature, and I even signed up for one creative writing course. I passed through it, and the rest of school, quietly. My father urged me to get certified as a teacher or to continue my studies. He had visions of his remaining daughter becoming some kind of scholar, or, I suppose, some kind of anything. But I had no such hopes.

The day I graduated from college, I walked in my black cap and gown because my father wanted me to. It had been nearly ten years without my sister, yet as I stood there among my classmates, strangers all of them, I cataloged the black-haired people in the audience. Henrietta, mid-twenties Henrietta, I was so sure just then, would have black hair, long and bohemian. She would have rings on her fingers and large silver earrings. She would clap for me, would lift me up, would hold my face between the press of her long, thin fingers and she would say, *Look at you. My god, Jane, look at you.*

We drove home quietly, the three of us. My mother asked

me if I might like to go out to eat, or if I would like them to cook up something special for dinner. *Is this depression?* I wondered, simultaneously shocked that anything on that day should feel particularly worse than all the others that had come before. Yet it did, because Henrietta, of course, had not come for me. I had done all my duties; I had finished school and gone on to college and I had finished that, too. Now an unplanned life that I was expected to enter on my own stretched endlessly before me.

With no other prospects, I took the simple path my parents suggested: I applied for and eventually accepted a job as the new receptionist at the dentist's office in town. The dentist had cleaned my teeth and given me fluoride and filled my cavities my entire life. He was a good employer. He paid me well enough and he gave me health insurance, and I had an hour off for lunch each day, after which he always told me to brush. He cleaned my teeth for free. I answered the phone and called patients to remind them of appointments; I kept track of his calendar. His office was in the front end of an old colonial in town. A family lived upstairs and an accountant worked in the back half. It was a small office, only the two of us. My desk sat just inside the front door, sandwiched by filing cabinets. The records, I suppose, were private property. I had never been asked to touch them. But one morning a few months into my job he was running late. I didn't have a key, so I waited on the front step. We always unlocked at 7:00 a.m., with the first appointment at 7:30. It was 7:20 by the time he pulled in. He said, 'You get the records. All the way through to noon, please.'

I knew what he meant – every morning, he made a pile of the records of all the patients he would see before lunch, each in their manila folder. After lunch, he did the same.

'Carol Clark,' I said. 'I can't find her.'

'She's in there,' the dentist said. He said she might be out of place, but she would be in there somewhere. 'Twenty years,' he said, 'I haven't gotten rid of one record.' And then, 'That just might be your next task, Jane.'

It occurred to me then. I opened the drawer for *A* through *C* once more and I did in fact find the file I'd missed, but I left it right there, pretended not to see it, and just began opening other drawers. *D* through *F* first, and then *X, Y, Z*. Eventually I dared open the drawer with *O* inside. I flipped through slowly. I felt terrified, as though I was about to encounter my sister, real and whole, after all this time. We were all alphabetized, so my father came first. *Olson, Charles.* I had recently had an appointment – it was how I knew about the job opening. I had leaned back in the chair and the dentist had sat down on his stool, and as he positioned the overhead lamp he had asked me what I was up to. 'Looking for a job now?' he'd asked. Which means that, for that appointment, he had just gotten my file. It had to have been him, because his old assistant had already retired by then. I never knew why he hadn't hired someone earlier. Anyway, the fact that he had gotten my file means that he had flipped past my sister in order to do so. She would have been second. What had he thought as he flipped that folder forward? Had he thought, *Henrietta, DEAD?* and just gone on and saved it anyway?

I put her folder at the bottom of my pile for him, and then

I placed Carol Clark's on top, and then I set the whole pile down and then I picked it back up, leaving Henrietta's folder still in place on my desk. I moved my datebook atop it, and then I delivered the rest to him. Later, while he filled a cavity, I pushed the folder into my purse, which, luckily, was over-sized. At lunch, I transferred it to my car.

That file I stole, it wasn't as good as a real tooth, but it was filled with X-rays of the living mouth of my sister. I held them to my window and stared as though they were her entire being. I memorized them. I knew that tooth 3 and tooth 19 had fillings. I touched the spot in my own mouth where these would have been. I guessed how much her wisdom teeth would have grown by now. I memorized the contours of her molars. For a while, those X-rays, the strange comfort they gave me, stood in place for my mercurial sister. But then they had another effect, too. They didn't just remind me of her. They pulled that ghostly form of her that I had done so well to squelch right back up into the woods.

It was late one afternoon while my parents were out that I walked to the living room as though in a trance and with-drew the old history book from the built-in shelf. It had been years since I'd touched it. I still remember the heave of it on that particular day, and its familiar weight on my lap. I felt I was doing something wrong and did not want to be caught, so as I opened the book and sank down in. I kept a corner of my mind buoyed above, attuned to any sound that might signal my parents' return. I flipped ahead, feeling it was inevitable to return to that story, as if I'd come home in a way I'd always known I would. I had tried to teach myself, since the day I'd woken up in my bed after nearly freezing to death, to believe, as Henrietta had, in nothing at all. To believe that life added up only to death. Yet as I breathed in the dusty pages of that book once more I began to feel the events of the past as currents that sprang forward to echo into the future. I began to read and reread that old shape-shifting coyote story and to feel, more strongly than anything else, that my life on our land could have been no other.

PART TWO

Elspeth

I

IN HER old life, she never rose before the sun came in, even if it meant her mother would scold her. But her sister, Claire, would cover for her anyway. Her sister had understood her – or, if not understood, at least loved her so completely that she accepted her faults, supreme laziness among them. Half the time her sister would do all the chores for them. She realized, in her new life, that it must have been a terrible burden – when she listed it, it all sounded like so much: Collect the water, clean the floors and windows, clean the laundry, tend the gardens, tend the chickens, buy the food, cook the food, that sort of thing, all on top of the spinning. Spin the flax, spin the flax, spin the flax until you lose your mind. But back then, even when she did keep right up with her hardworking sister, it never felt like so much at all. Never near as much as the burden she felt since she'd crossed the ocean.

But even she had to admit that this new life wasn't so terribly bad. For years she had kept a routine that her sister could scarcely believe – she rose with the 4:30 a.m. mill bell, and once her husband set out for work she sat at the table with her candle and wrote letters home until daybreak, when her boys stirred. Letters to her sister, to her parents, to the friends she'd left behind. It astonished her, sometimes, that there was an entire ocean between them, and sometimes it astonished her that there was only an ocean. She could just get on a boat, she thought sometimes. It was the 1850s, she thought constantly toward the end. People crossed the ocean every single day. She herself had crossed the ocean. To get back would not be impossible. Not like trying to cross into heaven or hell or some other realm she couldn't believe in.

It was in the morning, with her letters, that she had thoughts like this. It was when her boys – the three of them – were still sleeping. The oldest and the youngest slept silently, but she had always been able to hear the middle one's labored breath at night. It wasn't a snore, but something at once softer and more hard-earned. 'He sounds like a damn river,' her husband once said, but that hadn't seemed accurate to her, because a river never sounded like it had to try quite so hard.

She didn't mind the sound, though. Years ago, she'd asked a visiting doctor what might be the problem, or if in fact it was a problem at all, but he had said that in order to find out, her little boy would have to spend the night with the doctor for observation. That had been the end of that. Eventually the sound became a light blanket to her, a kind of steady comfort in this new world.

Her husband had come over first. Lots of people were doing that at the time, and she hadn't wanted to be like them in that way – or in any way, really – but it had been decided. He took a boat over, but when he arrived he learned that the mill he had meant to work for had just suffered a great flood, and so he followed another freshly arrived Scot north, to the country, to a small town with a new mill, where he found a job and home at once. Hardly three months later she received a letter saying he was settled in a place called Middlewood. She wasn't sure if it was luck or fortitude, but either way she was proud of him for getting there.

With that first letter, he had also sent a real present across the ocean for her – a brooch made of seed pearls. She had never owned such an exquisite piece of jewelry – not any jewelry at all, in fact – and the gift told her that mill workers in the new country were not like mill workers in Scotland; that in the new country they were of another class; and that when she left her home she would enter not only a new world but a new self entirely. That letter and that gift gave her the sense that she would no longer be of the weavers but a woman in a grand house with a library and a china tea set, woolen carpets, canopy beds, and artwork from France hung on the walls.

But it was all only daydreams. She liked to imagine it, but she never truly wanted such a life – it could not possibly be enough to make up for such loss. She didn't want to go. In those final days before she went she would walk up to the edge of the sand and lie right down – as much as she could despite her belly – and dig her fingers through the sharp grass, all the way into the ground. She would splash the ocean water on her bare face and hair. She would smell everything in those days, too – that grass and sand and water, but also the table they ate on, the spot of earth where the rosebushes grew, and the roses themselves, of course. Her mother's neck and her sister's neck, her pillow, her blanket, even her cottage wall. Cataloging it all before departure. It turned out that she would wish she hadn't done that, because those smells had been stored away, yet she would never be able to quite reach them. In the new country, it was enough to drive her mad sometimes.

Why hadn't it felt that way to her husband, too? He had come from the very same place. Surely he had known the land as much as she had. Yet not *as* she had, she came to realize. The land of home had never been his dream. Business, that's what he was interested in. You'd think she would have known it when they began, what with the way he'd talked about running the foundry one day, but then she had scarcely known a thing. There had never been a time they hadn't been acquainted, but then one day when she was sixteen years old she'd noticed he was standing across the street, behind the blooming lilacs, watching her as she pumped the water. The next day she noticed he was back again. 'What do you want?' she had asked him. 'Why aren't you working?'

'Lunchtime.'

'Why aren't you at lunch?'

'I came to tell you something.'

'Out with it, then.'

'I love you,' he had shouted across the oddly empty street, and she had laughed. He went red, of course, yet amazingly he had not skittered away, so she crossed over to him and apologized. Together they walked back toward her house, and when they got near enough they ducked into the yard. She had done plenty of reading by this time. Romance and horror, mostly. She thought of the helpless people in those stories and she looked at him and willed him to be brave, but nothing happened. She was due back with the water, but she didn't want to go back after such a letdown. She said quickly, 'If you love me, kiss me,' and he had. The kiss seemed to go on and on, though perhaps it was only one second. The bell for the foundry rang and he ran off to work. She picked up her water pails. Light as feathers, for she had been lifted right up. She practically skipped in the door. Practically spilled the water, too. Her sister scolded her but it did nothing to lower her mood. She hummed.

After that day the two of them met everywhere, every free moment they could find. They lied to their families to do it, of course. Said they were visiting this or that friend, or said they were slowed down with an errand because of this or that mishap. They met on the beaches; they met in the woods. She wanted to tell her sister, but then her sister might have called her a sinner. Though her whole family attended church, so far as she saw it was only Claire who prayed daily. Only Claire who dusted and polished the cross. Elspeth herself felt no such calling. Anyway, was love a sin? And if she were a sinner, why would she feel so wonderful? She promised herself that she would marry Thomas, and she comforted herself with the fact that though they would never admit it, her father and even her mother seemed to care more for Wordsworth than for the Bible.

Sometimes she and Thomas would meet in an old misshapen tree with branches long and wide enough to stretch right out on. She would lie back and he would run his hands over the length of her feet, up her legs, and in time under her linen dress. She eventually stopped wearing undergarments for this very purpose. He would touch her softly for a long, long time, and then something else would come over him entirely and he would throw her legs open and thrust his fingers up inside her. He would swear once in a while as he did this, all in exasperation, and she always liked that part, the way it stood out against his tender disposition and made him seem like a grown man. His body would be angled above hers, but her dress seemed to always be flung over her head, blocking her view, which turned out to be all right because frequently as they carried on she pictured some even more elaborate love story in her mind. Sometimes he would pull his hand away and push his mouth in, and then once, finally, after weeks and weeks of this, even though they understood just how a baby was made, they did what they knew they probably shouldn't do. They were seventeen years old by then. Nothing happened, not that time, so they had kept on. Nothing happened and nothing happened, and then suddenly something did. She told her family right away, and as expected, her father demanded that she get married. And then, after thinking it over for a few days, it was her father who had said she and her future husband had better take up with the group going to America.

Anyway, years ago now. In some ways the leaving wasn't fast, and by the time she was set to go she had been given plenty of time to understand clearly just why her father had made it so. It was no secret to their neighbors just when her baby had been conceived. Too many whispers in church to even attend by the end, and then their own neighborhood dairy had ceased to deliver their milk, and not long after that their own neighbor would not sell them potatoes. Because of the situation, despite their hasty marriage, she remained at her home and he at his own until he had enough money to cross over and begin a new life. It took only one month. Once he was gone, while she sat at home with that baby inside her, she felt that she must miss her husband, must be anxious to begin life with him. Yet she didn't particularly feel that way. She felt tired, incomprehensibly so. In the new country she would wonder, always, whether or not it had all been worth it, or even if any of it had been. But how ever to answer such a question? She could just look at her boys – three of them now, ages ten, twelve, and fourteen – she could look at their soft hands, their glowing and singular eyes, and that would be enough of an answer. Or to ask such a question – to even momentarily conceive of an existence that would erase theirs – no, she couldn't.

And yet. In truth, at least in the early days of her arrival, she could imagine a life without those afternoons in hiding with the man who would become her husband. She could imagine a life that had waited and, in doing so, had been allowed to remain back home.

A few months before Elspeth left, her mother sent her to the city so that she might get supplies for her journey. She was to ride the new railway there and spend the night, returning the next day. The trip wasn't necessary; she understood that this was her mother's treat – her very last – to her. Her mother had used up nearly half their stock of candles and stayed up half the night or more in front of the loom for weeks on end in order to earn the extra money so that her daughter might take this trip and choose a special gift for herself and her future baby in America. The money could have meant something to the family, but her mother was proud and it was no use refusing.

'Get a new pillow, a bit of sweets, a deck of cards,' her

mother had said as she hugged her on the train platform. She would be gone only overnight, yet the goodbye had felt real, and unbearable. A kind of practice. Elspeth had nearly not boarded.

The railway brought her within a block of the inn where she was to stay the night, and she went in and registered and found her way to her room, and she stayed there for two or three hours, looking down at the city streets, too afraid to venture forth. She had been here before but never on her own, and now it looked larger and busier than she had remembered. There were four single beds in the room but no other visitors. Finally, lonely, Elspeth forced herself to think of the new life she was about to embark on, and this gave her courage. She was a woman of America! She was about to be, anyway. She drew a deep breath and told herself to be bold, and then she went out to the street and walked up and down, alone, free. When she saw a shop she liked she just went right in. It was one of the ones for wealthy city ladies. She looked at the hats and dresses and then drew into her mind that pearl brooch that she now owned. It meant she was rich, she had felt sure of it. Settling in to the thought was like settling into a new skin entirely. In that skin she wove her way through the shop and eventually came upon the only real-life red dress she had ever seen. It occurred to her that it might be illegal. She picked it up and asked the lady if she could try it on, and then, in a moment, there she stood in a gown more scarlet than blood.

To think of that gown now, of the way she had loved it, it makes her sick, really.

Thank god she hadn't wasted her mother's money on the foolish thing – not that she'd had enough for it, anyway. But how could she possibly have thought for one second that she'd been headed to such a glamorous life in America? Thank god she'd had the sense to just buy some sweets with the money, hard ones that the shopkeeper told her would soothe her stomach on the journey over. She also bought a small framed drawing of the shores of her home, and in her new life that drawing became sacred to her.

It must have been something about the way she walked after wearing that dress, she still thinks sometimes. After all, she had been imagining, as she walked down the cobblestone street, that she was one of those women. One of the independent women such as she had read existed in America. The kind that lived in a boardinghouse and worked at a mill and earned her own money to do what she liked with, and had her own time at night to go out upon the street. The kind with a secret lover, too.

'Going in?' she had suddenly heard, and for a moment she thought it was a voice from her own thoughts. Yet there stood a man, holding the door to the pub beneath the inn open for her. How on earth had it all happened? A whiskey. He had asked her to a whiskey and she had acted like such a thing had happened before. What to talk about with a man from the city?

'Do you take *Blackwood's Magazine*? I think it's to die for and my father agrees. Have you read it?' She used to go red when she thought of herself sitting on that pub stool with a baby in her belly and saying that to him. Now she feels nauseated just thinking of it.

'A cottage weaver who likes to philosophize,' he had said with a smirk.

She had flushed. Was it so obvious, her character and her rust?

In the hallway he touched her hair and she giggled; she had had only a few sips of the whiskey, but all the same it had made her giddy. *I have no husband I have no baby inside I am not leaving this country, not ever.* So had it all been her fault? He held her shoulders from behind and turned her around and kissed her and the truth of it is that she kissed him right back. Next he led her to her otherwise empty room – how did he know where she slept? – and she let him right in, and it was only then, when she saw her suitcase, that she came back to herself. She said, 'I have a husband. I am off to meet him in America in two days' time.'

'Of course you are,' he had said, his hands on her hips.

Well, she had liked it for only one minute. But when he pulled at her skirt she knew she had to put a stop to it. Nearly four months pregnant now, but only showing if you looked closely. 'You have to leave,' she'd said. He didn't let go, so she said it again, soberly this time, slowly. She pulled away from him, and as she did so she happened to see her letter on the table, the one her husband had sent from America. She had brought it along with her on this journey because she had thought it would give her a strange courage, and just now it actually did. She glanced at it and decided it might get this man to leave. John Smith was his name. She waved it in front of his face. She felt a bit dizzy.

Why, why did she always behave so badly?

And yet, miraculously, it worked. He grabbed the envelope, looked it over, and left with it in his hand. She locked the door, and then, feeling unsure of her safety, pushed the nearest bed right over in front of it, just in case.

This new land was beautiful, anyway. Their home was deep in a forest of pine and maple and birch. There was a road a quarter-mile's walk through the woods, but by the time she'd arrived only one house had been built on that road. When she'd first approached it she'd thought it was to be hers. Such a large house! And that barn! But that was the home of just one man, Mr Josiah Bartlett, her only neighbor in this new land. In winter, when the trees were bare, she could stand at her door and see his high cupola in the distance.

Her own house was truly just a box. When she'd arrived some fifteen years ago and seen this she had understood that despite that pearl brooch they were not rich, that they were far, far from it. Her husband had worked hours upon hours splitting wood to earn that brooch. But no matter. The squareness of the house, the dampness of it, and that great big fireplace, it all suited her. Reminded her of her true home. Besides, her husband had assured her, buying this cabin had meant that within a year's time they would not owe a cent, that because they lived out there in the woods they were – or would soon be – free. She'd understood.

Over the years, nearly every day Elspeth and her boys would walk down to the river. Sometimes they would fish beneath that little bridge that led to town, or they'd cross the bridge, bypass the mill, and continue downstream to the train trestle, where they'd shimmy up the bank and then back down the other side and fish in the shade of those great trusses. Sometimes, while they were down there, a train would rush overhead and the ground would rumble and Elspeth would hold her breath, willing it to be over with, but her boys would delight in that iron giant. Other times the four of them would sit upstream of the mill, alongside the dam, and watch the water gush over the top. So she liked the little town just fine, and every single day she felt something more powerful than luck at the fact that they had landed here, and not in that city to the south. But she was lonely. Sometimes so lonely she collapsed. Even after more than a decade, even after she had the friendship of her neighbor, still when she woke up each morning she would keep her eyes closed to cast out a wish: *Let me be back home, let me be back home.* Like a child. But she never told anyone of her suffering. Anyway, who was there to tell? If she had said it in her letters, it would break her sister's heart. And her husband was so busy now. With all that work she would have thought he'd be rich, but he still wasn't, and she had long ago realized that he never would be.

She still did love him, of course. No reason not to. But then if it weren't for that, wouldn't she have never had to come here?

There was a stretch of time in that very first year, before she had gotten to know her neighbor, when she had practically no books, and what with the newborn baby and all the work that needed to be done on their little house she couldn't afford to order anything to read.

'Well, write something, why don't you,' her husband had said one day. The concept had been a shock to her, and she had told him she would never. But then one morning when she rose to write her letters, she found something else entirely spilling forth. It came out so fast and it felt so glorious, though she never would show it to anyone. In fact she wanted so badly to keep it hidden that she even considered stuffing the pages into the chimney, to the spot of missing bricks that she'd discovered when she had been using a broom to scare the bats out. But then of course she had no safe box to keep them in, and it would have been a terrible place anyhow. Instead she slipped the pages under her mattress – that's what she called the book in her mind, just *my pages* – and she found herself thinking about them day in and day out. *Maybe that's something good for my pages. Maybe that's what happens next in my pages.*

The story was a romance, really. Due to unfortunate circumstances a man and a woman were each lost in the woods at night, and fate had it that they literally stumbled upon each other. The woods were not Elspeth's woods in the new country and not the woods of her real home, either. They were woods like nothing she had ever seen before. They were at once dark and light. The air was black yet the trees glowed, and they illuminated a constant, creeping fog. The two loved each other at once. They found their independent ways home yet continued to meet. In those woods, they had to always be on the lookout for swift riders of dark, sleek horses. There were cliffs that dropped down to the ocean, and there were wild men – and even one woman – who could scale the cliffs, and there was a castle in the distance.

'More paper,' she had to say to her husband, over and over again, year after year after year. 'More ink.' Thankfully he was a kind, unquestioning man. She assumed that he assumed that she was just writing her letters, though her use of post-age had not increased along with the rest of it, and he hadn't asked why.

Anyway, by the time her second child was three or four years old, there was another project that took up its fair share of paper and ink, too. Well-Well Mountain Island, they called it. She could never even remember who came up with it, exactly. Sometimes, with that boy in particular, she felt both his mind and her own lift right up out of their respective bodies and meet together above to form an idea. She felt that when he talked in his sleep it was in reference to her very own dreams. 'You used to live in my belly,' she would tell this boy, though she had never said such a thing to either of the others. 'Right in there. We waited and waited for you, and one day you finally started to kick your way out.'

The island was a place that on one side was eternally in sunshine and on the other in snow. They drew hundreds of pictures of it. She had saved them all. Aside from the natural changes in Evan's drawings as he grew, the pictures were not really progressively more detailed, and nothing particularly changed with each one. Just picture after picture of a circular island with a line to split it across the middle, a sun casting its rays on the southern half, and snow falling down on the northern. It was the thing the two of them loved the very best to do together. They called it their club. Over the years neither of the other boys would ever join in, and both thought it was so stupid and strange the way she and Evan carried on with it. But there was something so exquisite about it, the way she set her pen down and nearly arrived in that perfect and magical land. She knew her son felt the same.

And the experience with her pages, the ones she wrote – it was so similar that Elspeth was astonished she'd never come to it earlier in life. Years into the project, she found that she loved all these people she wrote as she loved that place she and her son drew. In fact, in a way she loved these people more, because with them some real, tangible amount of loneliness could be abated. But at a certain point far into her story Elspeth realized not only that it didn't all fit under her mattress anymore – at least not inconspicuously – but also that there was a strange but sure pressure within it that something bad must happen. When everyone was out of the house she began to spread her pages under her sons' mattress, too, and she backed up. She made the woman married, but also from an island far off in the center of the ocean. Her husband had found her on a sailing voyage and married her and taken her to live in his castle in this new land, but she had never loved him, and in no time at all she met the other, poorer man of the woods, whom she loved tirelessly. The affair went on and wonderfully on until one foggy night the riders from the castle found the woman with her lover and flung her onto a horse and carried her naked all the way to her husband to expose her indiscretion. At this point in the story, however, Elspeth became utterly stuck. She wanted so badly for it all to end well, for all the people in the story to be good.

Her sister was good. Oftentimes throughout their childhood, Elspeth and Claire would go with the other neighborhood children to follow the lamplighter on his rounds through town, and when he was done, if it was a clear night, the two of them would go off alone into the fields or down to the water to gaze at the stars. It was as they entered their teen years that they began to have what they jokingly referred to as their *philosophy talks* out there in the dark. These talks frequently circled back to the fact that on these nights Claire – despite a belief in God – always felt only more insignificant out there under the majestic sweep. It was a feeling Elspeth could not understand. When she looked up at the stars, she didn't imagine herself as just a speck. Instead she felt called by that firmament, not necessarily singled out but at least seen. By the time she and Thomas had been at it, Elspeth had taken that irrepressible feeling that she mattered as just one more sign that she was not indeed a sinner, and so one night under the stars with her sister she finally told her all about taking her clothes off with him.

'No. Oh, no,' Claire had said, but Elspeth had assured her that it had all been wonderful, every bit of it.

'I don't think it's right,' her sister had said. And 'What if Father finds out?'

'Well,' Elspeth had said. 'God must know, and nothing's happened to me yet.'

'Maybe,' her sister had said. And then, to Elspeth's great shock, 'But isn't it possible that he doesn't care?' And then, even more shockingly: 'Tell me about it again. Tell me how it all happens,' and so Elspeth had tried, but of course the parts couldn't possibly represent the whole of the thing.

When Elspeth left, her sister had sworn she would stay on

forever with her parents, would care for them. 'But what if
you fall in love?' Elspeth had asked.

'I won't.' And then, 'Anyway, so what if I do?' This question, Elspeth had understood right then, had been what set
them apart. It was like a line drawn in the sand. Her sister on
the good side, she on the bad.

In some ways, Elspeth had always wished to be more like her
sister, though even back then she understood that the personality she'd been born to had afforded her much, much more
freedom. But once she had arrived in her new home, she wished
with every bit of her being that she had been more like her sister. That she had understood that something – the shores of
home, for example, that great wide ocean, even that small,
dingy kitchen of theirs – really ought to have meant more to
her than that hot desire she'd fallen into. Just the smell of her
family's linens, or the lilting voice of a person from her home –
she would give anything, now, to get back there.

Anything but her boys, that is. It was harder at first, when
they were just born. With each one of them, she had thought
she'd go mad. Only because she didn't have sleep, not a bit of
it, but understanding that hadn't made it easier. It had been
especially hard with the first, because it had all been so new,
and on top of that she wasn't used to not having her mother
and sister at her side.

But what good was it to think of any of it now? Better to
think of the gentle look they each gave. The feel of their soft
hands as they ran them down her face. Evan, the middle
one, had gone through a spell of hitting her across the face
when he was two. 'No,' she remembered saying, and, 'Please
don't do that.' Also, 'That hurts. That hurts my body and

my feelings.' But at a certain point when he was through hitting her, he would always take that soft little hand and run it down the length of her cheek, then back up and across her forehead, and then down her other cheek. Looking hard at her face the entire time. Testing, almost, if it would still be there, if she would still be there, whole and full of love even after such pain. And it was almost worth it, the hitting, to have him inspect her in this way when he was through.

When she was pregnant with the first she didn't want a second, and when she was pregnant with the second she didn't want a third, but she welcomed each one of them anyway, because what else could she do? But after the third she told her husband that she felt she would eclipse if she had one more. 'What does that mean?' he had asked. 'How can a person eclipse?'

She went to her only neighbor, who, by this time, had also become her only true friend. Mr Bartlett was some twenty years her senior, and had been born in the very farmhouse he still lived in. Apparently, as a boy he had helped to build the barn, which back then had been filled to the brim with livestock. Now he kept only chickens, three horses, two milk cows, five sheep, and sometimes a few pigs for slaughter. His parents had long ago passed, and his five siblings had dispersed to the south and west.

During Elspeth's first year on this new land, Mr Bartlett had been the only person in the entire town to knock on her door in order to welcome her. The first time, he brought a small basket of apples from the tree in his field. Her eldest had been a newborn then, and had screamed and screamed in her arms while she stood in the doorway of her squat house to accept her neighbor's gift. A week later, he returned with a jug of fresh milk. On and on this went, with scarcely a sentence exchanged between the two of them. It wasn't until her first son was nearly a year old that she finally ventured out to knock on Mr Bartlett's door. That day, her husband had been at the mill and her son had suddenly been struck with a burning fever. By then, because of his frequent trips to visit her, Mr Bartlett had carved a shortcut between their two houses. She ran that path through the woods, over the stone wall, and across his field, and knocked on his door while in her arms her child shivered and sweated.

'Elspeth,' he said, and drew her into the room.

Straightaway she saw what she had been missing. His entire sitting room, floor to ceiling, was lined with books. And there at the desk right by her side sat a stack of handwritten papers held down by a glass paperweight.

'You write, sir?' she asked him, then quickly remembered herself. She told him about her son's fever, and without a moment's hesitation he went to the barn and prepared his carriage to take them to the bigger town to the west, where, he said, his lifelong friend practiced medicine.

The ride took two hours, and they passed it mostly in silence, Elspeth terrified the entire way. Yet by the time they finally arrived, her boy's fever seemed to have calmed. She visited the doctor anyway, who examined the boy and applied a white paste that smelled of mint to his forehead and temples, then looked at her gently and asked if she didn't have any friends or family with children of their own. 'Children get fevers, you understand,' he told her.

'Mr Bartlett,' she said. She meant that he was her only

friend. The doctor nodded and said goodbye. On the way home, lightened with relief, Elspeth and Mr Bartlett talked and talked about the books they had read and, when she asked, the one he was writing. It was a history of the town, a lifelong project that his father had begun. When they returned to Middlewood that day, Elspeth went home with her tired child in her arms and a stack of books besides, and after that she walked the trail through the woods to her neighbor's house nearly every day for company.

So it was that some four years later she sat at the table with Mr Bartlett, another newborn in her arms and her two other children on the floor near her feet, and she whispered that she could not bear to have another. He understood. He suited up the carriage, and together they rode the two hours to the west, where once again she went into that doctor's home. This time Mr Bartlett left her there alone, and even insisted that he keep the children with him.

The doctor's home was dark and smelled of fresh-cut wood. On her first visit, she'd scarcely noticed a thing, other than the baby in her arms, but now she saw that dried plants hung in bouquets from the ceiling and that jars of dried plants lined the walls. The doctor sat down heavily and asked her if she was already with child again.

'No, sir,' she said.

'That's a relief,' he told her, and he crossed the room. He opened a drawer in the wall, withdrew a long slip of paper, and brought it to her.

'Pessary,' he said, and pointed to the word. 'Used to kill the sperm or block their passage through your cervix,' he said. 'You do know what that means?'

'Sir,' she said.

'Do not be shy,' he told her. 'This is no place for that.' He pointed again to the paper and showed her that she had a choice: a suppository made of honey and sodium carbonate, which would melt at body temperature to form a shield; or a sea sponge wrapped in silk and attached to a string.

'The cost, sir?'

'Mr Bartlett has paid,' he said.

'No,' she said, her face burning. To have her friend pay so that she might feel some pleasure. But then maybe it was solely protection against her husband's pleasure that Mr Bartlett thought he was paying for? She had changed, she knew, had become reticent in their bed, the fear of another baby overpowering every cell. But as she listened to the doctor an image of the abandon she'd once experienced with her husband passed quickly through her mind. Elspeth understood that what she had previously felt in bed was not what she had been taught to feel; that she did not simply endure; that since childhood she had *wanted*. She left the doctor's home with both options in her purse. When she stepped out into the blinding sun she had expected to see Mr Bartlett and her children waiting for her, but the carriage was not in sight, so she walked across the street, to the small park above the river. There she sat down on the stone bench, and just as she let out a long, relieved sigh, a man sat next to her.

'Lovely day,' he said. 'My name's James Baillie. Pleased to meet you.'

He extended his hand. Inside her purse, the small package from the doctor pulsated. *Should work every time!* the doctor had said, and to her shame she had lit right up.

Now, on the bench above the river, she took James Baillie's hand, then dropped it quickly. She felt there was a certain way he had of looking at her. Just the way the man in her pages, the lover, would have looked at his love. How to describe it? She knew when she saw him that she hadn't gotten it quite right in her story. She stared. Shining black eyes, that was part of it. Full attention paid to her face, her being. She would have to remember this, write it down. Something hidden behind that attention. But what was she doing, looking straight at this man? And with that medicine in her purse?

'Excuse me,' she said to him, and stood abruptly to walk closer toward the river.

'Let me walk with you,' the man said. She meant to say no, certainly not, but to her surprise he said, 'You are from my home, I can tell it in your voice.'

And it was true. He had come from not ten miles north of her Scottish home. Since he'd left, he'd been back and forth across the ocean four times in counting.

'How do you get the money?' she asked. They were walking now, no longer staring at each other, and she was thankful for that. She wouldn't have asked such a question had he been looking at her.

But he didn't seem bothered by her forward manner. He told her that he went up and down the river far to the west, the Mississippi. 'Spell it aloud,' he said. 'Teach your boys to spell it, it's a joy.'

'But your voice,' she said to him. 'There's nothing to it.' She meant of course that it did not sound the least bit Scottish, but the way the words came out made sense to her, too. Empty.

That's how the voices of this land, the ones that didn't sound like their old homes, so often sounded to her.

'Practice,' he said. 'There's more money for me if I have been here for at least a generation.'

'So you lie?'

'I fool,' he said.

Anyway, it led to nothing. She had of course told him about her husband, her boys, right at the start. They said goodbye and she returned to the street, found Mr Bartlett and her children, and that was that. The baby was sleeping in the carriage and the other two were delighting in the hard candy Mr Bartlett had bought for them. She climbed in and they rode home, crossing through the most beautiful country she had seen, on this side of the ocean anyway. Her boys surrounded her and she was content.

But the thrill of that short meeting! When she woke in her home the following day she thought suddenly of that other trip, that other man she had met. John Smith. She thought of the feel of his hands on her hips. The next time she sat down to work on her pages, she found herself writing a letter instead. A letter to him, that first man, but to this new one, too. Some fictional version of both of them combined. *Dear Lover*, she wrote. It would be a part of her book. She didn't yet know where it would fit in, but it would belong somewhere.

As Elspeth's boys grew, Mr Bartlett began to hire them, giving them a small sum of money in trade for feeding and watering the chickens, mucking out the pigpen, weeding the vegetable beds. He also dug up chunks of his perennials that fared well in the shade and gave them to Elspeth so that she might surround her little house in the woods with them. He had taught her to collect seeds from his vegetables so that she might plant herself a garden at no cost.

'But my house is so deep in the woods,' she had said. 'There's scarcely any sun.'

'Let's see what we can do about that,' he had said, and set to work digging up a plot for her on his own property.

Sometimes the two of them would sit in his parlor and read over his manuscript, which, nearly fifteen years into their friendship, he was still writing. There was a time, a handful of years ago, when he had been shunned by the town for speaking out against the church's support of slavery, but now it seemed his project had won him their favor once more. In addition to combing property records and the like, Mr Bartlett had also interviewed every willing resident and written down their stories, no matter the topic, and the town's newspaper had begun to publish bits and pieces of it. Sometimes the stories were so strange that he could not help but laugh with Elspeth about them. Stories of a man's oxen cart being upturned and broken on account of witchcraft; another of a mysterious body rising from the lake on a particular July 4 celebration long ago.

'"Incidences and Odd Occurrences,"' he told her. 'It is my favorite chapter.'

'But those stories can't be true.'

'And yet they are believed by so many,' he said. 'Surely that makes them a part of the town's history?'

'So you believe them?' she asked.

'I believe it is my job to accurately record the impressions of our residents.'

'And what if I told you I'd seen a ghost? Would that become a part of our town's history?'

'But you haven't, my dear,' Mr Bartlett said. 'Your place in this chapter shall be added as soon as you have something to add.'

II

ABOUT A quarter of a mile up the hill from Josiah Bartlett's was a house that carpenters had been building for more than a year. There was a lot of talk about it. The owner was not a man of their town, and no one seemed to even know his name. The house was not like the other houses around, either. 'The style of the queen' is what some people said. High, gabled windows, elegantly carved trim. Elspeth and her boys had liked to go and watch the construction, as had many others throughout town. When the work was complete, it was as though the town itself held its breath, watching that darkly painted house. It was well known that the current mill owner was sick and that he had no heir. Elspeth's husband, along with the other mill workers, worried almost daily over the fate of the mill. Finally, though, Thomas returned from work one day with news that the owner of that mysterious new home had arrived, that he had bought the mill, and that he would take over within a month's time.

'This man will make the mill big,' Thomas told his wife. 'He has bought up all the water rights and all the surrounding land. He wants to change our operations, Elspeth. To double our machinery and our power. Elspeth, he wants to open a foundry for the mill. He intends to carry us all into the next century.'

'I don't know what that means.'

'The best part is that he is from our country! He will understand us.'

'Fine,' she said. What did she care? She had never worried over Thomas's job; it had always seemed obvious to her that the mill would run and the workers at the top would tire those at the bottom right out.

Anyway, she was busy enough with her children. Her youngest had just turned ten, and Mr Bartlett had gifted them with snowshoes for the whole family. There had been an early November snowstorm, and the snow had stuck, and now in their spare time she and the boys spent long, glorious afternoons tramping through the woods, following rabbit and deer tracks. Once they saw the tracks of a wolf. They were sure of it, despite the fact that in their town it was said that the wolves had been killed off years ago. She and her boys kept a fold of paper as they hiked, and when they saw a new kind of track they would draw it down, and then – thanks to Mr Bartlett's books – look it up. So they were sure it was a wolf. Such a rare and wild discovery! They were all excited to tell their father. But when the night bell rang and he came home for supper, he said that Mr Eldridge from down at the mill had seen a wolf and was working on trapping it.

'For meat?' Elspeth asked.

'For kill,' her husband said. He told her that an entire flock of sheep had been mutilated by a wolf.

'No,' she said. 'One sheep. One.' It had been Mr Bartlett's. She told her husband so.

'Elspeth,' he said back, and she and her boys had all understood right then to not speak of the tracks they had seen.

But the four of them saw more. There must have been a pack, and they must have been living close to their house. Elspeth didn't say a word, but it made no difference. Soon enough the town was in an uproar over the animals. She and her children listened to Thomas tell about the pits the farmers were digging, covered with sticks and brush, filled with bait. Yet despite the traps, they continued to see multiple tracks day after day, until one terrible day when they couldn't find even one. Two days later her husband came home to say that Mr Eldridge and some boys had finally trapped a wolf in a hole and shot it dead. Not straight in the head, either. First they shot it in the legs, just to watch it strain and fail to get away. Then they shot it in the chest. They let it bleed and twist in return for the death to that livestock. The pelt, pock-marked with bullets but scrubbed free of blood, now hung right in the center of town. 'Scare off the whole lot of them, that's what for,' her husband said when she asked why anyone would do such a thing.

'What's happened to you?' Elspeth asked him.

'I don't know your meaning.'

'You sound like one of them,' she said.

'One of whom?'

She couldn't say, didn't know how to. It didn't sound real coming from him anyway, this aggression. She felt she could see right through it, could see clearly his need to fit in with the men who ran the mill. Also with the men of this country. His voice, she had noticed, had even begun to change, his sounds beginning to be cut off roughly from their own edges.

Her middle boy cried a little when he saw the first pelt hung in town.

'Do not be like them,' she whispered to him. She repeated it as the madness went on, as the signs went up: VOTED, TO GIVE TEN DOLLARS' BOUNTY FOR A GROWN WOLF'S HEAD, AND FIVE DOLLARS FOR A WOLF'S WHELP, FOR ALL THAT SHALL BE KILLED IN THIS TOWN. Soon, one wolf after another hung from a beam in the center of the street.

'You do not have to ever be like them,' she repeated to her children, each and every one of them.

When the new mill owner took up his post, her husband spoke often of him. John Smith. A common enough name. Still it put a little fear in her. What if he'd kept that envelope with her husband's address all this time and only now come all this way just to find her? Stupid thoughts, really. But then one day she led her boys through the woods to Mr Bartlett's, and when they came out from over the stone wall she saw a figure across the field, strolling up the road.

'Who is that?' she asked her middle child, for he knew more people than any of them did. It was his nature – he liked to traipse around through town and to call in on neighbors unexpectedly. Even as a very young boy he had liked to do so, and he'd always asked so many questions of people – where they had come from and what they worked at, what they enjoyed eating, what they enjoyed reading. The questions struck her as remarkably polite, though she knew he didn't mean it that way, or any way in particular.

'John Smith,' he said plainly. Elspeth watched the man strut toward his new home. That broad stretch of shoulder, that prominent chin, its downward tuck – was she remembering correctly? She became terrified with the thought. Had he crossed an entire ocean in order to take her? (And would she let him? *No. No, no, no.*) Was he here to expose her? Or was this some wild, unlucky chance? She couldn't sleep at night with all her fear.

She went to Mr Bartlett. 'The man,' she said. 'The new mill owner.'

'Trash,' he said.

'How do you mean?'

'He will ruin this village.'

'I'm afraid I know him,' she said. 'From before. From Scotland. More than I ought to have, if you know my meaning.'

'Watch out for him,' he said simply to her. And then, with a bit of a laugh, because at that point none of it had seemed so serious at all, 'He wants to rule the world.'

Well, she had to know if it was really him. She had to see him again to find out. Week after week she thought this, and at the start of December she decided it was time to reclaim her life. She bundled up and headed into town alone, told her boys she was just going for a stroll. Her plan was to stop in at the mill under the pretense that she had a message for her husband.

In all her time here, she had been inside that mill only
once, and it hadn't been so very long ago. Just before the new
owner had arrived. She had remarked to her husband that the
boys would like to see the machinery, so he had arranged a
visit. They had stood on the first floor, the machines roaring
around them, peering down into the wheelpit, watching the
two wheels turn. Her husband's face had lit up when he
pointed to the fly ball governor. His lips had begun to move
and she'd understood that he was explaining the mechanism
to them, but they could not hear him. Still, his face – for a
moment Elspeth remembered the young man she had married. She had forgotten how much he loved this machinery.
There he was, every evening, asking question after question
to her of the books she read, of the thoughts she had, and
she'd never even asked him for a single detail of his work. She
grabbed his hand then, gave it three quick squeezes.

On this day, though, when she walked alone to the mill to
try to glimpse this new John Smith, she didn't make it in. In
fact, she didn't even make it across the bridge into town
before being overcome with nerves and turning right back
around. Not the second or third time, either.

She had even asked her husband more about the man, and
he had simply remarked that John Smith was very efficient.

'What else?' she had said.

'Big ideas. He wants to change the way things run.'

'You've said. Boardinghouses, a foundry. What does it
really mean? When would this actually take place?'

'It's all so complex.'

'Well, what does it all mean?' she had asked.

Her husband had looked at her then. He'd put his

arms around her waist and pulled her in and said, 'I think it's all going to be good for us.' By which, of course, he'd meant that they would have more money to fix up the house, to clear out the land, to finally let some sunshine through their windows.

Over the years, she had schooled all of her children. All of them were now old enough to have some place at the mill – some twenty-five children worked there already – but she wouldn't have it for hers. She had told her husband so, and to her surprise he told her that was fine. 'I want them to be scholars,' she had said. 'I want them to use their minds.'

The children had all gone mornings to the schoolhouse in town, but she had also done as her mother had and taught them at the kitchen table in the evenings. Thanks to the neighbor's collection, she had taught every single one of them to love books. She had taught them many things, but the books had seemed like her greatest accomplishment. In the beginning, she hadn't the slightest idea how to teach someone to read, but then she had just gone along and done it and it turned out that she was quite good at it. So good, in fact, that other children had come to her, too. *How do you do it?* other mothers had asked, as though she had some sort of method or trick. She had been unable to answer the question. But in all her parenting, she thought that perhaps her favorite moment had been when the boys discovered that they could open a book and enter it entirely on their own. To suddenly be able to fit through such a passage! If she could remember for the rest of her life one single moment with each of her boys, one single expression, it would be that. For it had been a moment – with all three of them it had – a single second when the gears in their minds turned and clicked into place and the entire world unfolded infinitely before them.

Finally by mid-December Elspeth abandoned the idea of stopping in at the mill and instead she made her way up the hill to his house and then straight up his porch stairs. It was early evening, not long after the mill bell had rung. She had told her husband what she was doing and he'd thought it wise. A housewarming gift. She trembled as she trekked to his house, a basket of freshly baked sticky buns hung on her arm.

'Why, hello,' he said.

Oh. Red hair, greenish eyes, not him, not him at all. How could she have thought it would have been? All this time and all this fear and now to find she was disappointed.

'You are too kind,' he said. 'Come in.'

'My husband,' she said straightaway. 'He works for you. I have three boys. I heard you were alone.'

'You are too good,' he had said.

And she certainly was, to him. Next she made and delivered a Christmas meal. Six rolls, plus a ham from the very pig she and her boys had raised on her neighbor's property. Four oranges despite the fact that he was rich and she and her boys would have devoured those fruits with the greatest pleasure imaginable.

'Are you trying to buy your husband a better job, little lady?' Mr John Smith asked just then. A smirk, a short jolt of a laugh.

And really, what was she playing at?

Just harmless excitement, she knew that, but she also knew

better than that. She knew she was a woman; she knew what behaviors would and would not be tolerated.

A week after she delivered that meal, her husband announced that they were invited to a holiday party at the mill owner's house.

'All the workers will be there?' she asked. 'In his home?'

'He's different,' Thomas said. 'I told you. He'll run things differently.'

'And the children?'

'Dress them well and bring them along.'

The party was held on a Saturday. Mr Smith drew them in and straightaway he brought them through the crowd of people and up the stairs, saying he liked to give every guest a tour of the entire house. In the upstairs hallway he pointed to a rope that hung down from the ceiling. 'Trapdoor to the attic,' he said, and winked at the boys. 'Save that for another time.' Then he led them through his bedroom to a balcony, which, incorrectly – though Elspeth knew better than to correct him – he called a widow's walk. They stood there together in the cold night air, listening to the sounds below, and he said, 'Isn't it wonderful?' and Elspeth and her family all said yes, yes, it surely was.

Back in the living room, Elspeth looked around at the fine wallpaper, at the strong furniture that he must have had shipped in. And the food! She didn't know who had made it, but it was endless, and the lanterns, too. He had lanterns on every table. It was lovely, really, but then the strangest feeling came over her. Her eyes rested on all the workers and the children as though they were one moving sea. Everyone was dressed in their finest, everyone was smiling. She listened to the hum of their voices, yet she felt as though before her all of it had drifted into some other realm, leaving her behind. It was as though the people and their sounds were on one plane, and she on another, and even if she were to touch them she would not actually connect with them, not even with her own children.

Air.

She looked quickly around the party, then darted back up those stairs, through John Smith's bedroom and back to the balcony. It was a clear night and she stood there leaning over the edge, gazing upward at the stars. She didn't hear him approach. Suddenly, though, his voice was in her ear.

'Enjoying the night?' he said. Had John Smith followed her here, or had he simply happened to find her? She realized as she stood there that there was still a piece of cheese in her mouth, and it was much too large to chew politely. A daughter of a high-up millworker was playing the piano below, a Christmas song Elspeth recognized but never had learned the words to.

Finally she finished chewing and she breathed deeply and she came back to herself just a little bit. She said, 'Why is it that only the girls learn?'

Clearly she was referring to the piano; clearly he understood that. But he said, 'Is there something you would like to learn?'

'I don't know your meaning,' she said quickly. She did, though. She knew it right through. It was a good scene. She would write it down: the party below them something separate, the house and guests inside a snow globe. Or they themselves inside one, just the two of them. The moon full (which was not the truth, it was only about halfway there, but she would write it that way) and shockingly round and close. It would be snowing thick, perfect downy flakes. She would hold her hand out off the porch and catch one and show it to him.

She would write her sister about him, too. Maybe.

He said, 'I get so tired.'

That was it. With that comment, the fantasy passed. Right away she realized. Her husband – there was a man who got tired. This man, his big paycheck, his childless, warm house besides – she'd liked him better before he'd opened up to her.

She said, 'I'm sure you do.'

In the coming days, she would go over and over that phrase. She would lose sleep over it. She would say it aloud when no one was listening, say it in a thousand different tones. *I'm sure you do. I'm sure you do. I'm sure you do.* Had her meaning been so obvious?

He said, 'You watch yourself, missy.'

No one had ever called her that before. Of course, that too could be taken a few different ways. *Missy.* He could still be flirting. She could just giggle in return.

She did.

He said, 'A hundred men could do what your husband does. A woman could. I've eighteen women do already.'

She didn't know enough about her husband's work to know if that was true or not, but she feared it was. Her husband had never been called a machinist, always just a mill hand. She knew he worked the throstle, but now she found herself deeply ashamed to not know exactly what that meant.

She turned away from him. She would head back into the party, would sit in a corner with her ankles crossed and her hands on her lap, and she wouldn't say a thing until it was time to leave. And then only, 'Children, come along.'

'You think you're something,' he said to her before she made it in.

Was that so obvious, too? She did think she was something. She thought she was ages smarter than he was, ages smarter than most of the men around here, in fact. She would have liked to say so. Instead, only, 'It's a fine party.'

No, actually, the terrible truth, she had also said this: 'That's right. I do.' She said it, and then she looked right at him, right into his eyes. A challenge. He laughed in her face.

Her only hope, at the end of it, was that he was the sort of drinker who wouldn't remember in the morning. That night she asked her husband, 'Was it whiskey?' but he didn't even know, he had drunk only the cider from Mr Bartlett that they'd brought along. Unsure what to make of what had happened, for nearly a week she fiddled around the house, anxious over what to do. Even her boys asked her if she wasn't feeling all right. But then, finally, after her husband's full week's work, she calmed. Decided it was nothing.

Until, on Monday night: 'Mr Smith says I'm to take three days off. Says I'm not needed.'

She set right to work after that. In her mind she asked her sister what she ought to do, and on her own she decided that the thing to do was show him that she was nothing more than a woman in a house. She made the rolls, she made the roast. She packaged it all up in the basket and went to deliver it.

'Still trying to buy your husband a better job?'

He brushed his hand against her cheek when he said that. At first she thought he meant with the food. Buy a job by offering food and kindness. It wasn't until she was on the way home that she realized he was talking about another kind of comfort. How could she have been such a fool?

At night she thought:
Would he really try to do it?
How far would I go?
Could I do it?
What if I don't?
What if I do?
What if he made me?
Is there a way, in all of this, to get back to my own country?
And then back to the beginning of all the questions.

On January 7, 1852, Mr Bartlett reminded her of the date. The lunar eclipse! She had written to her sister months in advance to tell her of the event, but now she had nearly missed it with all her worry. She spent the afternoon preparing a picnic. Even her husband would come along. They gathered blankets and layered on all their clothes and stocked the fire and finally at eight o'clock the five of them set out into the cold, the snow creaking beneath their steps. The shadow had already begun to appear on the moon's edge. Their neighbor was in the field waiting with tea and cookies. They huddled up next to him and sank back in the snow, awed as their world shrank and the shadow grew. Elspeth would hold that feeling in the days to come, that sure knowledge that she could leave her body, that she could rise right up and meet her sister – who, somewhere, shared this very same moment and vision – and that in this way the two of them could float, held together by nothing but that vast sky.

The temperature hadn't yet plunged on the day she decided to quit letting her foolish mind get away from her, to quit imagining that any one thing John Smith said or did signified any other, and to just grab the courage to deliver another meal and make it all all right and be done with it. Turkey, squash, rolls, an apple pie. She packed it up and on the way through the woods she practiced her speech. *It was difficult for me, when I first arrived. And you without a wife! My husband and I would like to help you in any way we might.* She knocked.

'Elspeth!'

'Hello, sir.'

'Do come in. You haven't brought more food for me, have you? You spoil me, dear Elspeth.'

'It was difficult for me, when I first arrived in this land. And you without a wife!'

He cut her off then. Or his look did. A strange passage of transparent cold ran through him as clearly as if all the lights of the world had been put out. He said, 'I've just been going through some things. Won't you follow me upstairs? I've got the oddest old vase, Elspeth. It was my mother's. It's just up in the attic, I've stored all my extra things there, and just now I'm wondering how old the vase is.'

Had he ever spoken so much? Or so freely? She couldn't

seem to remember. 'Forgive me,' she said. 'I'm sure I know nothing about that sort of thing, Mr Smith.'

'But you'll come up, won't you?'

'There's enough here for a few meals at least, I should think. If you need more, please do call on us.'

'The vase is from France, I think. Fifteenth century? Sixteenth? I hear you like to school the children. Surely in all your reading you have studied some history.'

'I'm afraid I know nothing about artifacts, sir.'

'But you'll come up, Elspeth,' he said, and so, finally, she did. She went up the stairs before him, and when he directed her to pull the attic staircase down she did, and then she went up those stairs, too. She herself pushed the trapdoor open because he told her to. She stepped in and he followed her and then he dropped the door back down. Freezing up here, and dark. No boxes, no vase. When he pushed her down she fell easily, because she knew it was coming. That day, she could have not even gone inside his house in the first place. That was the worst of it, at least for a while. She could have just knocked on the door and left the basket and disappeared.

On the cold floor, she let it happen. Or that's how it seems to her, in retrospect. Because why did she just lie there, practically motionless? Why didn't she kick, scream, punch? She did bite him, at least, and hard, right on the shoulder. But what else could she do? She was too afraid to do anything else. Her husband, his job. Also, her life. Her boys who needed her. She should have known before. Mr Bartlett had warned her. She should have known. He pulled that skirt right up over her body. When he discovered that underneath the skirt she wore her husband's long john suit, he let out a vicious laugh. When the laugh was over he made a little joke of her dressing like a man and then he tore the wool right open.

'Why else would you come to see me,' he said while it was happening. And while she writhed beneath him, 'That's good, I like it this way.'

Which gave her an idea, somehow. Just a little way to survive. She had read about it in one of the journals her neighbor subscribed to. Just focus herself right out of existence, that was the task. Instead of this whole reality, just choose one piece. The bit of nail that stuck up higher than the rest and rubbed now into the base of her back. Just let her entire body fall into that cold, hard irregularity in the floor. Enter that feeling and no other.

When he was done with her he must have pulled her down the stairs, though she doesn't remember the descent. He opened the front door and pushed her out and at the edge of the porch she fell and tumbled down the three steps.

'Mama?'

Her middle boy. To the others she was only Mother, but Mama always to her middle one. The one who still wanted to fall asleep with his nose buried in her neck, his face covered with her hair.

Behind her, the door to the house had already closed. She stood herself up. *My basket,* she thought. Despite all else, she suddenly thought of how she had loved that picnic basket and that she would never see it again. She smoothed her dress. Evan. There he was. Her dear. Just here in front of her. Couldn't know what had happened. Couldn't possibly be able to tell.

'Mama?'

She leaned over and retched in the snow, and then she stood back up and she said, 'Do not tell your father.'

'What did that man do to you?' he asked.

'What man?'

They were headed up the hill now. Almost to the spot where they would turn off into the woods, onto their own path. She was shaking. 'Enough,' she said, when her son asked again.

When they reached their front door he gathered a bundle of wood from the makeshift shed to carry in and then he said, without looking at her, 'I am not a child, you know.'

She slept for three days. It snowed three feet. Evan tended to her. He told the others she had a fever. On the third day, she stood up. She said to him, 'I am better now.' They cooked a pot of chicken soup together, and while the other boys tramped back and forth in their snowshoes to make the path to the road passable, the two of them worked on their Well-Well Mountain Island drawings. She thought, as they drew together, that they had never drawn people on the island, and maybe it was time to introduce them. She asked him if she ought to and he looked up at her, pen in hand, mouth hung open, eyes somehow drooped in a way she had never seen before.

'Stupid idea,' she said. 'I'm sorry I even mentioned it.'

They kept on, drawing and drawing the entire day, and at the end of it she decided they should hang some of their pictures on the wall.

'Now you've really lost it,' her husband said playfully, and he helped them to nail an entire row of Well-Well Mountain Island pictures across the kitchen.

She slept better that night, less fitfully. But in the morning she woke before the mill bell to a freezing-cold house, but then there was something more, too. It took her only a moment to realize what. It was that strange, loud silence – Evan. His breathing was missing.

Right away she knew where to find him. Her husband was still asleep, and the other two boys. She pulled on her boots and coat and she ran. Thank god her other sons had made that path through the snow to the road.

Not a week before, Evan had beamed while he told the family of the odd schedule the new mill owner had pledged to adopt for himself. He had found it so oddly industrious. Of course Evan would be the one to know the schedule in the first place; of course he would be the one to have asked the questions. John Smith had a new plan. After the New Year he had moved a cot into the mill, and while everyone else was home he was there, pacing the silent floors, thinking, taking notes, envisioning a mill run twenty-four hours a day. Every three hours he would lie on the cot for one hour's rest. Evan had thought it grand, such passion and drive.

Evan. The sun had not yet risen by the time Elspeth reached the small bridge that led into town. From that bridge, she stopped to look around, and it was then that her sensation of fear was replaced with that of immense cold. She could have frozen right there in the shadow of the mill. She almost wanted to. But then the back door to the mill slammed shut and she watched as John Smith chased her boy away from the building.

'Evan!' Elspeth shouted. Her boy. He had been born breech and they had thought he would die, but he had lived. She ran up the back street toward him, and as she did it felt as though the echo of every single step of hers rushed up the side of the building and circled back down, encompassing her. 'Evan!' she shouted again. He had been caught. The man had her boy by the shoulders, but hearing her voice, he turned. 'Evan!' she shouted, and John Smith let go of him. She was twenty feet away, maybe thirty, and her boy had started to move in her direction. It was still not yet dawn, but it felt as though the cold made the dark glow. 'Run!' she called, and just at that moment, as though he had misunderstood the command, Elspeth watched as Evan suddenly turned back toward John Smith, ran, and with incomprehensible force slammed his body into the man. John Smith tumbled forward, onto the snowbank, slipped on the ice, fell, and regained his footing. Elspeth expected him to go back for her son after that, but he retreated up to the top of the small snowbank above the river. Now he stood there towering over her boy, ready to pounce. 'Evan!' Elspeth shouted. John Smith looked up toward her, and Evan grabbed his opportunity. He ran up the bank and once again slammed his full weight into the man. John Smith stumbled backward and fell. Elspeth did not hear a sound as she watched the new mill owner's body tumble down the embankment, over the dam, and into the gushing, ice-laden river.

'Evan,' she said, approaching him. She reached out, touched her mittened hand to his face. There was no evidence of what he had done, none but the atmosphere. It seemed to have inverted itself, overcome now by some dark absence.

And yes, now that she looked around, there was in fact some evidence. Footprints in the snow, clearly a scuffle, anyone would see that. She ran her feet back and forth over the tracks, and then, fearing her prints would be traceable, she lay right down in the snow and rolled back and forth in a fury. It wasn't until she tried to stand back up that she realized just how cold it really was. Her knees, she could scarcely bend them, and her fingers might as well have been cut off. She could not get up. It was like a nightmare in which she opened her mouth and could not scream. She held out her arm.

'Help me,' she mouthed to her son. The mill bell would ring soon. 'Help me,' she said again, and this time some sound came out, and he seemed to wake up. He looked straight at her. She said, 'Do you want them to hunt us like wolves? Do you want them to hang our pelts in the center of town?'

That did it. He pulled her arm and she rose, returning from her paralyzed state. Together they each put one foot in front of the other, faster and then faster still, and soon they had run down the length of the mill and crossed the bridge back to their road. Had they stopped to look, would they have seen the body running downstream beneath them? Or perhaps some blood? She led her son directly to Josiah Bartlett's house. Didn't even knock, just ran straight in and screamed his name.

'Elspeth,' he said, coming down the stairs in his gown, a candle held before him. 'Elspeth, my lord. It's freezing. What's happened?'

'We have killed John Smith,' she said.

'Mama,' her boy said. 'Mama, no.'

'I don't know,' she said frantically. 'I don't know what to do.'

'Is it true?' Mr Bartlett asked, but they did not answer.

'How?' he tried. 'Will they be able to find him?' When still they did not answer, Mr Bartlett gathered her hands into his own. 'I will keep your family safe,' he said. 'Tell me now.'

'You won't,' Elspeth said. 'You can't possibly.'

'There are places a person can go,' Mr Bartlett said without looking up at her. 'There are ways to hide a person.'

'I thought he would be sleeping,' Evan said.

'And he was not?'

'The dam,' Elspeth said now, unsure why she hadn't said it straightaway. 'He's been pushed over the dam.'

'It was I,' the boy said quickly.

'You've got to leave,' Mr Bartlett said. 'We've got to get you out of here.'

For a moment Elspeth thought he meant out of his house. She thought he meant to push them out onto the street and lock the door behind them. But instead he scribbled an address of a church in the West and handed the slip of paper to her. 'I have a sister there. She and her husband,' he said. 'They are good people.'

'How will we get there?' she asked.

'I will take you now to the city. From there you will catch a train.'

'There is a train here.'

'You can't be seen.'

'I don't have the money,' she said. 'My husband hasn't the money.'

At this her old friend went to his office and returned with a spread of blue fabric bound tightly around a stack of money. She peeked inside, said, 'God, no,' and then, knowing she had no other option, tucked it against her breast.

'Hurry,' he said.

'He can't have died quickly,' her son said vacantly.

She took the path across his field, over the stone wall. The mill bell rang just as they entered the woods, its sound so clear it was as though she could see it. Already it seemed the temperature had dropped some ten degrees since she'd found her son. It seemed she could see their breath freeze before them. The top layer of snow had gone completely solid, too, so that their feet would not break through even if they stomped.

'Water,' she said to Evan as they neared the well house. 'You need a drink.' She turned to head that way, but he told her that surely the water would be frozen, and anyway that they didn't have the time, and he was right. Just as their dark house came into view her husband came out the door. It was Friday, and though he hadn't been called back to work yet he was going to see if maybe he wasn't needed to keep things running on this freezing day. In the dim haze of dawn he saw his wife and son and he smiled wide. *This is his last moment,* Elspeth thought, and it turned out it was more or less true. She would never see him stand there so wide open, so free again.

'There you are,' he said thankfully. 'I was worried.'

'We have killed a man,' she said right away. No need to prolong it. No time, either. She couldn't believe how plainly it came out. 'We have killed John Smith.'

———

They packed only one bag – just enough food, just enough dry clothes. Her oldest stood at the door of their small house telling them to hurry, telling them the temperature would not stop dropping.

'It is not natural,' he told them, and Elspeth understood what he meant. There seemed to be no limit to it, as though the earth itself were falling into some cold, bottomless pit. Still, Elspeth went to the cupboard, removed paper, pen, and ink. The ink was frozen, so she found herself starting a fire and huddling before it in order to write. Her husband came to her, told her to quit, told her she had lost her mind, but she would not listen. Mr Bartlett might know this town and also know how to hide a person, but Elspeth would not ever forget those men's hungry, smiling eyes as they'd hung pelts in the street. She would not forget the beasts they could become. She called to Evan, who stood shivering before the wall of Well-Well Mountain Island drawings. He came, and she instructed him to hold her ink. The task seemed to steady him.

'What on earth?' her husband asked, furious.

Her nostrils were columns of ice. She could no longer feel her hands, could not even open her palm to let go of the pen. She did not look at the words she wrote, just moved forward, singleminded before the ink refroze. She asked them all, 'Are there still any wolves around?'

'Elspeth,' her husband demanded, but knowing he was powerless, he answered her question. Told her they claimed to have killed the last one just last month. 'A final bounty of thirty dollars, you remember,' he said.

'Is there another animal like them, then?' she asked.

'Dogs?' her youngest said.

'Dogs are pets.'

'Foxes?'

'No.'

'Bobcats?'

'No.'

Finally Evan tilted his head up toward her and said lightly, 'Coyotes?'

'What's a coyote?' she asked.

'It's that journal of the West he loves,' her oldest called from the door. '*Commerce of the Prairies*. It says there's a different kind of wolf. *Coyote* is the name.' He spoke calmly, and she understood that he was doing this with all his strength, that he believed his mother had lost her mind and that his acquiescence would be their quickest path to escape. So be it, she had a purpose. She said, 'Tell me quickly what you know about them.'

'Bloodshot eyes,' her oldest said. 'That's what Melville says, I think. I think they're the same as prairie wolves.'

'Well, what do they eat?' she demanded.

'Scavengers, I guess. Eat anything.'

She wrote and wrote. Her family yelled at her, but it didn't take long. When the freezing rain started her oldest demanded she come, and finally she listened. She folded up the papers and tucked them against her breast, alongside the money. The dim morning light that had arrived less than an hour ago had vanished again, and so had the moon. Elspeth rose and crossed the room, but Evan did not follow her.

'Come now,' she said to him, but he wouldn't move. 'Evan,' she said. Her husband looked at her and shook his head. He went to the boy, picked him up. Immediately the boy's arms and legs wrapped around his father, and his face sunk into his father's neck. In this way the two of them walked out. Elspeth was the last to leave. The cold air hit her like a wall. She turned against it and closed her door for the last time. Next she walked to the shed, took up one small log in each hand, and threw them at each of their two windows, breaking the glass in.

'Elspeth!' her husband yelled, Evan still in his arms. She told him to quiet, and then she stomped in front of him and led her whole family away from their home.

In the barn, Mr Bartlett had already suited up his horses.

'Cover yourselves,' he told them as they climbed into the cart. 'Every inch,' he said, and then, once they were all settled, he walked around the cart to make sure that not a spot of them was visible. Surely his care was in part due to the temperature; it was already so far below freezing. But as he took his seat, Elspeth heard him talking to himself. *Just out to deliver extra hay to the Johnsons,* he was saying. *Animals liable to die without it in this cold snap.* A little rehearsal. She understood. It was just in case they should meet someone on the road.

But there was no one, not the entire way. They reached their destination at around noon. The temperature was some 30 degrees below. Truly a wonder that Mr Bartlett survived up there in front, driving the horses through the frozen world. When they were stopped completely he came around and drew the blankets off of them, then pointed and ran against the cold into the station to purchase their tickets. When he returned to them, he stood before Elspeth to tell her the next step, but it was as though the ungodly cold had frozen their ears, or words. She could not hear him. It took three tries before she understood: All the trains had stopped; they would have to spend the night.

'You go,' Elspeth said, her voice high and loud against the cold.

'I can't go back in this.'

'You can't be with us,' she yelled. 'Goodbye.' She gathered her boys one by one, even her husband, and nudged them into a herd. All of them too frozen and shocked to protest. Then, before pushing them along toward the nearest hotel, she turned to the neighbor one last time and from the folds of her dress she removed the pages she had written. She handed them to him and leaned in close and gave him his instructions, and then she returned to her family.

'Elspeth!' he called, but she would not turn back.

PART THREE

Henrietta

SHE HAD wanted to go to Montana, but it turned out she wasn't ready for all the effort it would take to get there. Instead, at the bus station, she asked how far the next bus was going, and the woman said, 'Depends which direction.'

'North,' the girl had said, and Bangor, Maine, was the answer.

'Is it a big city?' the girl asked.

The woman shrugged. 'It's way the hell up there,' she said.

'I will give you one thousand dollars if you do not tell that you ever saw me,' the girl said plainly. She hadn't planned to say this, but it had suddenly struck her as a necessity. She was so cold. Cold right down inside her bones.

'Where does a girl like you get that kind of money?' The woman looked her over. 'Up to no good, written all over you,' she said.

'Take it or leave it,' the girl said, and thank god the woman took it. The girl told her to hang on one minute, and then she went to the public bathroom and opened her duffel and dug to the bottom, where she'd hidden the briefcase, and she opened that and counted out the cash and brought it back to the woman all folded up in a brown paper towel. No idea if the money was real or not. She had already worked for three hours cutting the bills and still only ten thousand of the dollars were cut. She could have done it faster, but she had needed to be so careful, and out in the woods she had only had that small pair of scissors from the twins' room, and besides, when the rain had started she had needed to tent herself beneath her jacket in order to continue cutting, and it had been an altogether terrible plan. At least five bills had been soaked through.

After she handed the money over and bought her ticket, she asked the woman for a few dollars' change in quarters, and then she bought two Snickers bars, a bag of potato chips, and a bag of peanuts from the vending machine. It hadn't been an easy task. She'd dropped her quarters over and over again as she tried to get them into the machine. She was trembling so badly. Cold, yes, but also afraid. Afraid the bus would not run, afraid it would. She is astonished, really, when she looks back on it, that she went through with it at all.

'I love you because you don't care,' Kaus had said one time. She thought of that as she sat there on the dirty blue plastic seat, waiting for the bus. She did care, didn't she?

Eventually she went to the water fountain and took a long drink, and then when she lifted her head back up there the bus was. It was 4:30 a.m. Outside, the freezing rain that would last nearly a week had already begun to beat down so loudly that she couldn't even hear the driver yelling to her. But she did see him calling out, waving his arms. His meaning was clear – he wanted her to stow her bag. She just shook her head and boarded. She would not let go of that bag for her life.

It was slow going, but because of the rain her view out the window was as much a blur as it would have been had they been traveling one hundred miles per hour. Better this way, she'd thought, easier to say goodbye to a landscape hardly visible.

She had almost been caught. In the woods she'd heard footsteps and had thought it was him, but then she'd heard her father's voice and she'd scurried across to the dip in the land, that old dumping pit that she knew her sister liked to spy on her from. Why hadn't her father looked there?

The bus slid a few times, its tail kicking out toward the ditch, and when they approached a stop sign the driver had to pump the brakes long ahead of time. It was a miracle that the bus still ran in that weather, though she wouldn't use that word. It was lucky; it was strange; no miracles here. She had been up all night, but still she kept her eyes open the entire trip. By the time they reached the coast the rain was softer anyway. Not so frozen. No one sat next to her; the bus was nearly empty. Just one woman spread out a few seats ahead, sleeping since she'd boarded the bus, and a long-haired man she didn't want to make eye contact with all the way at the back. She was directly in the middle. She wanted to ask someone – the driver, because who else? – about the place they were headed to. She had been such a fool. Used all her focus to get to this point, and she had forgotten entirely to look beyond it. When the bus stopped at a rest area she got out and asked in the gas station for a newspaper for Bangor, and even though they were still some three hours away they actually had one. She got back on the bus and spread the paper out over her duffel on her lap and began to look at the ads. All she needed, for now, was a place to live. And food, clothes. That would be enough for more than a few months.

At least she had counted carefully. So long as it wasn't fake, or so long as no one caught her with fake money, she had one hundred thousand dollars. She would be all right.

In the paper, there were so many ads – apartments, houses, roommates. Nothing like the occasional ad she'd seen in her own town's paper. Seeing it all, she felt suddenly and totally desperate. She left the paper in her seat, carried her bag, and before even considering what she was doing she scooted up toward the driver to ask about Bangor. How big was it?

'Oh, I don't know,' the man said. He was big, stocky and overweight, and for no reason at all Henrietta found this some-what comforting. 'I've never been good at that sort of thing.'

'Is it a city?' she asked.

'Course. Not so much as it once was, though.'

'Is there somewhere else I could go?' she asked. What was she saying, giving herself up like this? They'd be looking for her, she had better shut up. 'Somewhere I can . . .' she began again, but then she trailed off.

'What are you up to?' the driver asked, and caught a glance of her in his mirror. 'What's your name?'

She hadn't thought of a name yet, and she didn't particularly want to change her name anyway. So rather than answering, she said, 'I'm going to visit my grandmother, she's just moved up there, and I was just wondering if I might be able to escape the city with her to go see the ocean.' There, now. She was com-ing back to herself a bit.

Eventually, once she got him talking, the driver told her about a farm where his niece had worked. It was in a place called South Harbor. Sheep, chickens, acres and acres of flowers and vegetables. And right on the water. They plowed the fields with horses; they gave quaint little cabins to their workers.

Okay, she had thought. *A farm in South Harbor. I can get work there.* And then she'd thought, *Oh god, you can't work on a farm with a baby. And then: Well, it's not as if the baby will be born soon.*

Maybe, if she had a girl, she could name it Henrietta. And then it wouldn't be like she had lost her own name. But then that would be crazy, wouldn't it?

She had waited for him like they'd planned. She had wondered, as she sat there freezing by their sugar maple, if he had misunderstood the location. But he wouldn't have done that. Neither of them would have forgotten this particular spot in a hundred years, a thousand. As it got to be closer and closer to the time she knew the buses would start up again, she had been forced to decide. She had almost stayed. She had pressed the button to light up her watch in order to see the seconds pass. At 3:45 a.m., she'd felt more than anything else that she wasn't willing to lose another baby. Not that she wanted to have one, not at all, not really. But she wasn't going to not have one again. She ran down the road, past her field. She didn't look at her house. Better not to. Her parents' light would be on just then, her mother just sitting up in her embroidered flannel nightgown to say 'Where is she?' She ran over the bridge, all the way to the far side of town. Slipping the whole way, wishing she had had the sense to head down earlier. She fell twice, and she was freezing. By the time she got to the station she found out the bus was running late anyway – of course it would be – so once she'd dealt with her ticket and the woman behind the counter, she'd had a little time to get cleaned up in the bathroom. She had packed light – only the money, the one book, and three changes of clothes in total. But what to do with the soaking clothes? She didn't want to soak everything else in her bag. And she couldn't leave them, people would find them, and then they would find her. Finally she did the grossest thing she had ever done in her life. She took the trash bag out of one of the bathroom cans, dumped all its contents into another one, and then sealed her wet clothes in that dirty bag and put it in her duffel.

In Bangor, the buildings were big, as big as those in Boston, it seemed. The streets were wide, almost welcoming, and she thought that she might just like to stay on in the city. She could go to shops in the morning, drink coffee, that sort of thing. She could join some kind of club.

But then this was only based on that quick ride through town on the bus. She didn't really know a thing; she hadn't gone walking around, and now she was in a motel at the outskirts with a view of only parking lots. It was raining so hard here. In between looking out the window she watched TV.

She had thought she would see herself on the screen, at least on the news channel, but she didn't, not ever.

By the time she fell asleep, TV still on, she had been up for more than forty hours. She had a knife that Kaus had given her a long time ago, a small thing that folded into its blue case, and the case had a little butterfly on it. She kept it under her pillow while she slept. Her sleep was fitful, and she still felt so cold, even though she'd taken a hot shower. In her dream, she had stolen a baby from a grocery store and put it in a paper bag, but when she'd arrived home with it she'd been afraid to take it out and put it on the counter. She opened her eyes and stood and walked straight to the shower, took another long one, and then she packed up all the motel toiletries, including the soap she had just used, because it was what her mother would have done.

She had meant to venture out after that shower, but instead she took out the one book she had brought along. She hadn't read a book in who knows how long, but she had been so used to seeing her sister read that when she'd left the Hennesseys' and run into her house, claiming to be searching for the Ouija board but really packing, she'd just stuffed the book in her bag, a little reminder. *Flowers in the Attic.* She had found it in her own bedroom just that summer. It had been in her closet, on top of her little plastic set of drawers, and it had been so obvious that Jane had left it there in the midst of snooping. As punishment, Henrietta had hidden it and never given it back. She had thought Jane would have assumed her parents had taken it from her, and that she would throw a fit about it and maybe even tear the house apart, desperate to get to the end of the story. But then Jane never did say a word about it, and Henrietta more or less forgot. Now she lay down on the bed and opened it up. But instead of reading the words, she just rested her face right up against the pages and thought of Jane and fell asleep again. When she woke this time she got the phone book out and ordered a pizza with jalapeños on it. Twenty minutes later, the knock at the door made her heart stop for a moment. She peeked out from behind the curtain and of course it was just the delivery boy. She paid him much more than was due because she didn't want him to linger making change, didn't want him to see her face and recognize her from a picture. Not that there was a picture out there. But still. There must be one somewhere, mustn't there? She ate the whole pizza, and then she slept once more, and then, finally, she put her duffel on her shoulder and left her room. She held a newspaper over her head as she ran across the parking lot in the rain. It was 1:00 in the afternoon on her third day gone.

'Which way to the ocean?' Henrietta asked the woman in the motel office. There was a beaded door behind the office desk, and behind that Henrietta could hear a television. Incense burned somewhere nearby. The woman pointed to her left.

'Are there any beaches I can walk to?' Henrietta asked.

The woman laughed and asked Henrietta if she even knew where she was, and then she finally took out one of those little free tourist maps with all the shops and restaurants on it and showed her that they were some twenty miles from the ocean.

Henrietta just stood there looking at the paper. Pretending to inspect it, but really unable to see anything in front of her. What to do, what to do.

'Do you know of a farm?'

'Sorry?'

'One with sheep and chickens and vegetables. I heard about it.'

'I don't understand.'

Henrietta hadn't even cried when he never showed up. She hadn't cried when she walked by her house for the final time, hadn't cried when she'd fallen on the ice and gotten soaked to the core, hadn't cried in she couldn't remember how long. Had she even cried since she was a little girl? Now she felt on the verge of it. Maybe the woman could tell. She said softly, 'You mean a particular farm?'

'On the ocean,' Henrietta said.

'I suppose there are a lot. I'm sorry, honey.'

She had already booked the room for one more night, but now she just walked out of the office and back to the bus station. She didn't even hold the paper over her head. Didn't care if she melted right into rain, if she disappeared. At the counter she said she wanted to go to the ocean.

'Okay,' the woman said.

'Okay,' Henrietta said.

'Well, where?'

There was a map under the glass on the counter, no words, just route lines and blue dots to mark the destinations. She didn't want to take too long, look any more suspicious than she already did. Quickly she pointed to the biggest dot.

'Ellsworth?'

'Yes.'

In Ellsworth, her motel was at least a little nicer. A cleaner tub, softer sheets. She also got the paper every day, and even though there were lots of ads for places to live, she didn't call anyone. She just slept and watched TV. But then two nights in she woke up with a pain that made her double over. When she could walk she ran to the bathroom, sure that there would be blood, but there was none. She stayed up the rest of the night, checking. In the morning she found the phone book and called a taxi to take her to the hospital.

'I'm pregnant,' she said at the front desk.

'Well,' the receptionist said. 'What can I do for you?'

'I don't know what I'm supposed to do,' Henrietta said. She thought of running out of the place, but she did as she'd been told – fill out the paperwork, wait. She used her real name but had to invent an address. Already she was amazed at how easy it could be to disappear. Eventually the receptionist came over to her and said, 'Insurance?'

'No.'

The woman brought a flyer over to her. 'Go to this place,' she said. 'They'll take care of you. They won't charge you much. Probably nothing.'

'But is it a hospital? I want to have my baby in a hospital.'

'Well, you go to this place for your appointments and learn how you have it, and when the time comes you come in here and have your baby. Save you some money that way.'

'But can you check now?'

'Check what?'

'On the baby,' Henrietta said. 'I can pay.'

Soon a nurse brought her into a room and lay her down and lifted her shirt and said, 'Do you know how far along?'

Henrietta shrugged and shook her head.

'Do you know how many missed periods?'

She shook her head again and told the nurse that her periods had never been regular, and then she said, 'There was pain.'

The nurse said they would have to perform an early ultrasound. She told Henrietta to change into a gown, and then she left the room. A few minutes later a doctor came in, another woman, thankfully. She pressed and felt around on Henrietta's belly and she listened and said, 'Still too early to hear a heartbeat.' She put Henrietta's feet in the stirrups, and she felt around inside with the ultrasound probe while she kept her eyes on the computer screen. When she was finished she removed her gloves and washed her hands and patted Henrietta's arm and told her to sit up and get dressed. After she had left the room and come back in again she sat down across from Henrietta and she said, 'Do you want this baby?'

Henrietta shrugged, unsure of how exactly to answer.

The doctor told her the baby would be there by summer. 'You're in the first trimester,' she said. 'You're hungry. If you want this baby, you need to eat. Your baby is growing organs. It is building a heart and a liver and kidneys and lungs. Do you understand? Meat and vegetables and fruit and milk and cheese. If you want this baby you have got to eat and you have got to take vitamins.'

Henrietta nodded and left the room with a slip of paper telling her which vitamins to take. In the lobby she called for another taxi. At the grocery store she asked him to wait in the lot. Inside, she walked up and down the aisles wondering how the hell she would ever be a mother if she didn't even know how to cook chicken, fish, anything. And anyway, there was no way to cook in the motel. She bought her vitamins, plus four apples and a head of broccoli, and then she went back outside. Back at the room, she ate everything she had bought. Even ate the woody broccoli stalk. Then she looked out the window, across the street. She put her shoes back on and walked across to McDonald's.

There was one of those indoor playgrounds there, with a slew of children inside. Henrietta watched them for a while before taking her newspaper from her duffel. This time, when she looked at the ads, she stood right up and walked to the payphone and put her dime in and dialed.

A caretaker. A house way up the coast. On the phone, the woman asked lots of questions and Henrietta was reminded of just how good she was at lying. 'I've just finished college,' she said effortlessly. 'Veterinary science,' and, 'Hard work, I'm ready for a bit of a break.' They decided to meet the following day. As soon as she put the phone down she rushed to the counter and asked for a pen and paper, and she wrote down the time and the address of where they would meet, and the phone number from the paper, too, just in case. Then she walked up the road to the little strip mall and bought herself a new outfit for the meeting, plus a new winter jacket.

They met in a coffee shop downtown. The weather was cold, unbelievably so, and so windy and gray, but Henrietta walked there because she didn't want the woman to see her getting out of a taxi. It took her nearly an hour, just pushing against the wind. She had her duffel with her, of course. She had been a fool to not buy herself some sort of respectable bag while she'd been at the store. But then the woman didn't even seem to notice. Henrietta just stepped into the coffee shop and the woman flagged her down, ushered her into a seat, and said, 'I had a feeling that was you.'

She was old, likely in her eighties, and she said her children had kicked her out of her own house. 'They think I need to be in a home,' she said bitterly. 'I thought of getting a man for the house, but you know what, I like the look of an independent woman.'

Henrietta, she meant. Of course. Henrietta, an independent woman.

'You don't have to do much. My children want to sell it, but not over my dead body. Or over my dead body, I suppose. There's a list of everything you'll need. Plumber, snowplow man. You just have to keep the place warm, make sure the pipes don't freeze, keep the mice out. Get a cat if you want.' Then the woman laughed and said, 'Hell, get a lover.'

Henrietta turned red. Was it that obvious, the kind of girl she was?

The woman said, 'You have a car, don't you?'

'Yes.'

'Well, go on up there, why don't you. See if you like the look of things. Slide open the barn door, there's a key to the back door on the eastern wall. You just go up there and have a look and see if it suits you and then you call me again.'

At the motel, Henrietta showed the woman at the desk the address of the house. 'How long to walk?' she asked.

The woman shook her head, scoffed. 'That town's nearly two hours away by car,' she said.

'What's it like there?' she asked.

'Nothing is what,' she said. 'You like nothing? Better pack your groceries, that's what I say.'

For an entire day, Henrietta lay on the bed in the motel room, wondering what she ought to do. Finally she called that old woman back up. She said, 'My car broke down. Do you know where I can get another?'

The man who owned the garage was named Jaime. He looked her over and said, 'You don't look fourteen.'

'I'm not fourteen,' she said.

'Ha,' he said loudly, and then he led her to a little rusty blue two-door car parked in the grass behind his shop. It was a stick shift, which, luckily, Kaus had taught her to drive. It was one of the things no one had known, ever. That at night, when she snuck out, he would take his father's car and the two of them would drive right out of town, all the way up the river to the lake a half-hour away. They'd swim naked in the dark, and then they would just stand there in the soft night air and let their bodies drip off. Back then, Kaus had told her she would need to know how to drive, and he had been right. He had told her she would need to know lots of things, that she would need to know how to take care of herself. From the start he had been shocked by how little she knew about how to do that. 'You,' he would say. 'How do you know so little?'

It was also back then, on one of those nights when she took

the wheel and drove recklessly, laughing, filled up with a new kind of happiness, that he'd first told her she didn't care about anything. That he liked that about her. She had never said anything to him about it, but she thought of it still.

'You're not quite done, you know,' the man said after she had handed the money over and signed the papers. 'You've got to register it.' And then, 'You do have a license?' He kicked at the plates. 'These plates are ten years expired plus some.'

'Can I just drive the car over to register it?'

He shrugged. 'Your choice,' he said. 'Probably won't get caught, but up to you.'

She took the car and left. She stopped at a gas station and finally she bought herself a map, ashamed she hadn't thought of doing so until just that moment. It was more than a two-hour drive, plus some extra time to find the road, but when she did she woke right up. It was a dead end, a tunnel of dwarfed pines and gray-green moss that shimmered with dew, and it was actually more like a dirt driveway – her own driveway, soon – than a road at all. It was the sort of forest she imagined Jane would have liked. Magical, otherworldly. When it opened up on the other side it was to a high field of tall, sharp grass and that house that stood singular at its crest. Below was ocean in three directions. Henrietta, seeing the house, thought she must have the wrong address, so she turned the car around quickly and drove back down to the road and checked the mailbox number, then drove farther down still, retracing her steps all the way to the sign that announced she'd entered the town. Of course the house looked okay to her. Of course. When she got back to it she raced to the barn and slid the door open and found the key and hurried inside, feeling like she had finally gotten to the finish line of the terrible game she had started more than a week ago now. She let the door hang wide open as she raced around and tried every chair in the place, every bed. There was a sign on the front of the house, *1776,* and it had all been perfectly preserved – or restored, she never quite knew which. Thick, ancient windows, maple floors, a beehive oven in the brick of the fireplace. A woodstove in nearly every room, and quilts, and furniture upholstered in bucolic scenes: men with their hunting dogs, women and children out for an afternoon picnic. It was all too much. Straightaway she found the phone and called that woman up and said yes, yes. She said she felt she could stay on there forever.

In that house, Henrietta officially decided that in order to be a mother she had better know how to roast all the typical meats and to make macaroni and cheese, that sort of thing. There was no TV at that house anyway, so she didn't know what else she was going to do. There were lots of cookbooks, and there was a grocery store some twenty minutes away. There was also a little hardware store, and in addition to tools they sold some clothes and some things women would like: hand mirrors, makeup, glossy magazines. Henrietta bought herself light pink nail polish and a manicure/pedicure kit, and in another two days she went back to the store to buy a few more colors of polish. She also spent hours walking the property, and for this she'd bought some wool socks and rubber boots and some pants that were meant for a fisherman. There wasn't much snow, just cold, bitter rain, and keeping the house warm and dry kept her busy enough. She'd pulled a mattress out of one of the bedrooms and put it on the floor in the living room, and that way she had to heat only that room plus the kitchen. She would lie there on the mattress and look out the window at the ocean below for hours, thinking of nothing at all.

Every time she went to the grocery store, she got the paper from the city, and she'd sit in the car and flip frantically through it, searching for any mention of herself. There never was one.

She wasn't sure if that made her miss her family more or less. She should have left them a note, she thought. Maybe if she'd left a note, they wouldn't be as angry, which meant that maybe then they would look for her. But then one night she woke up with the realization that she had actually left one – or at least she thought she had. That practice one, the one she'd considered leaving but then decided against – she was sure she'd left it in that box in the fireplace in The Den. After she remembered that, every single day she would repeat, 'Please find my note, Jane, please find my note,' as though she believed in that sort of message or prayer.

But then why did she even leave? Had it even been necessary? Would her mother really have forced her to go through that whole terrible thing again? She sat up wondering that sometimes, too.

With her clothes on, it would still be imperceptible to others, but Henrietta could see the definite roundness of her belly now. Sometimes she felt that to admit there was a baby in there would be to make it disappear, and that was just one more thought that terrified her. Not that she wanted to have a baby any more now than she had at the start – she was only a child, after all. She knew that as well as anyone. But now the thing was in her, growing.

Sometimes Henrietta feels like all her life it has been her fate to leave. When she used to drive at night with Kaus she would always say, 'Just keep driving. Go far away.' He never would, though. Loved his grandmother too much, wanted to care for her. But Henrietta – even when she was younger, when she would walk in the woods or steal a ride on her father's horses, she would always think of just going and going and never coming back.

She had left her family in November, and by January she was certain she could feel a flutter. At first she knew it was just her baby spinning around in there, but then, all alone in that big, windy house, she convinced herself that it wasn't movement at all, but a signal of some horrible trouble within. Finally she called the place that receptionist at the hospital had told her about. The Birth Room. When the woman answered, Henrietta said, 'I'm pregnant.' In response, the woman practically jumped through the phone with congratulations. Henrietta told her quickly that it had been an accident, and then she made an appointment for the next day. She said she could feel something, and the woman said, simply, 'Well, there you go. You've got a baby in there.'

The place was all the way back in Ellsworth, which she

hadn't returned to since coming to the house. As she drove she repeatedly thought she must be headed the wrong way. It was that the drive was so much more beautiful than she'd remembered, the ocean so much grander. In one sense, she had become accustomed to such a view – in her new house, she could see the open ocean from nearly every window. But somehow, up in that house, she had come to see that ocean as separate, as water that encircled her spit of land and nothing else, as though even the earth's immutable features now held her apart from the rest of the world. Now, as she headed toward the big town, with the ocean at her side nearly the entire way, she was forced to admit that she was not nearly so disconnected as she might have thought. It made her want to pull over, to postpone the journey, because as she drove she could not stop picturing the people of the town below just waiting for her arrival, ready to trap her and drag her back off to where she belonged.

But then that wasn't an entirely bad vision. Besides the fear, there was a little seed of hope tucked into it.

But no matter – fear, excitement, she forgot it all. She went into that place and lay back on the purple couch and the midwife put some kind of speaker contraption to her belly and that little thing's heartbeat just filled the room. There it was, a whole, entire heart inside her belly.

The childbirth class at The Birth Room began in March, when Henrietta had been on her own for nearly half a year. By now she really could cook: She could make a pie and its crust, she could stuff and roast a turkey, she could bake a moderately good loaf of bread. It made her think of Jane. Really, so much of her life alone did. She'd even begun to read, and had already read every book the library owned on babies. She was excited to go to this class – felt an unexpected fascination in the growing baby. Before leaving she dressed carefully, as though it was her first day at a new school. She watched the tide coming in as she drove, and the sun gleaming off the water. It was a familiar trek by now – she'd been having appointments every other week since January – but the beauty of it continued to surprise her, and just now it filled her up, so that by the time she arrived she was wrapped in a new kind of feeling. Happiness, maybe. She was going to meet other pregnant people like her. The waiting room was lined with glossy photos of newborn babies and their deliriously happy parents, and for the first time as Henrietta walked in she could imagine herself up there among them.

She was late, though. She realized it as soon as the door shut behind her, ringing its bells, and faces from down the hall peered out. So many women were already there. And, worse, they all had their partners – their husbands – with them. They all had jobs and houses and plans, and surely they all had freshly painted nurseries and brand-new cribs. They sat snugly on the couches and chairs that lined the perimeter of the room. She stood awkwardly in the doorway as they went around the circle introducing themselves – name, due date, profession, that sort of thing. There was an accountant, a hairdresser, a few fishermen, lots of future stay-at-home moms. And Henrietta: single runaway. They had all already turned to her. She pushed herself harder against the doorframe, and when they still wouldn't look away she said, 'My name's Henrietta and I live way the hell up there.'

The bells on the front door rang again just then, and finally everyone peered past her to see who else had walked in.

And so, Alicia. Happy, perky, poor Alicia. She had a small frame, even smaller than Henrietta's, and a huge belly, and she wore a man's T-shirt and bright green track pants that snapped up the sides. Over the coming weeks the T-shirt would change but the pants would remain the same. She pushed herself right into that room and squeezed onto the couch, and when prompted she announced proudly that she worked as the clerk at a gas station. Her hair was a bright, shocking blond, which Henrietta assumed to be the result of bleach but later learned was pure nature. She too lived way the hell up there – she actually phrased it just as Henrietta had – and because she and Henrietta were the only ones without partners, they were paired together for the remainder of the monthlong class.

'What do you do?' Alicia asked Henrietta as she practiced squatting on a birth stool. In another few months, Henrietta would be holding Alicia's hands as Alicia moaned naked atop this very stool.

'The pelvis may be bone, but it shifts during labor,' the instructor said. 'The pelvis can do amazing things.'

'I need a job,' Henrietta said, because working did seem like the most normal thing to do.

Henrietta said she was twenty years old, but Alicia was honest about her age – or at least Henrietta thought she was. Alicia was eighteen. That evening, they moaned lowly together, and they practiced that quick, horselike sputtering, and together they were shocked to learn that after they pushed their babies out they would still have to push out an entire placenta. 'No fucking shit,' Alicia said in front of the whole class, when the instructor told them how much blood they would lose. 'My sister,' she said, 'she went all the way back to the hospital. She thought she'd lost an organ or something.'

Alicia's whole family still lived in the northernmost reaches of the state, and none of them knew she was pregnant. In Henrietta's mind, this put them in roughly the same boat, minus the briefcase of money, of course. So it was that they became friends. In the parking lot, after seeing the sad state of each other's car, they decided that since they both lived in roughly the same area, they might as well carpool.

Throughout the following week, Henrietta found herself looking forward to the next class, to some company. She even picked up Alicia's phone number a few times, considered calling just to talk or even to invite her over, but she decided to wait. When Wednesday finally arrived she drove early to the gas station and found Alicia waiting in front of the pumps. She had a bag of salt-and-vinegar chips to share and a bottle of iced tea for each of them. Before they pulled out, Alicia pointed out back to the trailer she rented, told Henrietta it was a shitbox but it was her own.

And then, 'I almost forgot, I found you a job! You know Josephine's?'

Henrietta did not.

'Fancy restaurant,' Alicia said. 'Least the cook thinks it's

fancy, but he's full of shit.' She said she'd known the man forever, and that he'd just told her they were looking for a
waitress. 'I told him you'd go in. What do you think?'

On Friday she went into the restaurant. She didn't need to,
not at this point, and what with the baby coming it probably
didn't make any sense, but other than wanting to appear normal, she also wanted to feel that way. Anyway, her father had
worked in a kitchen her entire life; to say she had experience
wasn't totally inaccurate. The cook called the owner, he came
in and shook her hand, and within five minutes she had a job.
No questions about the growing belly. She didn't see the
owner again the entire time she worked there.

The restaurant was the sort for tourists, opened only Thursday through Sunday, and it wouldn't get much business until
high summer. Just now – March, April – Henrietta rarely saw
more than five tables a shift. She was the only waitress. The
cook's name was Timothy Vallilee.

'Say it with me,' he said when they met. 'Val-li-lee. Like
Galilee.'

He had a brown wavy mullet and he wore fluorescent,
jungle-patterned chef pants. He was fifty-some-odd years old,
and he'd spent his entire career cooking at low-quality, over-
priced tourist restaurants that would keep him living where
the fishing was good. This particular spot was his favorite;
over the years he'd returned to it at least a dozen times. Most
recently he had returned to it from a 'mistake' in Alaska.

Timothy pronounced *marinara* sauce *mart-nara* without
knowing that was incorrect. He slapped Henrietta's ass with

his towel each time she walked by. Still, she liked him. She was on a barren spread of earth, beautiful but arctic, and aside from the loneliness, she always felt just one step away from being swallowed whole by the ocean. Knowing Timothy – just knowing one more person – seemed to help.

One time, Henrietta went to Timothy's cabin after close. She brought Alicia with her. It had been built as a vacation spot – a little summer shack in the woods not two minutes from the restaurant. This was still early spring, the air so wet and penetrating that Henrietta felt even her skin would never dry off. He'd hung woolen blankets over the windows to keep the heat in, so that while they sat there together in the living room it felt more or less like they were in a cave. Timothy smoked pot and played his electric guitar, and Alicia seemed to be having a good enough time, but after about an hour or so Henrietta was so disgusted by the combination of their pregnant bellies and the noise and Timothy and his smoke and beer that she told Alicia it was time to go and then she walked right out. Alicia took her time getting to the car. Once there, she suggested that rather than being driven all the way home, she could just stay over at Henrietta's. It seemed a good enough idea, and that's how it all began, at least in Henrietta's memory.

Because the next morning, when Henrietta woke, Alicia was already up, cooking. She'd been up for hours. She had doughnuts frying in the Dutch oven on the cookstove. When she saw Henrietta, she looked out the window and said, 'Isn't it just the thing, doughnuts on the ocean? I got back up last night to make the dough. If I lived here, I would make them every single day.' Also, 'Look at that view, if I lived here I'd have to pinch myself all day.' And 'So many rooms. If I lived here, I wouldn't be able to stand all the empty space.'

Still, it was at least another month of Henrietta alone. In that time, she met most of the men at the wharf and the people on the little main road less than a mile from her house. The job was emboldening her. She found she liked the people who lived up on this forsaken spit of land. Her kind of people, she felt. Not the sort to judge, not the sort to go thinking they were any better than she was. She told everyone her name, her real name, knowing it wouldn't matter anyway. No one was looking for her; no one ever had and no one ever would.

And she might have gone home if they had looked, she thought sometimes. But so what.

Also in that remaining time alone, after rereading all the library books about birth and babies, Henrietta went back to the books the house had – this time, instead of cookbooks, she read the gardening ones, and then as soon as the ground thawed she set right to it. First she weeded all the perennials around the place and heaped compost from the pile into the wheelbarrow and spread it out thick in all the spots she could think to spread it. It reminded her of that old foundation in her woods, of the remnants of plants that surrounded it. Her father had pointed them out: ferns, violets, day lilies, bleeding hearts. He'd said Henrietta and Jane ought to care for them, pour some compost on them and make them flourish. Now, in her new home, Henrietta cleared out the old vegetable beds and turned the soil over and stirred compost into that, too, and she felt so capable. Despite her big belly, it felt so good to move around and use her body in this way. She bought seeds and some starts at the hardware store, and in no time at all she had a garden ready to grow. She met a neighbor who sold sheep meat, so she bought some of that and taught herself to make and hang sausage. She even bought salt from a couple nearby who harvested it right from the ocean. She ate seaweed, she drank the raw milk from the farmer down the road, she taught herself to make a quick, simple cheese. And she grew and grew and grew, and imagined, sometimes, that the baby inside of her would be the strongest being on the whole entire planet.

Henrietta was at work when Alicia called the restaurant to say she'd lost her job. Summer was almost here; there were three tables waiting and the cook was snapping his fingers at her. Her baby was due in just over one month.

'Move in with me,' she said quickly, and by the time she got home that night, Alicia had. She'd just let herself right in.

Even by then, they'd never asked each other about the fathers of their babies. The only words they'd ever spoken on the subject had come from Alicia, and those had only been: 'I don't need someone trying to steal my baby.' Those words exactly. It was as if she had planted them.

Alicia had brought an old black camp trunk with her and that was it. When Henrietta showed her which room she should take, Alicia tipped backward onto the bed and spread her arms out on the quilt and proclaimed that it was so beautiful, that she would rise each morning and make the bed, that she would keep the place so, so perfect. And, in a way, she was telling the truth. She swept the floors, she dusted, she washed the dishes, and all of it while she sang. She was bubbling over with energy and happiness. So much so that one day not a week after she'd moved in she went down to the wharf and invited a man right up for dinner.

'Alicia,' Henrietta scolded.

'I'm not going to sleep with him, for Christ's sake. Who fucks a pregnant girl? And anyway, how?'

'From behind, I suppose,' Henrietta had said while laughing.

His name was Brian. He worked on his father's lobster boat, and he'd lived exactly one mile from the wharf for the entirety of his life – twenty-four years, so far. Henrietta had seen him around, had even been introduced to him, but she'd never really spoken with him. They heard his truck approach long before they could see it. He walked in carrying a case of beer, and he tipped his hat and said, 'I know this house,' and right away he told them the story. The woman, the one Henrietta was caretaking for, she had been a mistress, her lover a sailor. It was he who had bought the house for her. Supposedly he'd chosen this particular spot because it was the closest they could come to a 360-degree view of the ocean, by which she could watch for her lover's return.

'So, what happened?' Henrietta asked. 'Did he ever leave his wife?'

'Of course he didn't,' Alicia said, and she was right. Brian pointed west, said the old sailor and the wife still lived right there on the next peninsula.

Brian got a little drunk that night, but he was nice enough, and he was fun to have around. He'd brought a mound of picked clams with him, and they fried them right up. It took some time, but it was worth the wait, they were that delicious.

'What are you two, lesbos?' he asked as they ate. And then, 'Did the same man get you pregnant?'

Alicia feigned incredulousness, but Henrietta just sat there, pregnant and full with two strangers in this huge, empty house. She couldn't think of a thing to say. Soon she would have a baby here with her. She felt it – him, her – kick all the time now. Not so much throughout the day, but around two a.m., religiously, it would do cartwheels in there. Now she put her hands to that growing form that had made her leave her home, and she stared blankly ahead.

Though she'd always slept downstairs, when the weather began to warm Henrietta decided to move into a second-floor bedroom. The baby would be here soon and it just felt homier up there, despite the heat that she knew would come in August. There were two bedrooms on that floor, one just off the top of the stairs and the other at the end of a long hall. There was also a little bathroom with a curious internal window that overlooked the staircase. Once, Henrietta had asked Brian – who was now their friend, and who came over often – about the purpose of that window, and he'd said, 'Spying, I suppose.'

A painting hung in that stairwell – Andrew Wyeth's most famous. It was the very same one that had hung in Henrietta's own childhood living room, just above the couch. Though Henrietta's mother had been distant, she had taught Henrietta a few things, so she happened to know that that woman's name was Anna Christina, and that they shared the last name

Olson. As a child, this had made her sister love that painting. Jane used to stand on the couch and stare hard at it, willing herself to leave her own world for that eternal, fictional one.

'You know you'll just get there and have polio,' Henrietta had snapped at Jane one time.

'No,' Jane had said. 'No, I don't know that.' There was something about the way she'd said it that had always stuck with Henrietta. Her sister hadn't meant that she didn't know about the painting's subject. No, Henrietta was sure that Jane had meant it was foolish to place such limits on an imagined transcendence. Still, back then Henrietta had just laughed her sister off. Now, though, she found herself staring into that painting each time she mounted the stairs, willing herself to drop out of this life and into the unknown, boundless one that her sister had surely envisioned.

The painting wasn't the only thing that compelled this kind of thought that she'd always cast off as Jane's sort. Once, Henrietta woke in the night and sat up drenched in sweat, sure that she was surrounded by a pack of wild, hungry, desperate babies. A dream, she decided, but still the sounds would not quit. Finally she mustered the courage to stand up and walk across the hall, to the bathroom. The floor creaked with each step she took. Once there, rather than turning the light on, she found herself striking a match and lighting the candle that sat in a little iron holder. With it in her hands she tiptoed down the stairs and out the front door. Those sounds were still around her, but by the time she got outside and the candle flickered out she realized it was the ocean pounding on the rocks that she had heard and somehow transformed in her mind. Now, standing out there, the night sky seemed to curve around her so that only she and that house and that sweep of ocean remained, the lone contents of a snow globe. After that first time, she began to escape nightly, soundlessly, so that Alicia never knew. Out there she would stand on the edge of the cliff, the ocean roaring below her, and she would close her eyes and watch, every time, this encapsulated version of herself patting the inside of the glass like a mime, unsure of whether she wanted to emerge or not.

Alicia's baby was born first. Henrietta drove her to The Birth Room and it all happened so fast, took only two hours. A girl. Alicia wanted to name her Destiny, but Henrietta talked her right out of that. Instead she chose Robin. Henrietta said, 'Thank god your favorite bird's not a killdeer.'

Henrietta, when the time came, had Alicia drive her to the hospital, which turned out to be the right choice because the baby wouldn't come out. She lasted for twenty hours before they told her she would have to have surgery.

'No,' Henrietta said.

'Who cares?' Alicia said. 'You'll have a baby at the end.'

'But I never wanted a baby,' Henrietta said, delirious but sure.

'Well, then,' Alicia said, 'too bad for you.'

They wheeled her away. When they put a drug into her spine, she was sure she was experiencing the best feeling in the entire world. Time passed in some instantaneous but slow-moving block and suddenly a blue baby popped up over the sheet they'd used to guard her view from her own splayed-open, bloody body. The baby was rushed to the metal table.

Doctors crowded around, and through a heavy fog Henrietta began to yell after her baby, wanting to know if it was okay, if it was alive. Only then did she realize that Alicia was still at her side, dressed in scrubs. She was holding her hand and repeating, 'Your baby's here, your baby's here.'

Henrietta named him Charley, for her father, and she spent most of the next two months in a half-sleep with him at her breast.

But despite the exhaustion they had a good summer. Just a month after he was born, Henrietta went to the restaurant a few nights a week, while Alicia watched both babies. She was good at it, ridiculously good. She kept those little beings happy and calm. Sometimes Alicia and Henrietta would go down to the water and sit in the surf in their bikinis, nursing and shading their babies and talking away. During her pregnancy, as a safeguard against stretch marks, Alicia had doused her belly in pure cocoa butter – her most expensive possession – and she continued to smear it on, even after her daughter was born. It made her skin glow and the water bead right up, and one day as they sat there together like two beached whales with their babies on them Henrietta made a little joke about it. She said they could probably see her shiny belly from space.

'Good,' Alicia had said. 'Maybe that way someone will finally find me.'

Henrietta couldn't even bear to ask what she meant.

At a certain point, Brian came over to say he'd had a fight with his father, that he couldn't live with the man one more day, that he wouldn't be his dad's stern man on the boat anymore, and that he was now going to dig clams for work. He'd found a little place to rent, and he wanted Alicia and Henrietta and the babies to come see it.

'No,' Alicia said, the moment they set foot in the place. 'No. Live with us.'

And why not? Henrietta agreed that the place he planned to rent was not livable. Dirt for a floor, duct tape and plastic over one front window. Besides, it would be good to have someone as handy as Brian around. The kitchen sink had been clogging, Alicia's car wouldn't start, plus a million other small things.

Sometimes Henrietta wondered about the old woman who owned the house, wondered if maybe she shouldn't call her up to say that her beautiful old place was now a flophouse for young misfits. But what difference would that make? Brian moved in as quickly as Alicia had, but Henrietta liked him. He cooked them food, he did the dishes, he made them laugh, and he always picked up after himself. He was good with Charley, too, bouncing him around, singing, putting on giant, silly expressions to make him smile. Alicia and her baby had taken to long naps in the afternoons, but in the day-time Charley would only ever sleep soundly in his car seat, so during this time Henrietta and Brian began to take leisurely drives along the coast while the baby slept in the backseat. Sometimes they'd drive up into the blueberry barrens, where the land stretched on endlessly in every direction and they had to use a compass to find their way across. They'd go to diners and carry the sleeping baby right in in his car seat and people would mistake them for a happy little family. *And how far off is that,* Henrietta began to think. *Why not,* she thought.

Despite the fact that she was the one with a briefcase full of money, Henrietta, during this time, was also the only one who continued to work after the babies were born. Brian still hadn't gotten his clamming license and Alicia never had looked for another job after the gas station ended. Henrietta thought momentarily of quitting, too, but her job was only three nights a week and she liked doing it. She had a little breast pump from the hospital, and Alicia was happy to baby-sit, and anyway, she liked earning a little, not spending from that briefcase meant to last a lifetime. Plus, she had a good time with the cook. He was a bit lewd, but so what? One day, she told him she had a crush on Brian.

'Not the only one,' the cook said.

'What do you mean?'

'Alicia, duh.'

'They're friends. We're all friends.'

'Sure,' he said.

'What?'

'Two lovebirds at home alone while you earn a living is what.'

It wasn't like she would ever believe the cook about anything. Still, in spite of herself, that night Henrietta was anxious for her customers to leave, anxious to get home and – and what?

She drove home quickly. She found them sitting right up close to each other on the couch, watching the television that Brian had brought with him when he'd moved in. She racked her brain to remember if they had always sat so closely like that.

No good, she couldn't remember. In fact, just at that moment, she couldn't even remember what month it was. Alicia seemed fine, but since Charley's birth Henrietta hadn't gotten more than even one full hour of uninterrupted sleep, and it was doing insidious things to her mind. She often imagined backtracking, getting far enough back in her own existence to erase her son's entirely. It was a dream both terrifying and oddly addicting. Also, this: that high spot of cliff out above the ocean, on the far side of the field, just past the blighted apple tree, the one she would go to at night when she'd been pregnant. She could just step off it. That quickly, she could enter into the heaven of an eternal sleep.

When a local man was giving chickens away, Brian suggested they clean up the barn and move them in. This would have been October – nearly one whole year since she'd run away. Charley was four months old now, as sleepless as ever, but she'd lasted the summer at the restaurant and still, oddly, there was business.

'Leaf peepers,' the cook had said. This year more than he'd ever seen. He wouldn't stop talking about them. He wanted them to go home. He wanted to shut the restaurant down and go back to his cabin and play his guitar in peace. But even he had to admit that the trees were incredible this year, even up here in this land of pines. The tamaracks had suddenly transformed to gold, the pale aspens shimmered, and the blueberry bushes that lined the ground had turned a fiery red. It had all begun to glow, so much so that sometimes, Henrietta would look out the kitchen window of her home while she washed dishes and she would let her eyes rest and suddenly she would see that great big old barn bursting up into flames. Over and over again she would see this, yet she would do nothing to stop the vision. She would just keep on watching as a sailor moored out in the cove, rowed his dinghy in, and walked across the field. On his way his slacks would catch on the thorns of the rosebushes and tear; he would lean over to pick a late flower and get stung by bees; and yet still he would press on until he'd arrived at the front door.

'Go away,' Henrietta would say. And then this odd phrase, which was like a prayer of hers in this scene that had begun to replay itself in her mind: 'No good will come of you here.'

'What?' Alicia said once, because Henrietta had said it aloud. But she just shook her head, gave no answer.

One night, Brian went to Henrietta. It was past midnight. He slipped into the room so quietly that it could have been a dream. By this time, Charley was sleeping in a crib on the other side of the room. Still waking up at two-hour intervals for milk, but at least sleeping on his own in between.

'Don't make any noise,' Henrietta whispered to him, and he did not. He just stood there and let his pants slide off like water. And the rest of it, it was all so silent, so fluid. In the morning he was gone without a trace, but after that he snuck back into her bed over and over again.

The man with the chickens lived a few peninsulas over. Alicia stayed at home with the babies while Brian and Henrietta went to pick them up. On the way, they passed a line of trucks parked bumper to bumper, blocking the entrance to a road. Brian slowed down, peered over, then said, 'Hope they catch the fuckers.'

'Who?' Henrietta asked. 'Catch what?'

'Coyotes,' he said. He said that the road was the only entrance to a peninsula that had been overtaken by the animals, and that just now residents were chasing them down, herding them toward the land's narrow end. On their way, they would invariably cross the logging roads, and there they'd find men waiting to shoot them.

'Why would they?' Henrietta asked.

'You'll be shooting them yourself once you have chickens.'

'I've had chickens before,' Henrietta said. 'And coyotes. They lived in our woods. They never killed our animals.' It was the first time she had ever spoken of home, and she found herself wanting to continue. To tell Brian the story her father had always told her, about the family in the woods. To tell him about her romantic sister, who had always imagined that family had transformed, when clearly – because it had always been so clear to Henrietta – they had just gone off to some other life.

She didn't say a thing, though. Nothing more than that she had once had chickens and coyotes. Even that felt somehow

like too much. Like to speak of it would be to call it back –
and if she did that, how would she ever stay away?

At the farmer's house, Brian introduced Henrietta, and the
farmer said, 'Now, how'd you find yourself a woman like this?'
They lifted the crates into the bed of the truck and drove
home, and Henrietta had the distinct feeling that together
they were building a life. She almost said as much.

When they pulled in, though, Alicia came to the door of
the barn. She had a pitchfork in her hand. She wasn't doing
anything with it at that moment, just standing there, but
when Henrietta looked, Alicia struck her as the husband of
American Gothic. She had grown up with that painting, too –
it had hung in the upstairs bathroom her entire life, and it,
like *Christina's World,* had been a comfort. Now, though,
when Henrietta looked at her, she was filled with a very certain terror. Just there, with the pitchfork in her hand, Alicia
had claimed this land. She would not leave, not ever, not for
anything.

Henrietta told the cook about being with Brian. She felt that
comfortable with him. She could tell him anything. She told
him that at night, in her room, it was like magic. Like something so perfect she could scarcely remember it, like it hadn't
even existed.

'Maybe it doesn't,' the cook said. 'Maybe you're just insane.'

'Stop,' she said. 'That's not the problem.' The problem, she
explained, was that in the daytime – and particularly when
Alicia was around – Brian acted like they'd practically never
met. She said, 'What the hell is wrong with me? It's like he's

hiding it.' She took another drink of wine, which was their habit. She'd work the front of the restaurant, and in the back, he'd keep her glass full.

Finally he said, 'It's not you. It's Alicia, he and Alicia.' He winked at her and made a crass motion with his hands and she knew exactly what he meant.

'No,' she said. 'No, it can't be.'

Timothy Vallilee just smirked.

At home, Henrietta thought of that story of the sailor and the mistress that Brian had told them. Had it even been true? And did that make her the new mistress of the house? Or had Brian made the story up in order to prepare the two of them to share one man?

It was her house. Not hers exactly, but close enough. Brian and Alicia had moved into her space. And she would not be made a fool.

'I just want them to admit it,' she told the cook.

The cook shrugged.

'I have to know,' she said.

'Who cares?' he said. He told her to kick them out or let them stay. He told her to get on with her life.

'You have to help me,' she pleaded.

'Just don't sleep with him again. Who cares if they lie to you?'

She said, 'Whose side are you on, anyway?' It had just come out of her mouth, no thought involved. But now that it was out it occurred to her that she had hit on an important question. She studied the back of his head. If he doesn't turn around and look at me, she decided, he is hiding something.

He didn't turn. If he had, would it have meant that her son's entire childhood would have been spent in that beautiful, desolate place? And if so, would he have ever gone to meet his family, just six hours away?

Alicia and the cook had known each other *forever*, after all. Suddenly Henrietta remembered that. Obviously the cook would be on Alicia's side.

My father used to beat my mother, Henrietta lied to the cook one night. She hadn't planned to. It just came out before the idea took full shape. But then it did – the idea became a clear, solid plan. Because of course there was a certain way to gain the cook's respect. All it would take was a limited amount of harmless lies. She said, *I used to try to stop him, but then I'd just hide in the closet*. She said, *My high school teacher gave me a failing grade when I refused to make out with him. No one believed me. Eventually I dropped out*. She said, *I had a dog, but when he bit my father, my father made me shoot him myself.*

It worked. In two short weeks, Timothy Vallilee not only believed that Henrietta was the strongest girl he'd ever met, but also that she deserved to be treated better. He began to say 'You got brains, kid' and 'You might not had it easy but you done a good job,' and a hundred other meaningless phrases she had molded him to say. And then, at last: 'Those two, sneaking around, using you. Isn't fucking right.'

'It's not,' Henrietta said.

'We've got to get them,' the cook said.

'Teach them a lesson.'

'Show them who's in charge.'

Henrietta said, 'They won't tell me. Not ever.'

'Oh, those fuckers.'

'I know.'

'Alicia,' he said.

'I know.'

'We should get them,' Timothy said. He went on to tell some story about when he was in the army. He talked about the ways they used to *get* people – shaving cream, honey; Henrietta wasn't really listening. It was something benign, really. Nothing at all compared to what they were about to do.

She said, 'I just want them to admit it.'

'They won't.'

'No.'

'There has to be a way,' he said.

Unlike the list of destruction that Henrietta had kept for Kaus, she and the cook kept this list in their minds. They tossed ideas out as they heated buns and made salads and stirred pasta sauce and filled pitchers with ice. Henrietta could pretend to be at work but really hide in the closet to catch them at it. She could set up tape recorders in their rooms. Nothing much. Nothing harmful. Any one of the plans would have worked fine, and all of them, they knew, would never come to pass.

But then one night she said, 'If I took her kid.' Why, why ever, did she say it?

'No.'

'I don't mean forever. Just made her go missing.'

Timothy gave a malicious and eager little smile. *Go on.*

'Just to see how he reacts,' she said. 'Just to see if in the heat of the moment it slips from him. That he loves her. Alicia. That he loves Alicia.'

He said, 'Maybe he thinks the baby's in the car, and the car gets stolen.'

'Or Alicia disappears too, and then he freaks, says he has to find his woman.'

They went on and on like this. Hatched a thousand different plans to separate Alicia from her baby in a way that might make Brian mistakenly come clean. The little game echoed her terrible childhood one, and yet she barreled forward just the same. On some level, it was fun. Terrible but delicious. Besides, she would never go through with it.

'I got it,' the cook said one night. A Friday, early November, dark and slow. He tipped a giant box of bowtie pasta above a pot of boiling water, but his aim was off, and most of the dry pasta fell on the floor.

'Are you drunk?' Henrietta asked, kidding.

'Yes,' he said.

He proceeded to tell her his plan while she swept up the pasta and put it in the pot, lint and dirt and all. There was nothing complicated about it. She would creep into the room at night and take the baby. Call the cook when she had her. He would meet her at the end of the driveway, and from there he would take the baby to his house. It wasn't such a big deal,

ABI MAXWELL

Henrietta always remembers telling herself. They were going to be safe. She would bring the car seat.

'We have to do it tonight,' he said.

'No.'

'Now or never,' he taunted.

'This is stupid.'

'Your life is stupid,' he said, and handed her a glass of cheap, sweet merlot.

At the restaurant, Henrietta kept drinking wine and kept getting happier and happier. Charley was safe – even if she didn't trust her with Brian, she always trusted Alicia with her baby, always – and Henrietta was filled up with the thrill of it.

'Won't you make your baby drunk if you go home and feed him?' the cook asked.

She told him she had extra milk in the freezer. She told him she was prepared for this sort of occasion.

'Wait,' he said. 'What if Alicia's baby wakes up? What if she gets hungry?'

'That baby sleeps right through the night,' she said. 'I think there's something wrong with her.' She poured herself more wine, and then she slid so smoothly into this terrible and familiar role of hers. When the restaurant finally closed and she made her way home, she decided that they must have had a fight, Alicia and Brian. Or they must have suspected something, been afraid to be caught, because typically when she arrived home they would be awake, laughing, watching TV, sitting side by side on the stiff couch. But tonight they were both already asleep, Alicia in her bedroom and Brian in his.

No matter. It made the plan that much easier. Henrietta went upstairs, checked on her Charley. Sound asleep. She turned the monitor off and tiptoed back down, into Alicia's room. She was a little drunk. More than a little. The door creaked as she opened it and Alicia rustled. She, too, was a new mother, after all.

'Henrietta,' she said.

'Shh,' Henrietta said.

'Henrietta, I'm so sorry.' Her head was still on the pillow. Her eyes, from what Henrietta could tell, were closed. And because of this, she could tell herself that Alicia hadn't really known what she was saying at all.

'You're sleeping,' she whispered as she approached the crib on the far side of the room. Her words slurred a bit. 'Go to sleep,' she said.

'I'm so, so sorry,' Alicia said again. This time she sat up. She said, 'You were my only friend in the world.'

What was Henrietta supposed to do? She went to her, patted her head until she lay back down. Told her not to worry about a thing.

'It's a dream,' she said. 'You're having a dream.'

When Alicia nodded back off completely, Henrietta took her sleeping baby, slipped out, and tiptoed upstairs, peeked in at her Charley again, and then went to the phone in the hall. It was a wonder they all stayed sleeping. Even that little baby girl in her arms.

At first the cook didn't answer. And then, instead of waiting for Henrietta to call back, he called the house. She answered before the first ring was complete.

'What are you doing?' she hissed into the phone.

'Operation SBB,' he said. Henrietta had no idea what that stood for. She told him to come over but to not drive up the driveway. Charley would be fine; everyone would be fine. It would take only a minute to walk to the end of the driveway and back. She bundled that baby up and went out.

Henrietta has never been able to remember that moment when she handed the baby over to Timothy. She can't remember watching him drive away with that poor sleeping baby in the back of his car. But the night itself, that is clear: she stayed up all night, drinking water and tea and just watching her baby breathe. He woke up twice. Each time, she fed him warmed milk in a bottle, just in case she'd had too much to drink. While he slept she became overwhelmed with the fact that he was a person, his own whole person. That he would one day love someone. *Charley,* she whispered. She promised him a better life. It wasn't until two chickadees started calling back and forth to each other that it occurred to her not only how horrible of a person she was and what a scar she could leave on that baby, but also that she could go to jail for what she had done. That she had to undo it immediately, before anyone woke up, if she meant to make any kind of life.

Just then the door swung open.

'Henrietta?'

Alicia looked so childlike, there in her plaid pajamas and her loose ponytail.

'Henrietta, where's Robin?'

'What?'

'You have her, right?'

Did she answer? What, right then, became of her face? Her being? What had already become of it? What does it mean, really, for a person to lose her mind? Is it any less real than the full loss of her that her own family had experienced?

'Oh my god,' Alicia said.

Henrietta hadn't planned on this. Hadn't even thought of it. She'd only imagined the shame she could subject the two of them to, and somehow she'd ignored the fact that it would be Alicia, Alicia alone, who would suffer the worst kind of pain imaginable. When she said that, *Oh my god,* her skin paled and her eyes dropped and Henrietta felt certain, right then, that Alicia would never again be the same. Up until this moment, despite her lack of a foot up in the world, her personality had shielded her from any sense of real trouble. Now she had been forced to wake up. Henrietta had forced her.

'I don't know,' Henrietta said, in response to nothing, but Alicia probably didn't hear her. She was already turned around, had already begun to run through the house, open all the doors, and scream for her child. The baby was almost five months old now. She could roll over sometimes, but that was about it. She could not have gone anywhere unless someone had taken her. Still, Brian and Henrietta trailed Alicia, pretending it was possible that the baby had crawled out of her crib to a new place to sleep. Anyway, they couldn't have stopped her from looking in this way if they'd tried. She was fierce, directed, monstrous. Finally, Brian went to the phone.

'What are you doing?' Henrietta snapped, and when he said he was calling the police, Henrietta grabbed the phone from him.

'No,' she said.

'What is wrong with you?'

They looked at each other, and there it was, somehow. At least, Henrietta always thought so, thought that at that moment Brian had understood. Had seen right through her. He handed the phone to her without a word, then left her standing there, alone, while he helped Alicia to the kitchen, sat her down, got her a glass of water, and put the kettle on for tea.

Finally Timothy picked up. 'For the love of god,' he said. 'Come save this baby.'

On her way out, Henrietta went through the kitchen. She lied, of course, told Alicia she had called the police, that she would now go to the station to file a report. She said she was sure the baby was okay.

'How can you be sure?' Alicia demanded.

'I just can,' Henrietta said wholeheartedly, and it was the last thing she ever said to her. Charley was in his playpen, and before Henrietta left the house she swooped him up and gave him a spin, and then put him back down with a kiss. In that playpen he had a little crinkly book made of fabric that he liked to chew, and also a baby mirror to look into. Henrietta held that mirror up for him for one moment before it struck her that Brian had provided her with one last, final chance to be good.

She pulled back in a half-hour later. Alicia looked out the window and when she saw that Henrietta had a car seat in her arms, she came running out. She grabbed her baby and didn't so much as look at Henrietta. In that way, no explanation was ever needed. Henrietta packed her things quickly. She considered stealing one cookbook but decided to leave it, vowing that her days of dishonesty were through. She left the house while the three of them were playing in the living room. Didn't even say goodbye. The drive took five whole days. She stopped at motels to get what sleep she could, but she was always back up and on the road before the sun. She stayed off the highways because the car still wasn't registered and because she still had no license. She kept calling out to Charley as she drove. 'Hello!' she'd coo a little manically. 'We're okay!' Every now and then she reached back and dropped a handful of Cheerios onto his lap, and in fear of him entering into an inconsolable fit she sang a constant string of every childhood song she could remember.

It wasn't until they crossed into North Dakota that she finally felt like she could let out her breath, like she had gotten far enough away to know that she would make it. This was the last state to cross before she reached her destination. She relaxed a little as she drove, stopped with the singing and instead began to talk. She told Charley the story of the first time she'd ever sneaked one of her father's horses out of the barn and into the woods to ride. She knew he couldn't understand a story at this age, but still it felt so good to tell. She told him about playing house in The Den with her sister. His car seat faced the back, so when she stole glances of him in the rearview mirror she could only see his little feet inside his little pajamas, but he seemed happy. Maybe he was sleeping, but at least he wasn't crying. She kept talking. 'Once upon a time,' she said when her memories ran out. 'A family of five lived in a house in the woods. One night, the temperature dropped and the world turned to ice, even their windows turned to ice.' It was the first time she had ever told the story. She found herself trying to imitate her father – not what he told but the way he told it. That strong, full voice. But as for the details, she gave Charley an almost entirely different version. 'The parents had come from Scotland,' she said to her son. 'That's a country on the other side of the ocean. They came here for a new life, for freedom, but they didn't find it. They had to escape,' she said. She tried to think of a reason why this would be true, and finally she just decided to keep on. She said, 'I can't explain why. When you are older I can. But they had to escape,' she repeated, 'so what they did, they waited for a storm. There were coyotes who lived in their woods. When the storm came the family went to the coyote den and held out raw meat to tempt the animals. With the meat they led them back to their own home. *Make this your den,* they told the animals. They threw the meat on the floor and ran, and the townspeople, they thought the family had been—' But she stopped herself, not wanting to say something so gruesome to her boy, despite the fact that he would not understand.

The flatlands had given way to a kind of land that Henrietta hadn't known existed. Nearly treeless, but cropless too, and faintly red, with alternate pockets and stretches of green across the endless horizon. Little mountains rose and fell on all sides as she twisted her way through the strange land. That family from her woods, they would have had to run on their own feet. They might have had horses, though. What would it have been like to escape through a landscape like this one? Would they have stuck to the snaking riverbed? Would they have been able to hide?

'Charley?' she said to her son, though of course he could not answer. She approached a little gas station and pulled in, got out of the car, and walked around to the far side of the back seat. She opened the door, suddenly feeling like she had to touch his sleeping form, to check to make sure he was still in there, whole and alive. She leaned in, gave his forehead a gentle kiss. She swept her hand across his wispy hair. They would be in Montana within two hours, but she didn't yet comprehend just how big that state was, how long it would take to reach its western edge.

'We'll make our own life,' she whispered to her son. It was practice, saying that. By telling him, she was convincing herself, too. 'We can do this,' she said, and got back in the driver's seat.

It was the middle of the night when they finally arrived in the city she'd been headed to. She got a room at the first motel she saw. Within a week, she had found a place to live.

People were different here, it seemed to her. Friendlier. They said hello when she passed them on the street.

'You'll be a Montana boy,' she said to her son, though she had no real idea of what that might mean.

PART FOUR

Claire

27 April 1852
Dear Sir,

   Writing to you after my sister, Mrs Elspeth Ross, or
Mrs Thomas Ross, you could say. I never had a child
and do not know the demands it must put upon one
to have three; forgive me if I am jumping to conclusions.
Elspeth, my sister, has been a resident of your country
nearly fifteen years in counting and she has always kept
us in a steady stream of letters. Now four whole months
have passed and not a single word. Many times she
told me about you in her letters, and therefore I am
writing to you. You were her only friend, from what I
understand. 'Almost like she has a father over there' is
what our father said.

   Please, I hope to believe she is just up the road and
busy in her life, but please if it does not trouble you
tell her to send word to very worried family. She is
too independent ever since birth. She does not know
a woman's place is what father said, but not cruelly.

You see, we all love her dearly. Show her this letter if you must! I never left home and I still care for our parents and home, so I have a lot of time with my hands in the chores to worry. No doubt my sister will respond by telling me I am a fool.

> *Yours,*
> *Claire Mitchell, 95 Queen Street, Monifieth, Forfarshire, Scotland*

30 June 1852
Dear Sir,

    I pray not to bother you. Did my letter of two months ago arrive to you? It could have gotten lost overboard. I have never been aboard a ship but I presume it is difficult to keep track of mail in such a state, especially in the case of storm. Truly, just a slip of paper light as an ant to go all that distance, it is no wonder. I do not mean to bother. In the last letter which perhaps you did not receive I asked after my sister, Elspeth Ross, wife to Thomas Ross, worker at the mill, originated from Monifieth, county Forfarshire, Scotland. I begged you tell her to reach me or to tell me what news I need to know as I have not heard. Now I am thinking that even if you did get the letter perhaps you are busy in your farming and you have simply forgotten to just send a note to me to say she is busy and at peace; or perhaps you have something to tell me; yet either way it has occurred to me that you may not have my address. It is possible I forgot to include it. Here it is:

Claire Mitchell, 95 Queen Street, Monifieth, Forfarshire, Scotland. I have enclosed the postage.

Yours,
Claire Mitchell, beloved sister to Mrs Elspeth Ross

1 September 1852
To Kind Citizens:
I write to your newspaper in regards to my sister, Mrs Thomas Ross, Elspeth, and her three children, Colin, Evan, and Jeremiah, who were residents of your town for fifteen years now if they are still in residence. My sister has always been a faithful correspondent, and our family is now filled with anguish, as her habit of letters has ceased. I beg of you kindest citizens, if you have any shred of news of my sister and her family, please send immediately, address Claire Mitchell, 95 Queen Street, Monifieth, Forfarshire, Scotland. Include your return address and I assure I will repay double your postage.

Kindly yours,
Claire Mitchell

3 October 1852
Dear Claire Mitchell,
My name is Jonathan. I am a ten-year-old resident of Middlewood. When I was a younger boy your sister taught me to read and now I work as an apprentice at the

*newspaper. It was I who opened your letter. You
understand there is no need to print it in the paper. Your
sister was one of the kindest people I have had occasion to
meet. I hate most to tell you that she and her family have
disappeared due to an unfortunate event. Father says this
new land is wild. It is unlike the land of Scotland, at
least that is what Father tells us, though he is from
England and has never been to Scotland. This land is full
of wilderness and hungry animals such like you have
never seen. I suppose it is a risk that all who get on a ship
to come this way know. I am so very sorry to report this.*

> *In sympathy forever,*
> *Jonathan Kepper*

'I don't understand what this means,' Claire said to herself.
Her father sat across from her in the small, raw room. November already, and already so cold. She had been out walking
and taken a long path and not gotten home in time to get the
house warm before her father came in. Her mother gone for
the whole day and night, tending to a friend out in the country with a brand-new set of twins plus a two-year-old besides.
Her father didn't complain about the cold home, though.
Scarcely ever in his life had he complained about how his
daughters did – or did not – care for the house. 'You dote too
much,' their mother had said to him, again and again. Elspeth, Claire felt, had always been his favorite. She had no
jealousy, though. Elspeth had been everyone's favorite. Elspeth could make a dark room glow. Or if not glow, be cast in
the rarest kind of light. When she went off on that ship their

father had gone back to work at the loom and then he'd come into the kitchen to eat and then he'd gone to sleep and in the morning he'd gotten up to do the same, on and on like that for the next five days, and on the sixth he didn't get out of bed. Claire's mother went to him, asked him if he didn't feel all right, and he said that he wasn't sure how long it would go on. 'What?' she had asked. 'How long what will go on, dear?' And he'd said, 'Every day I picture coming into the room to see her, and every day I open the door to remember that I never will again.'

'She is still alive,' Claire had heard her mother whisper to him after a moment.

'How do you know?' he'd asked, but their mother wouldn't stand for that kind of misery. She gave his leg one brisk pat and told him to get up and get to work. He obeyed.

Now, with the letter in her hand, Claire looked across the room to her father. He looked at her, too, and he said, 'You seen a ghost?'

'Yes,' she said mistakenly, and then, 'No. I am cold.'

'What's that you have?' he asked, nodding toward the letter.

'Nothing,' she said, and then, quickly, 'a slip of paper. Nothing. I was writing something. It's nothing.'

He rubbed his hands together, so dry and cracked they sounded like the scraping together of kindling, and then he leaned into the fireplace to inspect the fire she had built. Nothing more than a smolder. He said, 'Claire,' meaning, of course, that she could do better than that. He pushed his hand right into the heat and moved the smoldering log off the top of the pile and pushed the kindling around, and then he took up the small ax and cut himself some more kindling and rebuilt the little fire, and he stood there blowing on it until it roared. 'There,' he said, and crossed the room to the counter. Claire remained in that same chair. He called to her, asked her what she had planned for dinner. When she didn't respond he thought of clapping his hands in her face and snapping her back to, but then he thought he would give her a rest. She had a little crush, he had heard, a little crush on their neighbor Alistair's son. Apparently she had been seen staring at him on more than one occasion. Had asked her friend Mary all about him. Mary had told her own mother that, and that woman had reported it to Claire's mother. Her father could have told her it was not a good idea. Now he suspected she might have learned for herself. So instead of bothering her, he decided to do the little cooking he knew how to do. He put the pan on the fire and cracked all the eggs in the basket into the pan, and he poured what was left of the buttermilk in, too, and he stood there stirring while his daughter sat blank-faced in the chair.

He had been a fool to make her go – Elspeth. He thought that now as he stirred, though he had no idea why he should think of it so sharply at just that moment. Of course he had thought of it most moments of his life since that time, but it had tended to be a murmur of a thought, a background noise in his mind that would not quit. He would say to his wife, 'This is a good pudding,' and underneath he would say, *Elspeth*. He would say, 'More work this year than ever,' and behind that *Elspeth*. 'Need to repair the roof' or 'Do you like that book?' or 'Samuel's wedding this Sunday,' and *Elspeth, Elspeth, Elspeth*. Why hadn't he himself gone to the new

country? Why hadn't he sent his own wife? They'd been grop-
ing in the dark long before marriage, too. What if that had
been everyone's punishment? Nearly this whole country
would have been emptied out, he felt sure.

'Claire,' he finally called, when he couldn't get Elspeth out
of the forefront of his mind. 'Claire, I can't get these damn
eggs to cook.'

She came to him then. Pushed him aside and looked into
the pan. 'Christ,' she said. 'You've made buttermilk soup.'

They ate it anyway, poured it over some biscuits that she
cooked in a flash. Her sister had probably just gone off with
some man. That was all she ever seemed to want, anyway. Claire
remembered once, when they were much younger, after Elspeth had been at it with Thomas, that she had said, 'It just
feels so good to be *fucked*.'

'Elspeth!' Claire had shouted, fear coursing through her,
but a delicious laughter welling up, too.

Elspeth let her own laughter out. She tipped back into the
sand and laughed and rolled and then sat up and said, 'It's
true, Claire. Why don't you go out and try it?'

'Elspeth,' Claire had said again. At once hungry and afraid.

'At least say it. It feels almost as good to say it,' Elspeth
said.

'You better be careful,' Claire had snapped, with no notion
whatsoever of just how true her statement was.

In the end, Elspeth hadn't been, but Claire herself had
been much, much too careful. Never any body pressing
against her own. Never even any approach of such a body.
'Fucked,' she had whispered to herself a few times, when she
was sure she was alone. *'Fucked.'* She wished only sometimes

ABI MAXWELL

that she had been born with a heart like her sister's, a wanting one, though she knew that would have meant treachery for her family.

They ate their dinner silently, and afterward Claire cleaned up, then went straight to bed. There, with the candle beside her, she opened the letter back up and reread it over and over again. She even read it backward, on the off chance that there might be a clue, that the child who wrote it might have crafted a secret map for her. No such thing, though. She thought of putting the letter in the fire, of convincing herself to believe that Elspeth had made an enemy and now someone was playing a terrible joke on them all. *That's it!* she said to herself. *This enemy is stealing the letters that my sister is sending home.* Elspeth got up and walked toward the fire, ready to go burn the letter and be done with it, but before she dropped it in she stopped and took a deep, slow breath and told herself to be reasonable, as she always had been. Her father just watched her from across the room. She could feel his eyes on her. What would be reasonable? To tell her father? No. Certainly not. It would be reasonable to keep on. She dropped the letter into the fire anyway, but not because she didn't believe it. She burned it because she needed to protect her parents from believing it, too.

'Any word?' her mother asked her when she arrived home the following day. Only her mother knew of the letter that Claire had sent to the newspaper. Their father knew that Elspeth's

204

letters had stopped – of course he knew, her monthly letters were like gold to him – but when Claire's mother had instructed him not to worry, that most likely she had herself too much work, what with the three boys and a cold winter to keep her from writing, he had if not believed her at least been able to stifle his thoughts and let the women take over. At the end of the day, he no longer asked if Elspeth had written. And when their mother asked, it was only out of earshot of her father.

Though she had resolved otherwise, now when her mother asked after Elspeth, Claire wanted so badly to say yes, that there had in fact been terrible word. She nearly did. Even opened her mouth to begin the sentence. But her mother's face – those cheeks so rosy today and a sudden brightness from those new babies filling her up. Claire could not bear it. She decided to move forward with her decision. 'No,' she said. 'No word.'

And now what would she do?

'Go live your own life,' her parents had said over the years.

Also, 'You know you could marry. It is possible to marry and make a life without leaving us. It is possible to live down the street.'

Honestly, though, if it weren't for her shaky belief in God, she might have become a nun. Sometimes she wanted bravery like her sister, but more than that she wanted order. She liked the clean counter. She liked the bare walls. Sometimes she and her mother would spend the entire day in efficient silence, and it suited her more than anything else ever had. She thought of children, sometimes, and certainly she thought of men, of what their touch might feel like – not just their gruff faces against her own, but even their strong hands holding her breasts and their other thing, whatever you call it, she couldn't say it, of that thing pushing right into her. She liked the thoughts, sort of. Not enough, though. She liked the clean house and the silence much, much more.

Claire had never expected Elspeth to miss home quite so much, and part of the shock of it was that it didn't seem like her longing came from any real-life suffering. Judging from her letters, her house had always sounded warm enough. The village nice enough. In time she'd had the friendship of a neighbor. They always had enough food. And eventually she'd even had enough books to keep her endlessly occupied. Her children had always been healthy and good. She had never been made to understand just what a famine across the land looked like. But the longing Elspeth wrote about, not just for her family but for the actual land – their particular dirt and sharp grass and their particular view of the ocean, their angle of the sun – all of this shocked Claire. She hadn't known her sister to care for anything quite so tangible and plain. Oddly, though, when Claire thought over it enough – because she had years to do so – she decided that her sister's longing for it came from a place not in fact tangible at all, not plain, either. It was precisely because her sister always had her head in the clouds that she cared so much about a thing like how the sun fell on her new home and whether or not her sons' voices would turn out to sound like her own father's, as she wanted them desperately to. Claire thought that if she herself were to leave the land, she might miss it, but not for that sort of reason. She might miss her parents. But a new way of life? If she had wanted it she would have taken it, and if she had taken it, as Elspeth had, then she would have wanted it.

In truth, Claire had spent years furious at her sister. All those years Elspeth had in the new country with new babies while at home Claire had to watch her father struggle to keep them warm and fed. Once during the first bad stretch he came home to announce that he would leave weaving for a job at the foundry, but her mother wouldn't have it. Instead, Claire and her mother had gone to the city and solicited more accounts for more work. After that had come the period of years when day after day it seemed the work would never end, and then once again a period – worse this time – when it seemed every minute like all of it would end, and they would be left with nothing. Now it felt things had evened out. No worry about hunger, and a steady enough stream of orders, and besides all that, it wasn't that she didn't like her life – just that she hadn't necessarily ever thought of it in those terms until Elspeth's letters had encouraged her to do so. Elspeth's letters, Elspeth's life, it had all seemed so rich and full.

In her last letter, Elspeth had written with a bit of information from an astronomical journal her neighbor subscribed to: on January 7, 1852, there would be a total lunar eclipse. Claire told the whole town. They were to all gather at the shore. She made biscuits and she kept herself half awake the whole night, just to be sure she wouldn't miss the eclipse in the early hours of morning. When the time finally came she got up, roused her parents, fed the fire, made the tea, and she folded a blanket and gathered her coat and hat. So excited she could hardly put her feet properly into her boots. They all set out together, and as they approached the water they could hear voices before them. At that point in the night, the moon still looked just as it always did, yet somehow it seemed also to hang at once more dimly yet more brilliantly. Claire handed the basket to her father and told her parents to go along without her, that she had forgotten something at home, and then, once they were out of sight, she ran toward the fields at the opposite side of town. She meant to watch the eclipse alone. She knew that on the other side of the ocean, just as night began, Elspeth would be watching it, too. In the most foolish thought she had ever allowed herself to have, she believed that so long as she was alone, as she watched the eclipse Elspeth would be at her side, watching it with her.

And she was, in a way. That night Claire believed, for the length of time it took the Earth to spin into its perfect line between the sun and moon, that it was possible to reach across all space and time, or to dissolve into it, and return to her sister, uncontained. When the moon was totally covered she left it there. She went to bed with her body humming with the life of her sister from all its edges.

In the morning though, no sister. She got up, started the fire, put the water on, put the oats on, returned to the ground.

'I don't know what to do,' Claire confided to her mother.

'Wait,' her mother said gently.

'I can't.' And then, 'It won't do any good.'

'I know.'

'I would like to go there.'

'You can't.'

'I can.'

'We can't afford it.'

'I have looked into it. We can.'

'We can't possibly.'

'We can afford one way.'

'And then what?'

'And then I will send a letter.'

'I won't lose two daughters,' her mother said.

Claire was nothing if not resolute, though. As a child she made up her mind to care for her parents, and since then she had never wavered. She had made up her mind to keep the cleanest house she had ever seen, and she had done that. To learn to make bread as well as the baker, to fix her family's clothing with the very strongest and neatest of patches, to keep them all in newly knitted socks, to read at least three hundred pages a week. Now she had decided to find her sister, and she would. While her father was working and her mother was helping the neighbor she went to Jacob, the son of Alistair. He was handsome and he was said to be trouble, though no one ever said exactly how much or even just why. She had, however, always suspected it. Impossible to look that good and to be that proud and not to be trouble, she had felt. Now she went to him for that very purpose. She found him in his shop – his father's shop, for he, too, had never married and never left home. As a teenager he had diagnosed the problem with the new railcar that none of the men could fix, and after that he had quickly become known for the mechanical skill that his mother had always claimed he held. Just now he was once again repairing an engine. She called from the open shop door. So nervous she thought she would be sick. She said, 'I need to go to America and back and I only have money for one way.'

His head was tucked into the engine and he didn't look up at her. Only called out, 'Well.'

The truth was she actually did know precisely why he was trouble. She had been told. It had been after church service. Mary, the only friend she ever confided in after Elspeth left, had told her. They had stood outside in the sun, looking over at him, and Claire had suddenly been overcome with the sort of bravery – if you could call it that – that Elspeth had always had, and she had said, 'He sure is handsome.'

It had been a shock to all of them that he should show up. His parents weren't there, never attended anymore, and he had dropped out of school and church ages ago, and not been quiet about it, either. Supposedly he had joked about all of them, of what fools they were. Now Mary guessed at why he was there: 'Atoning, I should say.'

'What for?'

Mary's mother had heard it from Jacob's own. Jacob had gone off for an entire week, and while he was gone he'd spent his father's whole jar of savings besides. When his red-faced father told him that if he wanted to get drunk he might as well have done it at home where it wouldn't cost all the damn money, Jacob had looked right into his father's eyes and told him that it hadn't been liquor he'd been after. His father had understood and left it at that. 'Do something,' his mother had begged, but what could be done? 'He's a man,' Alistair had told his wife, chuckling.

It took Claire a while to understand. Actually, she didn't,

not standing there at the church looking at him, but later, thinking about it, she realized what he had been after, what he had spent his money on. She wasn't sure what she thought about it. That kind of need he must have felt. She wasn't sure at all what to think about it.

Now, in his shop, she said his name. 'Jacob,' she said. She knew Mary had run off and told her own mother that Claire thought Jacob handsome. She knew Jacob might have heard the gossip by now. Rather than humiliate her, it gave her a little courage. She felt as bold as Elspeth. She said, 'Look at me.'

He stood up behind the workbench. Light gleamed off the metal before him. 'What?' he said, not moving closer. Not really interested at all. Just bothered, she thought, and only a little.

She said, 'I am willing. For a fee.'

'Sorry?' he said.

Her face was red, she was trembling. It was possible he didn't want her. That she wasn't good enough. Which would be worse? Whatever tool he had held now clanged against the table. At first she thought he had dropped it, but then his hand was still upon it, so he must have set it down harshly. He let go and crossed the room to her. Oh, no, what had she done? She had been warned. Her mother had told her that once a man starts he cannot stop. *That's how I feel*, Elspeth had whispered to her later, and Claire had pretended to be appalled.

'Claire,' he said. Really, so kind, the way he said it. 'Claire,' he said again. She looked away from him, turned around slowly, walked out of the shop, and as soon as she was out of sight she ran, her tears blinding her. He never said a word about it, and for the rest of her life she believed he was one of the gentlest people she had ever known.

'Mother,' she said now and then, as the weeks dragged on. She kept the days without Elspeth marked on the calendar. Nearly Christmas now; nearly one whole year. 'I don't know what to do.'

'Add the oats,' her mother said.

'Mother,' she said as the new year began. 'I don't know how to find her.'

'I know.'

'I can't live like this,' she said as winter deepened.

'You can.'

And then one day in March: 'I promised myself I would find her. I have to know. How can you not know?'

'Okay, then.'

'What?'

'Here,' her mother said, and went to the cupboard and returned with a tin. She had to pry the top off with a butter knife to see what was inside. 'It's enough,' her mother said, as Claire counted. 'There and back. Your father knows. You might as well pack.'

12 March 1853
Dear Sir,

    Writing to you just before my passage. Coming for news
of my sister. Will be at your door within four weeks' time
from this day 12 March, 1853. Pray that you will have me.

     In hopes,
     Claire Mitchell, sister to Elspeth Ross

The passage over was nothing like she expected. There were kind people on board, hopeful people and sad, but for the most part there were just people, packed so tightly she could scarcely make sense of where her own skin ended and the next person's began. She had understood that people were leaving for America in droves, but she hadn't exactly pictured what that meant. The ache and stench of it, the horror. When waves came she clung to her narrow, hard berth and watched her midsection rise and fall in the air. She vomited – she and the rest of them – day after day after day. Thank heavens her mother had sent her with cans of water (and her own hard-tack and boiled eggs besides), though when the fear of dying of seasickness or ship fever subsided she thought she would die of shame at the fact that she sipped her own clean water while others waited for it to be pumped from barrels, praying there would be enough and that it would not spill.

But a few days in she discovered something new on board. At night, when all ship noise had quieted, she would sneak up on deck to be filled with the most untamed feeling she had ever known. Those stars bent around her in all directions, as though she were flying through the very sky. What a thought! She let it overtake her, so that she slipped into a sort of trance, wishing away hours of day only to be greeted by night and stars and that endless firmament. It occupied her entire being, and in memory her passage over became nothing but a blur of sea salt, uneven footsteps, and starlight.

The ship docked in Boston. She had some trouble setting foot on land because the officers refused to believe she would be going back, so finally she withdrew her fold of money and bought her return passage right there. She had given herself two weeks. She stepped outside into the light, but she did not waste a moment. Her luggage was not heavy. She carried it herself. She had done her research. The train would take her directly to her sister's town in less than four hours. All she had to do from there was walk onto the main road, pass the mills, and then cross the bridge and continue up the hill. Her sister had described it in her letters, though Claire hadn't understood just how well. Mr Bartlett's barn, for example. She had thought her sister must be exaggerating.

At his door, she said her sister's name by way of introduction, but she didn't need to. He knew it right away, the two of them so clearly cut from the same cloth: top lips so deeply curved, eyes set just wider than other people's, just enough to give their faces an unfamiliar, slightly wild look. He looked up and down the street as he ushered her in. My god, what was she doing here? As he pulled her through the door it occurred to him that he oughtn't to have looked up and down in that way, that had someone been watching, then they'd surely become suspicious. Suspicions coursed through this town like a plague these days.

'Tea?' he said calmly, carefully locking the door after her. 'Take your boots off. Here,' he said, and he hurried to the closet and found her a pair of slippers. April and still so cold.

'Sit,' he said, and then, 'My goodness, you look as she looks.'

'Sir,' she said.

'You must be hungry. I've got nothing planned. I'll just run to the cellar and see what we have. I suspect you won't find the food so very different.'

'Sir, tell me now. I don't mean to stay. I have come a great distance and not for your meals, if you'll excuse me. Please tell me now.'

'I lost my wife years ago. Wife and child, childbirth. I'm sorry, I don't know why I just told you that. Your sister was a great friend to me, you see. A daughter. I received your letter. I have been up nights wondering whether or not to believe it. And here you are.'

When she didn't respond he kept on. He said, 'Also your earlier letters. Asking for response. I thought and thought. In the end I decided it was not wise. What if someone should find my response? Your sister could end up in a great deal of trouble. But now you have come all this way. I'm afraid I don't know what I've done. Or how I could have done otherwise.'

'You mean she could *have*.'

'Sorry?'

'You said she could end up in trouble. You mean she still can? Or that she could have and can no longer?'

'I'm sorry, I still don't know your meaning.'

'Sir, tell me if my sister is dead.'

'Oh, heavens, Claire,' he said. He was sweating and at the same time adding another log to the fire. Once it was on he took up the poker and began to stir the red coals. Finally he said, 'Your sister had a terrible time.' Something about the way he said it, the way he stopped moving and looked past her, couldn't meet her eyes while he said it, made Claire sure she understood.

She said, 'She was always getting herself into trouble with men,' and then immediately she regretted it. What did she think she meant by that? She said, 'Was she badly hurt?'

'Her body was still healthy, if that's what you mean. There was no serious harm to her body.'

'And now?'

'It's been over a year, hasn't it,' he said.

'Where is she? A boy sent word,' she said, and she recited those words she had memorized. *Disappeared due to an unfortunate event. This new land is wild.* 'What am I to make of this?' she asked.

'Oh, Claire,' he said. He had lit the candles. In a moment he would leave her alone in that candlelit room and go out to the barn to tend the animals. Now he told her that she had to watch to not be seen in town. How much she looked like her sister, like her sister's children – people might suspect something. He went to his desk and withdrew a stack of papers. He said, 'I am writing the history of Middlewood. You'll be interested to see this part.'

'You'll forgive me,' she said. 'Elspeth, if you will.'

He put the book down and looked straight past her, toward the window. He said, 'Her Evan was a good boy.'

'I'm sure.'

'The mill owner,' he said. 'I never knew the details. The boy said it was a mistake and I am inclined to believe him.'

'I have come a great distance,' Claire said again. 'Tell me plainly.'

Mr Bartlett pursed his lips and breathed carefully, in and out, in and out. He closed his eyes for a moment, then opened them back up and looked into the fire as he said quietly, 'It was the mill owner did that to your sister. Next her Evan killed the mill owner.' He looked quickly around the room after he said that, as though to make sure no one could hear, and then he added in a whisper, 'Pushed him over the dam. I gave her a good deal of my savings and I sent her family to my sister's parish in the West.' Once more he took up the manuscript and pushed it toward Claire, but she held up her hands and urged him to continue with his story. He set the pages down again, rubbed his hands briskly together just as her own father always did, then rubbed his eyes deeply. Finally he said, 'I have not heard from her.'

'And your sister? What does she say?'

'I can tell you where she lives. But she has not seen her.'

'Her husband? Her children?'

'None. Claire, I am so sorry.'

'I don't know what that means, sir.'

'If there's anything I can do.'

'You can help me find my sister,' she said.

'You understand this town thinks her dead. You understand there's been a report of her death.'

'I'm afraid I don't understand.'

'Claire,' he said. Again he picked up the manuscript. 'Just this one page,' he said. 'It has my name on it, but it's not true, I didn't write it. It was your sister's doing.'

'Sir,' she said, a bit harshly. 'Sir, my eyes are tired. Read it aloud, if you will.'

Mr Bartlett straightened the pages and his back. He cleared his throat. 'January 19, 1852,' he began. 'Cold Friday.' He stopped then, put the pages down, and said, 'You understand I don't know the truth. I deposited your sister at the station, you see. She had already written these pages, but I did not know it.'

'Mr Bartlett,' Claire said gently.

'Forgive me,' he said. Once again he sat up straighter in his chair and took a deep breath, and then at last he began:

'All alive in this town will remember that on the night-fall of January 18, 1852, the temperature of Middlewood remained in its typical place, but that by sunup on Friday, January 19, the mercury had begun to plunge until it hit a shocking 31 degrees below and then froze in its gauge. As time goes forward we will hear of others in our fine state dying from the cold, but this tale in our own town will remain the saddest and surely the most mysterious. You will know that scarcely one hundred rods from Mr Josiah Bartlett's, across his upper field and into the woods, is the squat home of the Scottish family Ross, the parents, Thomas and Elspeth, immigrants, the children Colin (fourteen), Evan (twelve), and Jeremiah (age ten) born here.'

He stopped, looked at Claire, then continued:

'One half-hour before sunrise, that house gave way to the violence of the day, the windows being blown in, exposing the whole building to destruction. Mrs Ross huddled with her boys on the bed while Mr Ross started for his nearest neighbor's house, Mr Josiah Bartlett's, reaching there at sunrise, feet and face badly frozen and barely able to stand. Seeing the man could venture no more, Mr Josiah Bartlett suited up his horses and drove his sleigh back through the snow to rescue the family, leaving Mr Ross to warm himself. Mr Bartlett pushed through the violent, piercing wind. When he entered the woods he had a mysterious, some would say religious, sense of something amiss, and his senses proved correct. He descended quickly from his sleigh and rushed to the door but did not enter, for the family had vanished, and in their place sat five wild, hungry dogs, their backs hunched, their mouths dripping, their eyes at once cold and bloodshot. Mr Bartlett ran his sleigh home.'

'This is what the Kepper boy wrote me about?' Claire asked. 'This is what I was to believe happened to my sister?' Her voice was loud now, her entire body shaking with fury.

'There is more,' he said gently, and when she nodded he went on:

'All of our town will remember the scare we have had with wolves. Mr Bartlett, being both a farmer and a scholar, is surely a man capable of identifying wolves, and that these animals were not. No, these animals are coyotes, the scavengers of the western prairies. How did they arrive here? And what exactly have they done to this innocent family? No trace of the Ross family remains, nor any trace of this vicious new predator from the West.'

'That's it?' she asked. 'This is rubbish. This is why no one has found my sister?' She grabbed the manuscript from him and shook it in his direction. 'How did people hear this rubbish, anyway? Your book has yet to be published, no?'

'Yes, I am not yet through. I have printed this section in the newspaper, Claire. I have claimed this as the truth.'

'But this is nonsense,' she said.

'Your sister wrote this. She believed this would work and she was correct. There was a great hunt for wolves here, you see. They killed them all, but they wanted to kill more. So far as they can see, your sister and her family were mauled to death. Coyote is sport now, the whole of Middlewood is wild for it, though of course they haven't found one, the damn things don't exist here, they'd know that if they ever read.' He breathed deeply and held his hands out for the manuscript. She passed it to him and he tucked it back into its folder and said, 'If only she could know her story worked so well.'

Claire had been given a room on the second floor, where the bed was positioned right up against the chimney, so as she lay there she was warmed in the most wonderful of ways. She closed her eyes. Silence, and then wind, and then silence, but a new kind here. A new land. She drifted off into it, and when she woke again it was to the dim darkness of morning. She heard Mr Bartlett moving around beneath her, so she dressed and tiptoed downstairs. She thought of her parents. *This is the trip of your life,* they had said. Mr Bartlett had told her to be afraid of the town, of causing them to call her sister's story into mind, and then perhaps into question, but she would not waste such an opportunity. She said, 'Please, I want to see where my sister lived.'

He gave her a pair of boots that were much too big, but with extra twine they cinched down enough. It was just dawn when they set out.

'You understand it is ruined,' he said.

'It is no matter,' she said, and they were mostly silent for the rest of the walk. He led her across the field, where the sheep had already been set out to graze. At the edge, he held out his hand to help her over the stone wall, but she refused. The woods were wet with snowmelt and the trees had just begun to bud and in spite of herself she felt happy for her sister, to have at least lived in such beauty. As they walked, he kept looking back to be sure she still followed, and when he did that she had the strange sense that she herself was her sister, accompanying this new, adopted father on a little walk. After some time he stopped at a stream and then turned sharply uphill.

'A detour,' he said, and led her to a little well house. A bucket sat at the side, attached to a rope. He lowered it down and pulled it back up and offered it to her.

'Sir,' she said. They had scarcely been walking five minutes. She had no need of water. She said, 'I would like you to take me straight to her house, please.'

He clapped his hands and continued on. It wasn't but a minute more, up a little knoll. Before it came into sight she said, 'There is no road?' And then, 'Do others in your town live like this? In the woods?'

'I'm afraid not.'

She might have asked why, but just then they arrived, and she comforted herself with the thought that when he had first come to this new town, Elspeth's husband might have had the choice of any number of houses, in any number of places, but had chosen this one because it would remind Elspeth of home. Not that the setting was anything like home. This house was so deep in the woods that it would never be bathed in the kind of light that Elspeth would have wanted. But the smallness of it, the squareness. That at least was like home. She knew that Mr Bartlett had expected her to stand there in shock. The door had fallen loose off its hinges and the windows were blown in and no one had picked up the glass. Oddly, though, Claire wasn't upset. The sun was parallel to them now, and braiding its light through the trees, and she could see well enough to make out the details of the place. A little garden here, its greenery poking up through the spring cover. A tree with notches in it. She counted them and knew immediately it was for the years her sister had been here. Had there been a particular day, the anniversary of her arrival, that she'd notched the wood? Had she done it the first day she arrived, or had she waited an entire year, marking the completion rather than the start?

'I didn't want to,' he began, but she shook her head, meaning to say that it was all all right. She pushed the door a bit, and then she decided that it ought to come off, so she enlisted his help and together they pulled it loose. He led her across the way to a dip in the woods and they threw it down in.

'Your sister's and mine,' he said, meaning the dumping pit.

She went back to the house. One room inside, and freezing. One large bed in the middle and two more smaller ones against the walls. He said, 'I've cleared some of it out. You understand that I don't want people to wonder.'

One table. Six chairs. On the wall, one faded picture. She took it down and held it against her heart as though the childish drawing were her very sister. For the most part, though, the place was empty.

'What did she do?' she asked. Her voice seemed so loud in here.

'I have gathered all the books,' he said. 'Your sister read a great deal. I have also gathered the kitchenware piece by piece.'

She walked across the floor to the fireplace and held her hands out in front of it as though there was a fire within. She squatted down. The structure was so big, and must have kept her sister warm enough. She kept squatting there, imagining that warmth. He said, 'We ought to be going,' though there wasn't any real need to.

She stood up and turned to follow him out. But then she turned back. She went to the bed, patted one of the mattresses, almost flipped it up but changed her mind.

He said, 'Claire?' and she turned back to him, followed him out of the house. When they had reached the edge of the woods his massive barn came into view. The sun was as high as the tops of the trees now, and it shot straight to that barn, casting it in a blazing light.

'I want to see his house,' she said before she left.

'Whose?'

'The man who did this to her. The mill owner. I want to see his house.'

'Claire,' he said.

'Then I will go on my own.'

He insisted she could not, and he led her there the following morning, before dawn, when once again no one would see them.

'Sir,' she said. 'Is going at this hour not more suspicious?' Yet he did not answer. Though they could have walked just a few minutes up the road, he led her across the field and over the stone wall and through the woods again, past Elspeth's fallen house, past the dumping pit, over another stone wall at the far edge of the woods, and across the carriage road. When they finally arrived at the mill owner's they just stood there silently in front of it. After some time she said, 'Did it happen there?'

'In the top floor. The attic.'

'And the murder?' she asked.

'At the mill dam. It is lucky. His body was found within the week and the town believes he fell in.'

'Will anyone move in now?'

'I don't know.'

'Shall we go in?'

'No,' he said. 'I should think we should not go in,' and

then he turned and led her directly back down the hill, this time on the road rather than through the woods.

The two weeks passed quickly. She told him, during that time, of the feeling she had, that despite the sure fact that her sister was missing, at least on this side of the ocean they now shared the same piece of earth. Now, rather than needing a boat, Claire could just put her shoes on and set out walking to find her sister.

'You can't,' he said. 'It is such a large country. There is nothing to be done.'

Alone in his guest room, she thought of all the ways he might be wrong until finally she admitted he was right.

Her parents, when she arrived home, were not disappointed. Not in her, anyway. They were proud of their brave daughter and they seemed to love her all the more for the fact that she had made it back. Or for the fact that they had worried she would not. They showered her with attention, so much so that she had to remind them that she was not an infant.

'I just want to understand,' her mother said only once. Claire had returned home with the awful story of what had happened – she could not bear to keep it to herself. Other than that, she had returned with nothing but that one strange pen-and-ink drawing that she'd taken from the small house, drawn, they presumed, by Elspeth and her children. It was of an uninhabited island that on the one side looked tropical and the other soaked in rain or snow, they couldn't tell which.

They framed it and hung it in their kitchen, but really it was nothing. It meant nothing, and given the tragedy she had learned of in America, her parents struggled to understand the change that had come over her. But Claire couldn't explain it, the feeling that had finally encompassed her on her last night there, as she'd lain awake in the warm bed against the chimney in Josiah Bartlett's house. The feeling of peace when she had waved goodbye to him. The odd vision that as she left Elspeth tumbled toward her in her wake. How ever to explain such a thing?

Yet not some two months later, a package arrived.

June 6, 1853
Dear Claire,

I pray this arrives safely. Soon after you left I did what I should have done long ago. I do not know why I was afraid in your sister's house. What a fool! I told myself. It was as though the story your sister had written had become real to me, too. I went back to your sister's house and I cleaned every nook and cranny, as they say. It was freezing but that only made me work all the harder. I took my broom and stuck it in the chimney to scare the bats and swallows out, and then I flipped the mattresses up to carry them out. I have enclosed all that I found beneath. You will see. The mattresses themselves were ruined by rodents and it is a wonder these pages were relatively untouched. Were it not for your trip and the thoughts of you that lingered I may have been such a fool as to never clear out the house. There is no title, but thankfully she numbered the pages. I know you will be astonished as I am. I packaged it up to you the moment I finished reading. The drawings were also found beneath the mattresses, and as you can see, they all appear to be of a sort.

> Sincerely yours,
> Josiah Bartlett

'Mother!' Claire called. Her mother rushed to her, but Claire didn't speak, just handed the letter over, and as soon as she was done she handed the first page over, too. Her mother sat down across from her at the table. Neither said a word, they just read as quickly as they possibly could. When her father came in and saw them there he asked what had happened, but they could not stop long enough to explain. Claire simply found the letter and the first page again and handed it to him and he sat down in the third chair. All three of them sat in this way until the early hours of morning, reading. It was as though Elspeth had sent it straight to them – or, better, that Elspeth herself had entered the room. They took turns refilling the candles. For dinner they ate leftover rolls, raw carrots, and an entire batch of biscuits. They could not stop. Claire was the first to finish. When she was done she set the last page down and then picked up the bundle of pictures, more than thirty of them, all of varying detail but depicting that same island, the one they had framed in the kitchen. Claire flipped through all of them and then set them back in the order that Mr Bartlett had sent them in and then she just stared forward, waiting. Finally her mother picked up that last page and read it. Only then did Claire look at her.

Immediately she knew that her mother did not understand it as she did.

Claire said, 'She has escaped, she will come home.'

'Claire,' her mother said, so suddenly so full of sadness. As though she had thought that in those pages there would be an explanation. That if only she reached the end she would know where her daughter had gone. But it was only fiction. She said it aloud. 'It is only fiction.'

'No,' Claire said. 'No, she will come home.'

'There is nothing about home in this book. This book is about doomed lovers.'

'No,' Claire said. 'No. Did you not read it? Read it again. She gives it all up, her lover, the husband she doesn't love, her castle, all of it. She gives it all up to return to her home. There.' She took the last page up again and shook it in her mother's face. 'See?' she demanded. 'Elspeth will return.'

Her father reached across the table then. He grabbed the page out of her hand. She was afraid she would be reprimanded. Elspeth home, it was not a thing to speak lightly of. She and her mother sat silently as he read it. When he was done, he put it back down on the table and he stood up, went to the fireplace.

'George,' her mother finally said. It was so serious, but oddly it felt like a game, too. They were all so excited. 'George. George! Tell us your opinion.'

'It is a story,' he said plainly. He returned to the table and leafed through the pictures that had been sent. 'Fantasy,' he said, and put them back down. He pointed to a tiny detail in the corner of one of the drawings; only this one had it. A title: *Well-Well Mountain Island*. 'She was always full of fantasy,' he said.

'Yes,' Claire said, all excitement suddenly gone from her. She stacked the pages neatly and returned them to their envelope. It was a story. She set it on the shelf by her bed, where she also kept a copy of that other story her sister had written, the coyote story. Mr Bartlett had transcribed it for her before she left. One day soon, she would save her money to have all of Elspeth's writing, plus those strange pictures, bound together into a book, as she imagined her sister would have wanted. For now, the shelf it sat upon needed to be repainted. This home looked so much smaller and damper to her after she had seen America, but so much more like *home*, too. That word, after that trip, had taken on a new meaning, one that Elspeth had certainly understood once she'd left.

It was only a story. And yet. After that story arrived, Claire began to imagine just where, exactly, Elspeth was in her journey homeward. Whose house did she sleep in, or what barn? What forest, what ship? How far, exactly, from the ocean, and on which side of it? She would go down to the waterfront and look out across and she would will herself to see a ship appear on the horizon, her sister and her family waving from deck. Yet she never did see that. Instead, sometimes, especially in the rain, if the light was just dim enough and the water just dark enough, Claire would see that other story her sister had written. Not the romance but the disappearance. She would look out to the sure vision of a pack of five wild, doglike animals rushing across the ocean, staying afloat at every crest of wave, their heads low and their legs fast, headed definitively home.

PART FIVE

Jane and Henrietta

Henrietta

THEY LIE on their backs in The Den, her shirt lifted, his warm hand on her flat torso.

'I'm so sorry,' he says. She had been looking overhead, at the August leaves that glowed even in the dusk, and had been able to see a blur of his profile in her peripheral vision. But now she turns her head away, looks only at the stone of the foundation. Granite, she knows that, has known that practically her entire life. She imagines the people who came before her digging up these rocks, rolling them over to their place. But is that how it would have worked? Or would there have been a quarry in town, and a rock cutter? She would like to ask her father, but it is late summer of 1991 and soon she will vanish, having never bothered to ask.

'We couldn't have anyway,' he says. 'Henrietta. Look at me.'

Very slowly she turns her head again. The leaves crunch beneath her hair and she can feel a stick snap. She knows there must be ants on her, but she has trained herself to be still, to not reach for any itch she feels.

There, she allows herself to look at him. It has been one week since her mother took her to the doctor in Boston. One week since she lay on that cold table and told them simply that she didn't want to do this. That she wanted to raise her child. One week since her mother held her hand so tightly that it bent the cheap clatter ring she wore on her ring finger, the one that Kaus had bought for her at one of those little stands in the middle of the mall a few towns over.

'Did you steal it?' she had asked him caustically when he gave it to her, then she noticed his red cheeks, the embarrassment he felt as he dropped it into her hand. She noticed the sincerity of his gesture.

'I won't let you ruin your life,' her mother had said, and squeezed Henrietta's fingers so hard that months later, when she tried to remove the ring, she would have to pry it off.

'Did I ruin your life?' Henrietta had snapped back at her mother as she lay there on the table, legs splayed open. But then she had closed her eyes, ridding off the possibility that her mother would answer. That her mother would say, *Yes. Yes, you did.*

Just then the door opened and a nurse came in and placed her hand on Henrietta's hair. Henrietta opened her eyes wide and said clearly, 'I don't want to do this.'

'Shhhhh,' the nurse said. 'There, now.'

And so she did what Kaus had told her to do when something hurt. To focus herself right out of existence. To find one spot, one feeling, and pour all of her consciousness into it. The spot of cold metal beneath her pinkie finger on her left hand, the spot that the sheet had somehow failed to cover. She let that spot exist and nothing else. She released herself into it until she slipped right through, into the other side. No time passed and it was over.

'What would we have done?' Kaus asks, there on the floor of The Den. 'Henrietta, where would we have lived?'

She still doesn't speak. She knows that he knows that this is punishment. She hadn't told him about it, not any of it. That she had been pregnant, that she had wanted to keep it, that she had told her parents, that they had made her terminate it. He had called and called and she had avoided his calls until she could no longer. Until she felt that only he would know her, only he would understand what she felt now. Now, such shame, such regret at not telling him before. But then when she had said it, had opened her mouth and let it all come out as quickly as it could, he had yelled at her. Had said, 'Fuck, Henrietta! Fuck!' as though it had been her fault. Which, perhaps, it had. She had not been tied down. She could have sat up. She could have run.

An hour or so later, though, he is calm. She has made him this way, maybe, with her absolute silence. Only just now, this very second, does she finally look him in the eyes.

'Anyway,' she says. 'You cheated. You're a rotten piece of shit.'

He doesn't look away, doesn't get angry. He simply moves his hand from her empty belly to her face and says, 'Have you lost your mind?'

She explains. After their first night, her first time, the night in the barn. The next morning. She had gone to his house and he hadn't been there, no one had been. She had gone to the trestle. The other girls had laughed right at her, then, seeing her face, had offered her a cigarette. *At least he liked you for a little while,* they had said. *Anyway, we saw him with Kristi this morning, so you might as well get over it.*

'They said that?' he asks her, there in The Den. 'Why would they say that? Why didn't you tell me?'

Henrietta comes to this moment often in her new life, nearly twenty years later. All these years she has come to it over and over again as she sits with her son in the woods on the edge of a trail, or as she lies on the banks of a river. Even though the forest floor in Montana is so dry, even though its scent is so piney, so unlike that sweet, fecund smell of The Den, still it sends her right back there, lying next to Kaus. It is like a dream, but of course she is awake when she enters it. Of the thirty-three years of her life she had known him for four months, maybe five. She had not known him at all. But then she had, completely. Jane, her own sister, Henrietta had never been able to tell if she was lying or not. About the fire, for instance. Had Jane really seen him in the glow of the flames? How could she have seen him so clearly, so surely that she felt she could just announce it like that, without reservation? She had surely known what it would mean for him, to say that.

Before the fire, Henrietta had searched for him. That afternoon they had said goodbye in The Den, she had eaten dinner with her family and then retreated to her room, and then, after they had all gone to sleep, she had snuck back out and walked to his house and just stood there, looking up at his window, willing him to come see her. It was late at night but early for him. Usually he had a light on, but just then his entire house had been dark and still. So had he even been home? Or had he been at her house, waiting for her just as she was waiting for him? Or – she had to ask herself – was it possible that he had gone home that evening and realized his anger and then returned to the barn to punish her parents for his lost child in the worst way he could imagine?

But he wouldn't have done that. He could not have. Anyway, why had Jane said another word first? Why *coyote* and not *Kaus*?

Kaus, she knew he was telling the truth. Knew as they lay there together in The Den that he had not cheated, that he would not, that he loved Henrietta, that he would not leave her.

'I'm sorry,' she says in the dream. Had she said it in reality? Sometimes she imagines there is a way to slip back into that time. To float above it and observe every word, every moment, every turn. Which turns led to her future? All of them? And which might she have changed, if she could? 'I should have just run away,' she says on the floor of The Den, just hours before the barn burns to the ground.

'No,' Kaus says. 'I would have missed you too much.'

Jane

'WE'LL BE an hour away, maybe two,' my father said to me, as though I was still a child. But I was in my twenties by then. I had graduated college; I had taken care of myself, somewhat. We were in the kitchen when he said this. They had called me down from my bedroom. My father had made a dinner of waffles and eggs, which had been a favorite of mine since childhood. When I saw that, right away I suspected something.

The house had been paid off for years, my parents said. I would only have to worry about the taxes and upkeep. They told me I had nothing to be afraid of.

'I don't understand,' I said. 'Will you rent a place? Where will Dad work?'

'Your father already found a job,' my mother told me. And then to my father: 'Show her.'

'We'll take you this weekend,' he said, and lay before me photographs of the small cottage they had bought on the coast.

'We didn't want to worry you before we were sure,' my

mother said, and it struck me then just how fragile they must have believed I was. I would not let on that they were right.

'Great,' I said. 'It looks great.' And just like that, my parents packed for a life I never would have expected them to live. The air in their new town is always wet and salty. One row of cottages separates them from the coastline, but you can see a square of ocean from the living room window. It's a ghost town in winter and full of fancy out-of-staters in summer, and it's the kind of place I would have thought they'd loathe, but they have their own life there, and they seem to enjoy it. The cottage is a tiny place, less than eight hundred square feet, but since it's right near the ocean the only reason they could afford it was because it was liable to fall over. They are fixing it up. Main Street is close by, and my father works there, at a French restaurant, while my mother paints in the kitchen. She hangs her artwork up now, too, enough to cover all the walls. She hangs it heedlessly, with no attention to height or alignment, but it looks artful in the way that everything she does looks. The paintings themselves are an odd mix – not together, but each individual painting. They are pictures of our home – our field, our woods, now and then an unnamed yet decidedly New England building. In that sense they are comforting. But there is a trick of light to them. When my sister and I were children, our mother used to say she liked the Romantics best. Henrietta and I imagined that meant she was up in her studio painting some great love affair that had escaped her own life. It wasn't until college that I saw how wrong we had been. The paintings are dark, but somehow, within them, there's some untraceable source of light that makes the whole of them glow. Walking in and seeing them for the first time, I felt cheated. Why hadn't she shown me these before? Why hadn't she told me that she saw our land as I do?

It wasn't long after they moved that I began swimming. In the late nineties a little development was built up the road from my house, a maze of roads peppered with A-frame-style houses for people who like to come to this area and ski, and they also put a little hotel up there, where I swim laps. The pool is long and wide, and I am almost always alone in it. The eastern wall of the pool room is floor-to-ceiling glass that faces a downward slope of woods, and the first floor of the pool room's interior wall is typical enough – white concrete, doors to the locker rooms – but above that, the wall becomes a row of windows that looks right into the hotel's restaurant, so diners can watch swimmers below. It is an odd arrangement. Back then I would swim at four o'clock every day, and frequently as I swam a man sat up there, watching. Not eating, from what I could tell. I assumed he was a worker, perhaps the owner, sitting in his empty restaurant, looking at his nearly empty pool, contemplating his failed venture.

Before my parents left, it was they who always grocery shopped. Twenty-five years, and for the most part I had never had to perform the simple task of planning my food, of restocking my toilet paper and dish soap. Once they were gone I found that I was not so good at it. Frequently I would be left with eggs or a bowl of cereal for dinner. So it was that one night, after swimming, I decided to go up to that empty restaurant and see what they were serving. It wasn't the sort of thing I would typically do, but I liked the idea of it, of feeling unknown and capable. In the wake of my parents leaving, I had resolved to be brave.

I ordered a hamburger and french fries and even a soda. The waitress delivered it to me, and just as she began to ask if there was anything else I might like, a short, dark-haired, middle-aged woman walked in, and my waitress said, 'Excuse me,' and then in a little whisper, 'New hotel manager.'

I must have been eating as I stared. I looked down and suddenly all but a bite of my burger was gone. I knew exactly who it was before she approached my table. She had sold the house years ago, after a divorce, and I knew from my father that, strangely, she had bought a smaller house in town rather than returning to the city, but I had never seen her around.

'How is everything?' she asked, indicating the food.

'Les,' I said.

'I'm sorry?' she said, and then she lowered the glasses that sat atop her head. 'Oh, my,' she said.

'Jane,' I said.

'Of course I remember. Jane. How are you?' She seemed nervous, from my view. Was it because of what her husband had done to, or with, my sister? Which was, exactly, what? For years I had imagined their tryst. Had Les imagined it, too? Or was she nervous about the money? They had never said a word about it, and that fact had sealed for me the impression that they had it by some illegal means. 'How are your parents?' she asked, her voice unnaturally loud.

'They've moved,' I said absently.

'And you?'

'I stayed,' I said, and then realized that had not been her meaning. She had again meant to ask how I was. But how to answer that question? I had always seen my sister's disappearance as a series of dominos falling, with Les's husband – her ex-husband – standing there to ensure that final, definitive fall.

'And Henrietta?' Les asked. She looked the same, older but somehow better than I had remembered. Maybe not so tired. I should have asked about her girls, but I did not. I pictured them off to some fancy college, one that meant their mother could no longer live off checks from her ex-husband alone, that she had to take this job. Though maybe she worked because she liked it.

I said, 'Excuse me?'

'Your sister,' she said. 'How is she? Did she ever come back to this area?'

Had she not asked that question, I might have just gone on in my timid way. But that question – its casual air, its suggestion that my sister had done nothing but simply gone away – made me fierce. I looked right at her, the way my mother – or Henrietta – would have, and with all the hatred I could muster I said, 'No.' And then, adjusting my voice to just the right false pitch, 'And what about your husband?'

'Ex-husband,' she said quickly, with no reaction whatsoever to my tone. 'The crook.'

I went red with guilt, imagining that briefcase. 'Crook?' I asked innocently.

'And I thought we moved to the country for the fresh air,' she said. 'Idiot.'

'I don't understand.'

'Look it up. It was all over the Boston papers. Dr Jack Hennessey, the great embezzler,' she announced like a newscaster. She leaned over me as she said it, took my empty cup, and asked simply, 'Would you like a refill?' and when I shook my head no she turned away, but then turned back. 'I'm sorry about Henrietta,' she said lightly.

'Thank you,' I said. I couldn't look at her when I said it, couldn't move my head or even my eyes. I just focused on breathing, on pulling air in and letting it back out. My father had told me to do this in those after-college years when I had returned to The Den and then week after week hallucinated my sister beneath every maple, at the edge of every stone wall, hallucinated her strolling down every single sidewalk. It had gone on and on until I no longer dared leave my room, scarcely dared open my eyes. I had called for my father. 'Breathe,' he'd said. 'The entire day. Just one breath after another,' he had said. He reminded me daily, until the visions that I had spent so many years warding off finally retreated back to their hiding place. I listened, I breathed, but never did I tell him the whole picture. That it was not only Henrietta who I'd seen. That inside every car that passed me on the highway, painted on the inside of my lids every time I closed my eyes, had also been Kaus, real and whole and innocent. Kaus and the treachery of what I had done.

When I had taken enough breaths I leaned over and pulled my wallet out from my gym bag. I found a twenty-dollar bill and placed it on the table. Les had disappeared into the kitchen. I steadied myself and walked out.

I didn't have much in the way of expenses, as my parents had said. I found a seasonal job with a plant nursery and I learned to take care of the gardens around the house that had become my own. I learned to stake up the peonies and to separate the lilies when they got too cramped. I learned to cut back the raspberries. I built a little coop myself and got chickens for eggs. I had a good, lonely life. I kept swimming, determined to do as my father had told me and not let the past stop me. But I never ventured out of the pool room, and Les never came down. That man who I believed to be the owner continued to sit up in the restaurant, yet I began to envision it was Dr Hennessey up there watching me. Still, every single day I swam my one long, slow mile. I promised myself I would keep a firm grip on my mind.

One evening not long after encountering Les I went out to the mailbox to mail some bills, and just when I put the flag up I looked across the driveway and saw that I was staring at a fox. It was small, silent, reddish, with a face framed in gray. The animal startled me, and when I took a step toward it I knew – a chicken had been killed. The fox and I stared at each other while my mind raced through the details of the other chickens – where they were, whether or not they were safe. I moved toward the backyard, where they like to roam, and off the fox ran, across the field and into the woods.

The previous week, I had come home to find the chickens in their coop, fighting over a dead bat. I had kept these particular layers for two years and this had been my very first problem with them. I suppose that logically it might not have even been a problem – they are animals, there is no reason they should not peck at another dead animal – yet the incident disturbed me. And then the very next week that smart and beautiful fox crept in to kill my least favorite of the brood.

There are – or were – five of them, and I had named them all. Circus, Helen, Egg, Betty, and Dinosaur, who died. Even though that chicken was always bullying the others and pecking at me, her loss made me feel overcome with my responsibility to keep these beings safe. Short of locking them all in the coop all day, which I didn't want to do, I wasn't quite sure how to protect the others, and since I had no books on chicken husbandry, I went to the library to try to learn a little.

'You might like this,' the librarian said, seeing the books I was checking out. 'Next Thursday night at six o'clock.' I took the flyer home, wrote the date on my calendar. *Living with the Eastern Coyote.* When the night arrived I walked to town. I sat at the back of the room, riveted. The room was full – maybe forty people – which was more than I had expected. The speaker was a man in his late twenties who had begun his career studying wolves in the Midwest.

'I saved their teeth,' I remember him saying that very night. He said it had been on his first job, taking care of pups that would be tagged and reintroduced into the wild. They would lose their teeth, and if he was lucky enough to find them he would save them like a parent would a child's. 'Now my collection could fill a whole mouth,' he said.

So it was that anecdote, I suppose, that first drew me to him. I thought of those X-rays of Henrietta's teeth and instantly I felt I had encountered someone who understood.

That night, he talked about how the coyote we see in the East is different from that of the West, of how our eastern animal is the unlikely product of the gray wolves to our north and the coyotes formerly of our land. He shone as he spoke of how, unlike any other predator, coyotes alone have flourished in the face of our efforts to eradicate them. *Opportunistic scavenger,* he said. The phrase startled me. For a moment, I thought of Henrietta. Was she the opportunistic scavenger, or was it I?

When the talk was done I waited for everyone to trickle out, and then I went to the front of the room. Without even introducing myself I said, 'What is it that coyotes do that wolves don't?' How was it possible, I meant, that coyotes could flourish in the face of wolves' near extinction? He understood my question right away. As he answered – diet, adaptability, genetics – he asked me if I would walk him to his car, help him carry his things out. He had a box with some footprints and fur and of course the tooth collection, which was now half wolves' teeth and half coyotes'. In the parking lot, he told me the story of a couple who had walked all the way home from a movie – two whole miles, on neighborhood streets in a small eastern city – and the entire time they'd been tracked by a coyote without even knowing it. His colleague had been studying the animals of that particular territory – that's how he knew. This colleague had videotaped the entire episode.

In response, I told him my coyote story. The house in our woods, the disappearance. And then, at the end of it, without meaning to at all, I said, 'And then the same thing happened to my sister.'

'What?'

'I don't know,' I said quickly. 'I'm sorry. I don't know why I just said that.'

'What happened to your sister?' he asked.

'She didn't turn into a coyote,' I said lightly. 'I mean, I guess I used to think she did.'

'And now?'

'Now I think she turned into nothing?' I said as a question, knowing as I spoke that I sounded like a fool. But he just kept looking at me, no laughter, no pity, just a little bit of a smile. Waiting.

I shrugged and finally said, 'She vanished.'

After that he held out his hand. 'Clarence Shute,' he said. I told him my name. When I turned to walk home, he asked if I didn't want a ride. I got in, and a few minutes later, seeing my house, he said, 'You farm?'

'I pretend,' I said. 'Just chickens.' And then, once again by mistake, 'I burned the barn down years ago.'

He asked me how.

'Cigarette,' I said, shocked by how simple it could be to lay a secret bare.

Again he just looked at me, waited, and then he said, 'That's how they all start, isn't it.'

The next day, he was back in the driveway, wanting to take me out. I shepherded the chickens into their coop and left.

We drove an hour to the north, mostly silent together. He didn't tell me where we were going – just said he had something he thought I would like to see. We stayed off the highway, and instead stuck to bumpy back roads lined with stone walls. I watched them as I rode along, and imagined some ghostlike version of myself running along the top of the walls, leaping from the last stone of one to land gracefully at the start of the next. I kept up the entire time.

We parked on a dead-end dirt road that had one truck off

to the side and no buildings in sight. I wouldn't have seen the trail had Clarence not led me to it. It was spring and green and wet. I followed him through the mud and unfurled ferns, and it wasn't five minutes before the trail opened up to a tucked-away field with a small, rough cabin at its edge. Clarence knocked, and as if in response to the knock I suddenly heard the yips and howls. An older woman opened the door, came right out, and said, 'I'll lead you straight down.'

The woman's name was Penny and she was the owner of all the land in sight – some one-hundred-plus acres. She had spent the bulk of her life on it, rehabilitating animals and then sending them on their ways, back into the wild or sometimes to some kind of animal-preserve facility. Usually, she said, she had at least a few barred owls and a couple animals that people thought were cuddly, like skunks or raccoons. Just now she had only the two coyote pups, found orphaned and weak thirty miles to the north.

I had told Clarence, the night before, that I had spent a lifetime thinking of coyotes yet had never seen one. On the drive up he had said, 'It couldn't have been coyotes, you know.'

'I know,' I'd said, a bit regretfully. I had expected him to say as much the first night we spoke, but he hadn't. He had waited until the drive.

'Really,' he'd said as we rode along, '1852. There is absolutely no way. Not in New Hampshire.'

I hadn't responded. Now, as I stood in the woods, fingers wrapped into the chain-link fence that separated those injured coyotes from me, it seemed that the fact that I had never actually seen the animal before was just as impossible as the fact that it couldn't have been them on our land all those years ago.

'Take your time,' Penny told me, and then continued deeper into the woods. Clarence stayed with me for a moment, but then he, too, walked on, and I was left alone, staring at those animals. They had quieted by the time we'd arrived, and now they were huddled together, eyes closed, from what I could tell. I stood there staring at them, beckoning them to wake up and come look me in the eyes, to howl.

By that point in my life, I had been with only two men. I hadn't really known either one of them at all, and none of it had been as I had expected it would be. No merging of bodies, of consciousness. Nothing miraculous, as in the books I read or the time I'd spent spying on Henrietta. Instead, it had felt clumsy and prescribed, some kind of shared duty that we knew we were supposed to undertake. With Clarence, though, at first I thought the difference was that I wanted something, my body wanted something. But after some time I realized that wasn't it at all. I realized that with him, I could just float right up outside of my body and, at least for a time, enter some elemental existence, the kind I had so dreamed for my sister.

After he took me to see the coyotes, I woke in the middle of the night and walked across the hall to Henrietta's room. Before they left, my parents had cleared it out. Though they'd never said as much, I had understood that they were finally doing what they knew I could not. They had waited so long, and I was never sure if that wait had made it easier or harder or if throwing the cut-off flannel shirts and jean shorts that Henrietta had worn for what was, from our perspective, her last summer into a garbage bag was always as hard as it would ever be, on any day. I also never understood how they chose to save what they saved. Her jewelry box with a ballerina that stood up and spun in circles when the lid was lifted, for example. She had never cared about that except for the fact that it provided a good hiding place for things like that list about all the ways we could destroy Kaus. They kept the porcelain doll that sat on her dresser, which I'm sure she would have given away. They kept her diaries, which was an obvious choice, but they emptied everything else out. Walking through her space when they were finished, I had been shocked by the sparseness of it, by the bare walls and empty closet, but then what would I have suggested they save? What, if anything, had meant something to Henrietta?

The dream that had woken me was of those captive coyotes, barking and baring their teeth at me. In the dream, I put my hand up to the gate that surely I could unfasten, and then I looked at the wild dogs once again. They were not there. Instead, Kaus. I turned and ran, leaving him locked up.

In Henrietta's room, I took out everything that my parents had left. The box of diaries, the one sweater our mother had knit for her, scratchy blue yarn that Henrietta had hardly ever worn. Her Christmas stocking. I laid it all out on the bed. Clarence was across the hall, sleeping soundly in what would soon become his home. I could show him all these things, but it would never be enough. *Kaus,* I wanted to say. *Kaus,* I wanted to tell that man who lay in my bed, and see what it felt like to unearth my final secret.

———

Clarence moved in quickly. At first, I worried now and then over the thought that he loved me just for my house and land.

'But you don't even have a barn,' he reminded me. 'If I chose a woman for her farm, I could have at least chosen one with a barn.'

But within a year we had made plans to rebuild the barn, to fill it with animals. And within three years we had actually done this, and gotten married in the courthouse.

Clarence keeps a flock of sheep. It's for his research. When I met him, he had been working for years on a book about the development of the eastern coyote. I learned in his first talk that a part of a coyote's survival has to do with their reaction to threat. Under normal conditions, a coyote will give birth to a litter of five, maybe six. But if the pack is threatened, the size of the litter will suddenly double. Clarence wants to prove, then, that farmers can live peacefully with the animal – that in fact it is to their benefit. He has fenced our field and filled it with sheep that each night we dutifully bring in. Throughout the day, we collect our urine in a bucket, and after we bring the sheep in he spreads the scent along the perimeter. And his theory works – we have never lost one animal, though he has arranged things specifically so that their blood might be smelled.

Clarence travels often, though, giving talks, crawling headlong into dens, researching and taking notes for the book he dreams of completing. During these times I do the season's chores. If there are lambs, I tend to them. Each year I call a professional shearer from the north, and together we shear the sheep, a job I have worked for years to learn. It suits me, such tasks. A busy life is better than the one I lived before.

In this town, in any town like this, I suppose that encountering people from your past must be the natural course of things. It must be inevitable. Yet perhaps because Henrietta left so cleanly, so completely, or because my parents left with virtually the same amount of swiftness, my encounters, to my mind, always seem fated. Why, for example, after years of surely circling around Les Hennessey, did my space finally clank up against hers just weeks after I was left to myself? It seemed like some kind of test. To interact with her was to interact, on some level, with the self that I had been at that time. Could I do that? Could I do that and not curl up?

I do not mean that I believe in a plan. Yet I have read a little about time, about the theory of relativity and about black holes. I think about it often. I understand how a scientist would explain it, but still I cannot rid myself of the thought that if it is conceivable, according to relativity, to somehow burst forward into the future, then that means the future might already exist. And what then for the past? Sometimes I imagine all of time – everything that has existed and could potentially exist – as a series of innumerable floating planes that we are all just hopping along on.

Take this one particular day. A Friday. Throughout the week I was generally unaware of how any one day differentiated from any other, but Friday was the day that family had disappeared, and Friday was the day Henrietta disappeared; I always knew Fridays.

I went to the mailbox, found a slip for a package. I took Clarence's truck down the hill, to the post office. For my entire upbringing, the woman who works the counter and I were in the same grade, but we do not really speak to each other. I wonder, though, when she sees me – when anyone from my childhood sees me – just what she remembers. Does she see my sister's face in my own? And what feeling, exactly, does this fill her with? Pity, surely, but it has always seemed to me that there's some amount of righteousness, too. *Slut got what she deserved,* I always imagine people saying.

But I have no grounds for such a hateful thought. In fact, I said exactly that to myself, and then I said hello, and I handed her my slip. She brought my package – a new pair of rain boots for Clarence – and I bought a book of stamps. For some reason, just as I took the stamps into my hand, I had the strange thought that I would use each and every one on a letter to Henrietta. It was as if for a moment I believed I had some address to send such letters to. I gave my head a little shake and I turned around.

There. All this time and all this anguish and he was just there, sharing the same moment and space as me. Just pushing a P.O. Box closed. My first thought, shamefully, was that he still looked good. He wore a cowboy hat, which no one out here wears. He dropped his hand from the box, turned, tipped his hat to me, and sauntered out.

I said his name under my breath. 'Kaus,' I said. I should have had the wherewithal to run out after him, but I had nothing.

Clarence was reading in the kitchen when I returned. I gave him his package and told him I felt oddly exhausted. I went upstairs, lay down atop our quilt, closed my eyes, and then got right back up again. I packed my swim bag and returned downstairs, but at the door I decided to leave the bag, to abandon swimming altogether and to just walk.

I went into town first. I pretended I didn't know where I was going, pretended I didn't know why I had gone out to the streets and not to the pool. Yet who was I hiding my purpose from? I walked over the bridge, past the mill, and toward Church Street. I was thirty years old now. Henrietta had been gone for nearly seventeen years, my parents for nine. I had been with Clarence for eight. I had avoided this road for my entire teenage and adult life, and though I had always known exactly why, now I felt the reason in my body. Every car that went by, every voice, forced me to turn and search. By the time I made it to that little house my body ached with tension and my brain was a constant series of misfires that I could not quiet. I stood there and looked up at the house and into the time so many years ago. There was no car in the drive, no sign of movement within. The house's red paint had chipped considerably. I took in one deep breath and then I turned on my heels, just as Henrietta had done in just that spot, and I headed for the trestle. I climbed right up the bank and walked out onto the tracks, unafraid. I stood in the place where I had first watched my sister be touched. I looked downward, imagined jumping.

I must have walked for more than two hours that day, retracing my sister's teenage paths. Clarence had already made dinner by the time I returned. But my stomach was anxious and uneasy, so I told him I could not eat. I left him in the kitchen, and I went upstairs, lay down, and passed into a heavy, dreamless sleep. Yet when I opened my eyes to the shock that morning had already arrived, I felt entirely unrefreshed. I scarcely had the energy to bathe, to dress, to go downstairs and put the coffee on. I was weak as I helped Clarence herd the sheep out, weak as I cuddled the lambs. Clarence recommended I lie down again, but I felt I could not; despite my exhaustion, I felt that all I could do was walk.

It occurs to me, when I look back on this time period, that I was having an affair, though it was not a physical one, and the object of my obsession was not so much a person as a time and existence. Yet that spring I quit swimming and I quit reading and I basically quit talking to Clarence, and instead I walked and walked and walked, continually placing myself in a path that he – Kaus – might cross. Was this what Henrietta had done at fifteen? Like her, I could scarcely eat. Pounds dropped off seemingly by the day, and on the occasions when I was able to swallow a reasonable amount of food, I immediately felt sick to my stomach. Still, I walked to town, to the trestle, to the woods. I walked to The Den, where I lay on the bare ground and gazed above, imagining my body as hers, and his next to mine. In this way my world tunneled and the man that I saw at the post office ceased to be the man I had wronged and became, simply, my sister's lover. Or my own, for I was doing my best to sink into her. On those walks I felt her, I heard him, I smelled the oncoming fire. Every action, every word, every sound, it all came back. It was like I had finally succeeded; I had jumped off my plane of time and effectively landed on another. It came with a certain amount of darkness, though, for I had, more or less, ceased to live.

———

One afternoon in early fall I came in to find Clarence on the couch with my book open on his lap. *The History of Middlewood*.

'This is so strange,' he said. 'This makes no sense.'

I had just been in The Den, digging my fingers into the soil and clearing the leaves out from around the few sad plants that still showed themselves each year. I had just been thinking of that very story. I had never seen that book in anyone else's hands, save for my father's, and seeing it in Clarence's lap like that, in his possession, made me defensive. I told him I of all people knew that the story made no sense.

'That's not what I mean,' he said. 'Josiah Bartlett. He lived in this house? He's the neighbor of this story, the one who goes to rescue the family and finds the coyotes instead?'

I nodded.

'But he wrote it in the third person. Why would he do that? I've read almost the entire book. He uses the first person all the time. Why wouldn't he here?'

'If you don't like it, don't read it,' I snapped.

Clarence didn't even respond to that. He just kept on. It's one of his best qualities, the ability to press on happily, taking no offense. He said, 'The style is totally different. Didn't you ever notice that? The voice in this one story sounds nothing like the voice in any other section. Not even like the voice in the rest of the chapter.'

'What are you trying to say?'

'You could probably find out what really happened to these people, you know.'

'I know what happened to them,' I said.

THE DEN

'You know what I mean,' he said. He closed the book but kept it on his lap. He said, 'What do you do all day, Jane?'

I shrugged.

'Why do you go out there?'

'Where?'

'Maybe it would help,' he said.

This, I think, is the other best quality of my husband, though it can be hard to accept it in the moment. He works and thinks and does whatever it is he does all day, and he scarcely asks me a question, and he gives no indication that he knows what I am doing, but all along he understands.

He said, 'What if these people didn't really disappear?'

'But they did.'

'Maybe,' he said. 'What if you found out where they went?'

'It's not like I'm thinking about them,' I said.

'Well, then, what is it, Jane? You don't eat, you don't talk to me, you walk around all day like you're some ghost. Maybe you'd feel different if you knew.'

'Knew what?'

'I don't know,' he said. 'There're programs now. On the computer. You could look up their birth and death records. Passenger lists. I don't know, Jane. It's just an idea.'

I asked him if he thought these records would tell me what happened to my sister.

'Jesus,' he said. 'You're the one who put these stories together in the first place. What if one of them isn't true? Or what if it's different than you thought? I don't know. I just thought you'd like to find out,' he said. He took the book from his lap and set it on the table and left the room. I looked at the clock. Almost 3:00 p.m. Almost the hour when I had seen Kaus in the post office. I grabbed my jacket and hurried out, and maybe it was because of my anger at my husband that I finally had the nerve to ask the woman at the post office about him. I asked, and as she answered I swear I could see her trying to hold a little smirk in. I like to pretend it was in reference to our shared moment of imagining this remarkably attractive man waltzing through our town, and not because of any memory she had of his connection to my broken family.

'Just moved back,' she said. 'Course I'm not supposed to tell you that.' She looked away from me then, picked up a stack of packages, and went into the back room. I waited a minute for her to return, but she didn't, so I walked out, and I kept walking. I walked all the way through spring and into the sticky days of summer. I didn't mow the lawn, didn't plant a garden. I just roamed the streets, and then one aimless day I roamed in after getting the mail and I complained to Clarence that they'd sent another new telephone book, and that it was such a shameful waste of paper this day and age, and before I had even finished my rant I found myself opening the book, flipping the pages, and reading through all the *S* names. His came early. *Saengsavang, Kaus.* I ran my finger back and forth over the name of the one person I could find – save, perhaps, for the doctor – who potentially knew my sister more than I had. Thirty-eight Mountain Drive. It was right there, right up the hill from my home, in that little development where I'd gone nearly every day to swim.

The first time I walked up to his road, I noticed a pileated woodpecker in a silver maple at the corner. I stopped and watched it for a long time. I'd read once in the daily paper that birds are like people in that they eat three meals a day, and that if you want to see them you can look at breakfast, lunch, or dinner. I'm not a birder, but in this case it seems to work. I frequently walk up to that spot at mealtimes now, just to see him. It's male, I know – I looked it up. His red crest goes all the way down to the base of his bill. Sometimes, a car drives by while I am standing there, just one hundred yards or so from the driveway that leads up to the A-frame-style house that Kaus lives in. It's the sort of house that I imagine will fall right off the rock ledge it's built on when whatever is coming for this world comes. I walked up there that first day, all the way to the top of his driveway. It was late on a humid afternoon. There was a broad, high porch above me, with what must be a fantastic view of the woods below. His truck was in the driveway. I stood there for a while, just letting the mosquitos swarm, not even swatting at them. I thought of how I deserved every bad thing that had ever or would ever happen to me, of how my apology would mean nothing, change nothing. I took a deep breath, turned around, and walked home.

The next day I was standing in my kitchen with my hands in the dishwater when I saw a fox bolt into the yard. Though my reaction must have been instant, I remember a moment in which I had the time to think of how unlucky I felt. A coyote is what I wanted. Why in all this time had I not been allowed to see even one wild coyote? My chickens were out, but I knew I had a chance. I ran out the back door, grabbing a log from the remains of the year's woodpile on the way, and I hollered as I got outside, and threw that wood at the animal. My aim was good. The wood hit her right on the back. She yelped and spun around. I spun around, too. There was a voice.

'Sasha,' it said. 'Sasha, come!'

'Oh my god,' I said.

The dog limped to her owner. He still wore the same hat I had seen him in that day in the post office.

'Oh my god,' I said again. 'I'm so sorry.'

'Jesus Christ,' he said.

'Is she okay?' The dog was at his side now, nudging her head into his legs, and he was leaning over, petting her and at the same time pulling her back out of my yard. 'My chickens,' I said. 'Her color. I don't know. She's so small. I thought she was a fox.' I looked up at him. 'Kaus,' I said. I had said his name in my mind so many thousands of times, but had I ever actually said it to him before? 'Kaus, I am so, so sorry.'

The dog had returned to her bounding self, and Kaus began to turn around and head for the road. I imagined myself letting him go. Behind me, I heard the barn door slide open. Clarence. He would see us, would join us.

'Kaus,' I said again, but he didn't turn. 'Wait,' I pleaded. 'Did you see me?'

He stopped then, finally. 'What did you say?' he asked as he turned around. His question felt so heavy that for a moment I wondered what my initial question had even meant. What, exactly, had I been referring to?

'At your house,' I said quickly. 'I looked you up. I walked by your house. Is that why you came here today?'

'I didn't come here,' he said. 'I was just walking by.' He didn't look at me as he spoke. His voice was at once quiet and pointed. He turned away again and whistled for his dog, who had gone up the road without him. 'Sasha!' he called, and then he left my property before my husband had even made it across the lawn to us.

Henrietta

BEFORE HE could even talk, it seemed unfathomable to Henrietta just how much her son had his own independent mind. Like the way the drain of the bathtub or sink or any drain at all, really, amazed him so fully with no prompting whatsoever. When he was a young toddler they used to take walks through the neighborhood, and had she not eventually picked him up and carried him home she felt he would have lasted out there all night, just staring down the city drains, plopping rocks through the grates and clapping in delight when he heard their splashes. It used to be that she thought he enjoyed the sound of it, that maybe he would even turn out to be a musician. But as he grew and began to speak it became clear that it was strictly the plumbing that he loved. He wanted to know how the water in the city got to their house, wanted to see the path it took when it left. He wanted to know what exactly happened when the toilet flushed. Eventually she bought him a flashlight and a stool, and after that he would spend hours at the bathroom sink, just staring down, exclaiming now and then that he saw something. She never did know what it was he saw, if anything. But when he drew pictures, more often than not it was tubes and pipes. *Well,* she would say to him now and then, *at least I won't have to call a plumber when you grow up.*

She wasn't so sure he loved those things now, though. She'd even asked him, 'Do you still love pipes?' and he had laughed right at her. Still, his understanding of the way things worked had never left. She liked to think he'd inherited this mechanical sense from her own father, though she wasn't convinced her father possessed that sort of mind. Maybe her grandfather. Because she didn't like to think very often of what parts of him might have come from his own father.

He was sixteen years old now. Henrietta said, 'You sure are spending a lot of time with Annika.' And, 'Maybe it's time you slow things down with Annika.'

'God, Mom,' he said. And then, when he was angrier, 'God, get off my back, as if you know what it's like to love someone.'

She went to the drugstore and bought a box of condoms after that. He scoffed at her and refused to touch the box, so the next day while he was at school she brought it into his bedroom and put it in his underwear drawer. After that he never said anything about it and she never allowed herself to check to see if it had been opened. But a few weeks later she did bring Annika outside to see the daffodils, and while they stood there marveling at the giant patch that had grown forth from just a few lone plants a handful of years ago, Henrietta said, 'Don't you get pregnant, you understand me?' Annika, predictably, just blushed, and then she actually turned to leave, but Henrietta grabbed her arm. She said, 'Does your mother talk to you about this? Are you taking birth control?'

'No.'

'No she doesn't talk to you, or no you're not on it?'

'I'm not having sex, Ms Olson.'

'Henrietta.'

'I'm not.'

'You will,' Henrietta said. 'And do you know whose problem it will be? Yours.'

Yours alone, Henrietta thought. She would have liked to believe otherwise, would have liked to imagine her Charley as good enough to stand by, but she had spent his entire life thinking about the opportunity a man was afforded to go the other way. What, exactly, had that opportunity looked like for his own father? Had it been a string of decisions that led inevitably to an open door that he could not help but choose? Or had it been an unexpected and shining path that had appeared before him like an apparition?

In their first few years in Montana, Henrietta hadn't retold that coyote story to her son. She'd told him other stories of her childhood – sneaking out to ride the horses had been the main plot – but for some reason she had always stayed away from that particular one. But then one day when he was four he noticed a picture of a wolf on the front page of the newspaper on their table and he said, 'Why is that coyote there?' She told him it was a wolf that had been spotted on the edge of town but he wouldn't believe her. She said, 'Where did you learn about coyotes?'

'I just know,' he said.

'But who told you about them?'

'I just know,' he said again, and when she asked a third time he grunted and said, 'I don't want to talk,' and he walked away.

That night, though, at bedtime, he wouldn't stop asking her questions. *What is a wolf? How is a coyote different than a wolf? Where do the animals live? What do they like to do?* She told him to stop with the questions and to close his eyes, but he would not. By this time he had of course read many stories of the Big Bad Wolf, and had always delighted in that wicked animal, but now it seemed to her that he must not have ever fully realized that such an animal really existed. He sat up in bed and said, 'Are there wolves and coyotes outside now?'

Finally, in order to get him to just lie down and be quiet, she said, 'I will tell you a story about coyotes if you promise me you'll close your eyes.' He promised and she said, 'This might be a bad idea. What if you get scared, Charley?'

At that he let out a little mocking laugh and told her that coyotes didn't scare him.

'Of course,' she said. 'Once upon a time,' she began, 'in the place that I am from, a family of five lived in my woods.' She told the story slowly. It was the second time in her life that she had told it, and once again she found herself rewriting it as she spoke, saying that the family had needed to get away, that they had lured coyotes into their house and then disappeared. 'So the coyotes helped the people, and the people got to go free,' she said as her son let his breath out, cuddled in to her, and eventually fell asleep. After that, the story – her version of it – became a favorite, one that he wanted told right alongside all the others from her childhood.

———

Once, she and Charley checked out a copy of *Little Red Riding Hood* from the library. At home, Charley sat transfixed as she read it to him. She had forgotten the ending – that the girl and her grandmother were eaten, and then, when the hunter arrived, cut free from the belly of the wolf. When the story was done he sat quietly for a long time. She asked him if he liked it and he didn't answer. She asked if he had been scared. He had just barely turned five years old. Finally he said, 'Why did our family in the woods have to go?'

It was the first time he asked for the information that she had promised him – though of course he couldn't remember that – on their journey west. Now she thought for a while about what to tell him. She didn't want to make up any more specifics, but she could say that they had done something bad, or something that other people thought was bad, but neither statement felt quite right. Finally she said, 'It's a total mystery, we will never, ever know.' She thought that he wouldn't accept it for an answer, but actually he seemed to love that added dimension of the story. 'Tell it,' he urged, and so once again she told him what had come to feel like their very own creation story.

In late spring, Henrietta dropped Charley and Annika off at a trailhead twenty minutes out of town and said she'd pick them up again four hours later. They'd planned to hike through a burn area, where Charley thought there would be lots of morels to pick, and then continue three miles onward, to a waterfall, where they would have a picnic before hiking back. When the time came, Henrietta sat at the trailhead, waiting. An hour passed, another. Thank god it stayed light so late. While Henrietta sat there on the old logging road she saw a bear. Just a black bear, a big one, lolling along with its head low. A minute later she saw a deer. Just as that animal jumped over the small incline at the side of the road and darted back into the forest, a moose walked out. Next an elk. It was uncanny. The animals just kept coming and coming. Henrietta thought for a moment that she had lost her mind, even been drugged. It took her some effort to calm down. She reminded herself that she had never felt safe here. It was nothing like where she'd come from. Here, the wilderness went on and on, and it was filled up with animals that could kill her. She reminded herself that that particular unrest had always suited her, had always been part of what she loved about this landscape. Now, though, with her son out there, she found herself terrified.

Anyway, they returned. They had a full bag of morels with them. They said they'd seen a wolf on the trail, that they'd decided to stay still and wait for it to retreat, and then after it had, they'd waited another hour just to be sure. She probably would have thought it was just a story, that really they were out there having sex and losing track of time, but because of the animals she herself had seen, she believed them. Plus, part of the story was that Charley had been the one who was scared, the one who'd insisted they wait. It seemed to Henrietta that had they made the story up, they would have kept Charley as the brave one.

Charley's birthday was a few weeks after that hike, and on it Annika gave him a book. An old paperback copy of *Never Cry Wolf*. In the past, Henrietta had scarcely seen him read, but once he began that book he would not put it down. She asked him over and over again what he loved about it, but he wouldn't say. Lately he would scarcely say a word to her.

The hardest part of mothering, she thinks, has been the loneliness. Long ago, when she first came to this big state, she'd seen a little article in the paper for a new group for teen mothers. These days, that seemed typical enough, but back then she'd been shocked that there were enough of them to step out in public and form a group. Henrietta had been seventeen at the time, and she'd kept the article and thought almost daily of joining. She'd even driven by the house where the group met, but she hadn't had the nerve to stop. Because what if people saw her going to the group? What if, somehow, she was found out? Even though she'd promised herself that she would be honest she had still lied about her age, said she was twenty-one. She'd used that lie to buy a house. She had at least used her own name and Social Security Number, because what did she have to lose? She wasn't quite sure. Her son was healthy and her life was surprisingly good, and the possibility that anyone would ever come after her for the money had long ago evaporated from her mind. Still, in the long weeks after the forms for the loan were turned in there was one small but sure thread in her that wondered hopefully whether or not she would be found. When the papers were returned and the signing was done she was once again shocked by how easy it could all be. Now she had a mortgage payment, and what kind of teenager had that? She wouldn't fit in with the other girls in the teen mothers group. Still, she'd saved the article, which had been printed with a photograph of seven girls standing at a rose-filled park with their babies.

Her job had kept her going, anyway. Early on, after she'd bought the little ranch house, she'd had the sense to know that the money wouldn't last, so she took the first job she found, at a coffee shop in the center of town. She'd thought she'd stay only temporarily, just until she figured out a way to go back to school. But then it turned out she had loved that calm little shop with its coffee bar and regulars who came in and sat at the booths every day. At first, Charley went to daycare while she worked, but it cost her nearly her entire paycheck. Luckily – actually, it seemed much too great for luck alone – when Charley learned to walk her boss took a liking to him and offered to have him come into the shop for half of the day. He'd been allowed to climb up on a stool and help wipe the counter, that sort of thing. Somehow, for the most part, it worked, and Charley kept coming back. Customers liked him and he had been entertained by all the activity and treats, plus his trucks and crayons. The other employees were good to him, too, and they helped Henrietta out in that way. They'd take him for walks on their breaks, and one particular woman would even take him to the park if she finished before Henrietta. It had been a good sort of life. In fact, Henrietta had more or less loved her life.

Yet when Charley started kindergarten, she had seen that other mothers didn't like her. The way they looked her up and down, the way they nudged her right out of conversations – those mothers made her feel as skinny and poor as she had in her old life. She was some ten or even twenty years younger than the rest of them, and she felt certain that in their eyes, she couldn't possibly be a good mother.

But even then, she had a good time with her son. They'd swim together in the rivers, and sometimes they would eat too much ice cream together. They'd go to the movies, they'd cook, once they'd even painted pictures all over his bedroom walls. She had never known such happiness. But oddly, not so much loneliness, either, particularly when things were rough. When Charley was sick or inconsolably fussy or when she was exhausted. Sometimes she felt so much loneliness that she'd find herself looking out the window that faced east and thinking of her family and wishing she could leap across the land right back to them.

But how to ever go back? How, how ever, to cross such a distance?

Charley finished the book from Annika in three days, and when he was done Henrietta picked it up, read the back, and asked if it had reminded him at all of the story about the coyotes that she used to tell when he was a boy. She couldn't recall the last time she had told it to him, but it had probably been when he was about six or seven, and had learned to read and wanted to go to bed on his own, with a flashlight and a book. Now it shocked her to hear that he didn't remember the story at all. She said, 'But it was our story. You loved it so much.'

Charley shrugged and said, 'Tell it, then.'

'Don't you be rude to me,' she said, and then she told him that she had come from a farm where coyotes stalked the woods, and that the story she had told him had actually been her father's favorite story, though when he was young she'd told him her own version of it.

'Tell me the real one,' Charley said now, and so she did. She told him that the temperature had dropped – she even said what her father had, that the *mercury had begun to plunge* – and the wind had blown in the windows and the father had gone for help; she said that the neighbor had returned to find no family, but five coyotes instead. 'The father was gone, too. Cold Friday, 1852. It happened in the woods behind my child-hood home. The neighbor in the story is the man who lived in my house back then,' she said. Then, because her son had been so cocky lately, and would probably point out that the story was impossible, that coyotes hadn't even been out east back then, she said it herself. But he had no response to that. He just sat there, transfixed in that way that he, and she and Jane, had been in childhood.

'I don't know what I think about the coyotes in the story,' she said absently, and it was as though she fell down into her childhood dining room as she said it. Those overgrown plants hung in the windows, blocking the light; the maroon stencils at the borders of the walls, which her mother had painted one winter in a fury. She could almost hear her mother, that soft but aggravated way she would chide her father when he told it. About the coyotes, Henrietta had never believed or not believed. But the story itself was another matter. She told her son. She said, 'I always imagined that the family just ran away.' She'd told him that before, of course, but now, when she said it so plainly, it split her open. Her mother. 'My god,' she said. She was talking to herself, not even quite sure her words were coming out. 'My mother would have thought those poor fools had been eaten.' Her eyes welled up as she said it. How could she have gone on this long and not realized that simple fact? All these years, what would it have meant for her mother? Sylvia was not a religious woman, and there would be no memorial for her daughter. Would there be pictures? Would she still be searching for a body? 'Charley,' Henrietta said urgently, suddenly overcome by a need to hold her son. He had wandered to the far side of the kitchen by now, and when he came back within reach she pulled his tall frame onto her lap and tried to take in that smell of him, as she had when he was young. It was buried beneath so many other smells now, but she could still find it, that essence of her one boy. But he wouldn't let her, of course. He pulled away and, put off by her sudden neediness, headed out of the room. He was almost to the hallway when she stood up and said, 'My sister. Oh my god, Jane.' Charley watched as his mother looked frantically about the room, as though she expected to find someone there. All color had drained out of her. She sat back down. Jane had thought those people had transformed into the coyotes, she had always thought that. She could see her sister now, pacing the woods, calling out, looking for some shape-shifted version of the sister she had once had. Would it have ever even occurred to Jane that Henrietta had simply left?

Charley was heading back to her side, at least. She was hunched over, her elbows on the table and her head in her hands, but she heard his footsteps and now she could see his feet out of the corner of her eyes. Those long, broad, masculine toes. She'd paid sixty dollars for the flip-flops he was wearing and they were already fraying. She thought he might place a hand on her back or offer to get her some water or crackers, but he just stood there. Finally she gathered herself up and asked him what he should have asked her. She said, 'Charley, are you okay?' He didn't answer, but he wouldn't stop staring, either. It unnerved her. 'What?' she said. She sat up straight. She was still so good at shifting gears. Like riding a bike, she thought a bit darkly. 'Do you sort of remember the story now? That's really not the way I used to tell it. I used to say the people tempted the coyotes in and then ran away. That they set up the whole thing.' Every word took effort, but something in his eyes told her that she had to keep going, had to find the right thing to say to pull him back up. 'Goddamn it, what?' she finally demanded.

That did it. For a moment before he spoke she thought stupidly that he might tell her which version of the story he believed. She wasn't prepared for his anger, and in fact had never quite experienced that sort from him before. The kind so pure it was glacial. He kept his eyes right on her and his voice completely steady as he said, 'You have a sister?'

'Yes,' Henrietta said plainly, realizing what a fool she had been. She looked out the window, stood up abruptly, and then walked out the back door, into their flowerbed, where she fell to her knees and began to weed.

Charley had read the book about wolves in July, and in September Henrietta saw a flyer in the coffee shop – a wildlife biologist, coming to give a lecture on wolves and coyotes at the university. It wasn't such a coincidence; out here the wildlife biology department was exceptional, and she thought she'd probably seen this sort of flyer on the bulletin board of her work at least a few times a year ever since she'd first arrived. Still, it struck her as unusually lucky. She wrote the speaker's name down, went to the college, and bought her son a copy of his book plus three tickets – she, Annika, and Charley would go to the lecture in two weeks.

During those two weeks, she assumed her son read the new book, though he really didn't say anything about it – he was too busy in a sudden spell of fights with Annika. Yet, even though her son wasn't talking about that book, Henrietta found herself entranced by the man's flyer, so much so that when no one was looking she quickly ripped it off the bulletin board and folded it up and put it in her purse. At night she would take it out and smooth it against her pillow and prop herself up on her elbows to stare at it as though it were a painting. In the picture, the man stood at the edge of a field. A faint outline of a stone wall was just behind him, and decidedly eastern woods rose above. Those woods, that particular sugar maple – no, it couldn't be. Still, the flyer had the ability to send her right back. She would place it beneath her pillow, and lie atop it, and close her eyes, and sink.

Charley, during this time, had begun to ask about his father. Henrietta believed that his sudden questioning on the subject was somehow connected to her recent retelling of the coyote story, which had obviously reminded him that his mother had come from somewhere, had fled from somewhere. He had asked about his father before – first when he was just a young boy hearing about other fathers at school. Back then she'd been able to deflect the questions with simple distractions – an offer of an ice-cream cone, a trip to the park. But then when he got a little older she'd been forced to give a legitimate answer. At first she'd gotten angry and snapped at him, told him to stop prying and just leave her alone. He had been totally dumbstruck. Finally, a few days later, she'd said, 'He was smart, but at least back then he wasn't kind.'

'I don't want to find him,' eight-year-old Charley had said immediately.

Around the same time, though, he'd also begun to ask about his maternal grandparents. He wanted to know if they were alive, and where they lived. 'It's hard to explain,' she had said for a while, and then, 'I don't want to talk about it,' and finally, because she wanted to be better for him, 'New Hampshire. I am from New Hampshire. I had a hard time as a teenager, and in order to take care of you I had to leave.' That had seemed like enough information. But now, suddenly, he was asking if he could go back east, if he could see where she was from, if he could look for his own father. So far, she had not responded. What in the world could she even say? She would have to start with the first pregnancy, the one that had been terminated. But where to go from there?

I do know what it's like, she imagined herself saying to him. *I know better than you.* To love someone, she meant, though even as she thought that she wondered at its validity. Was what she'd felt at fifteen anything even close to what love truly was? To be physically sick with thoughts of someone, to lose all interest in anything that had ever sustained her before, to dream up paths for destruction and then throw them right out, was that truly what love was? In those days, her entire self had been eclipsed, but then Kaus had never seemed to feel as she felt. He had never seemed to lose what direction he had, not until they took it from him. Her son didn't, either, though she worried that Annika might. Was this the path of girls, then? Obsession, and complete loss of power? She had been trained for such a fate, she thought sometimes. All the stories had trained her for it.

Still, though, she remembered that time with Kaus as a true, shining seed that she could cup in her hands. She would not ever have traded that time, would not ever let go of it. She still had his letter, his very last one, stuffed at the back of her closet, in the duffel that she had left home with. She hadn't read it in years, but now she found herself crawling to the back of her closet and reading it there, on the floor, in secret. *Dear Henrietta.* Why had he written it in pencil? Had they not allowed pens in that place he'd been sent? The years were making the words fade. Eventually the entire thing would be blotched out.

> *I got your letter. I don't think it is a mistake that it happened. It was only three weeks ago that I came home for the weekend so are you sure? Even though it is so early? I still mean I want it. Maybe it is saying something that it happened again. I mean maybe we were meant to have a child Henrietta. You are right they can't do that to you again and I will do whatever you need. I earned another weekend home for good behavior so my mother is picking me up and I will be home on Friday night of next week. November 15, don't forget the date. Meet me in your woods where we met in October. I can sneak out like last time.*

*My grandmother doesn't go to bed until after 10 so meet me
at midnight just to be safe. You don't have to do it again. We
can figure out what to do and we can find money. I know
it is tiny in your belly but it will be our child and I will not
let them do this to you again. I don't have much longer here
and then I can work. I don't care what I do all I care about
is you. You are too brave to be scared so don't.*

Reading it now, she wondered at the fact that she hadn't
burned it rather than carrying it around all these years as
though it held some clue as to what had happened to him,
when what had happened was so totally obvious: He had
abandoned her. That night, out there in the woods with that
briefcase of money, she had laughed at the fact that after all, it
really was she who was the braver one. She had never quite
believed it. Of course, over the years she had changed it in her
mind a little, had rearranged things so that he knew she stole
the money, knew that she planned to escape. In truth he didn't
know anything of that. He knew only that she was pregnant
with his baby again, that she intended to keep it, and that she
was in the woods, waiting for him to show up. He never did.

The woods – Henrietta even got her son's old magnifying
glass out one night to look more closely at that flyer, to no
avail. Another night when Charley was out she went into his
room to look for the book the speaker had written, but she
couldn't find it. At dinner on more than one occasion she
said, 'Have you enjoyed that new book?' and 'Can you tell me
about that book I bought you?' and 'Where, exactly, does it
take place?' But her son would only shrug and look at her as
though she had lost her mind.

And maybe she had, because when the night of the lecture arrived, Henrietta felt sick with nerves. Thank god her son was going with her. But then he almost didn't go – another argument with Annika, who refused to come along.

'You go,' Charley snapped at Henrietta. 'Why do I need to go to some mind-numbing lecture?'

'Charley,' she said. 'Charley, you'll love it.' And then, finally, 'Damn it, Charley, you're coming with me.'

Anger, at him and in general, had been a very, very rare occurrence, and when it happened it always shocked him a bit, made him listen. So he went along with her, but while they sat there side by side she wondered if she might have done better to come alone anyway. She felt oddly nervous, and out of place in a way that she thought she'd outgrown. There were at least one hundred people around them, and they all seemed to be students or professors. She and Charley had arrived early, and while everyone in the audience seemed to talk comfortably to each other, Henrietta just pried at a loose string on her sleeve while her teenage son stared at the ceiling and now and then turned his head in her direction to ask her why the hell she was being so strange.

'Strange?' she repeated like a fool.

Finally, the man walked out onto the stage. He was larger and softer than she had expected he would be, and his plaid shirt wasn't tucked in quite right. He walked slowly to the podium and he said, 'I've always wanted to come out here,' and then, after talking for a bit about how beautiful the rivers and mountains and big sky were, he said, 'Back in New Hampshire,' and Henrietta felt her heart stop. She thought of this later that night. That stopping heart, it was almost like a second premonition – the first being the way she'd stared at that flyer – because really she had met others from New Hampshire; it was no great thing. It was an entire state, after all. But her heart had been right to be warned, to seize up, because the next thing he said was 'I live on a sheep farm,' and then, 'used to be the home of the largest barn in the county, but that burned down in 1991.'

'Oh my god,' Henrietta said, and clapped her hand over her mouth. The young couple in front of her turned in their seats to look at her and her son slapped her leg. She stared forward. Had her family left her? If she were to return home now, would she find this strange man in her home? Or was this man her family?

Yes. Yes, of course. She had never considered what sort of man Jane would end up with, if any man at all, but now as he stood there bumbling about the book he had written and the animals he studied, she knew. She stood up in her seat and her son tugged her back down. She looked behind her, to all sides. Suddenly she felt dizzy. She leaned forward, put her head between her knees. Was Jane the sort of wife to travel with her husband? Would she sit in the back row or the front? Henrietta sat back up and held her hand to her heart. It was beating so fast that she worried she might have a heart attack. Her father's mother had died young of a heart attack. If that were to happen to her right now, who would take care of Charley? Before it happened, before she died right here, could she somehow leave a message for her son that told him his family was onstage? Could she tell him to follow this man back east to that farmhouse?

'Stop,' she said aloud, by mistake.

Her son nudged her again. He looked at her, leaned over, and whispered. 'Mom,' he said. 'Mom, are you okay? You're sweating. Mom?'

Finally, she thought, and she felt tears emerge. Finally her son was at least being kind for a moment. He hadn't been kind in a few months. 'Charley,' she whispered back to him, but of course she couldn't say any of it. She put her hand on his leg, gave a little squeeze, and then moved back into her own space.

Okay, she was whispering to herself. *You can do this.* Just as she had said to him all those years ago. But this time, what was it she was saying she could do?

'Mom,' Charley said. 'Mom, get up.' She looked around. The lecture had ended. The clapping had turned to a trickle and the people were standing, filing out. Those in her aisle were waiting for her to move. She cleared her throat and stood and said loudly, 'Do you want your book signed?' When he didn't answer she said, a bit too enthusiastically, 'Well, I want it signed!' and she rushed away.

In the lobby they were greeted by the contained echo of all those milling bodies. This July there had been forest fires, and the smoke had hung on in the valley for two weeks, and she felt now as she had felt then. Breathless, like no matter how hard she pulled in air there just was not enough oxygen available.

'Are we getting in line?' her son asked her. She scanned the room, searching, and then she pointed to the far side.

'Wow!' she said, and dragged him over. It was a taxidermy moose head that she had no real interest in but thought she could stall Charley with, but it turned out that of course he had no interest in it, either. 'Hors d'oeuvres!' she said, trying again, and she pointed back across the room. She dragged him that direction, to the table of crackers, cheeses, and grapes. 'Charley,' she said as she filled a plate, 'do you want some wine?'

'I'm seventeen,' he said blandly. 'Can we get in line already?'

The line for the book signing snaked around the room, and it took them some time to find the end of it. 'Forget it,' Henrietta said once as they walked, but thankfully her son didn't hear her. She really couldn't forget it. Charley was carrying the book. When they finally took their place in line she pressed her little paper plate of cheese on her son and told him to give her the book. She held it against her chest. She imagined that its heft would hold her heart in. She saw her sister everywhere. Her long braid in front of them in line, the top of her head at the front of the room, her sandaled feet standing there by the drink table. She heard her sister's voice.

The line moved slowly, and a few times when people got behind them she surreptitiously moved out of her spot and back to the end of the line once again. Charley rolled his eyes at her every time she did this, but she just shrugged and said, 'What? I want to be last.' Eventually, though, there was no place to move. The line tunneled its way to the front tables. First she saw the display of books and then, of course, the writer.

She already had one book in her hand, but now she reached for another, and then a third and a fourth.

'Hush,' she scolded Charley, though he hadn't even commented yet. With the stack of books in her arms she inched her way over one more foot until she stood face-to-face with the man.

'Oh, no,' she said to him.

'Hello,' he said. 'Did you enjoy the lecture?'

'I just realized I don't have cash,' she said, and she put the three new books she had picked up back on the table. 'I'm sorry,' she said. 'I love your book. I mean, I didn't read it yet, but this one is already mine. I already bought it.'

'And who would you like me to sign it to?' he asked. His voice was so plain and kind. His face. It was so open, so unassuming, that she could practically fall right into it. It was like her father's, in a way. It reminded her of her father. This man knew her father.

'Jane,' Henrietta said, and suddenly the room seemed to go silent. Whatever weight on her chest that had been pressing in seemed now to fly outward; a thousand birds flew outward from her when she said that.

'What are you talking about?' Charley said.

'That's my wife's name,' the man said.

'Oh my god,' Henrietta said for the second time that night, and then she grabbed her son, pulled him in front of her like a shield. 'This is my son,' she said frantically to the man. 'This is Charley.'

'Mom,' he snapped at her.

The man closed her copy of the book and stood up slowly. He put his hands out in front of him – proof of his harmlessness – and he said, 'I'm sorry. This is going to sound crazy.' Then, with great care, as though she were a horse who could be spooked, he began to come around to her side of the table. Outside, the clock tower struck.

As he approached, Henrietta imagined her feet sinking into the tiled floor. She imagined staying put, not running.

Slow, she told herself. *Breathe.* Charley was still in front of her and she squeezed his arms as tightly as she could.

'Ouch,' he said, and suddenly the spell was broken. *No,* she thought, and then she said it aloud. 'No, no.' She had to unfreeze her feet. She had to not be caught. All these years. No, it would not happen like this. It would not happen on someone else's terms. 'No,' she said, and she grabbed her son as tightly as she could, turned around, and ran them out of that building.

'Jesus fucking Christ,' her son said when they finally stopped on the far side of the campus quad, beneath the shadow of the mountain.

'The wind's shifted,' she said plainly, as if nothing had happened. 'A few days ago. Did you notice? True fall is here.'

'Don't talk to me,' he said, and so she didn't. They drove home silently. He called Annika when they got there. Henrietta went to her room and took from her shelf one of the very few things she still had from home: Jane's copy of *Flowers in the Attic.* Over the years, when she was in her better states, the book had made her laugh a little bit – why couldn't Henrietta have been wiser, chosen a kinder, homier sort of story to carry with her all these years? Why couldn't Jane have left *Anne of Green Gables* or *Little House on the Prairie* in the closet while she snooped?

She lay with her head on that book as she had so many times before, and thought once again of that night she had left. Long ago, she had tossed the briefcase out. She'd thought of throwing it in the river like some criminal – which, of course, she was – but finally she'd just put it in her trash bag and, the next morning, watched it get thrown into the garbage truck with all the rest.

Since she'd left, she'd thought often of the doctor. Had he ever looked for her? He had been the first one she told. He was friendly, he liked her, and she'd always felt seen by him. He was a doctor who would know about this sort of thing, and on top of that, from what she understood, whatever she told him would have to be kept confidential. So one night in October she'd sat in his car while her sister stood there on the porch imagining some secret love affair between the two of them, and she'd said plainly, 'I'm pregnant and I don't know what to do.' He'd said he could help her. Right away he'd said that, without even missing a beat. She'd gone on, told him what her parents had made her do the first time, and he'd practically shouted. 'That is not okay!' he'd said. 'How is that okay at all?' When he'd calmed down he'd said again, 'I'm not that kind of doctor, but I could help you. Whichever way you choose.'

Whichever way. She had waited for a path to open, pretending she didn't already know her path. But if she didn't understand the passing of time, her body did. Every day she felt it change and she knew she could not keep waiting. Finally one day after school she just did not get on the bus. Instead, she walked straight to the hospital. She told him she didn't have a choice, not under her parents' roof. To that she had watched his face go tight with rage and then sink back to its normal state. He told her he would talk with them, and when she said no he'd said, 'You're your own person, you know. You could do this on your own.' And then, 'I have money, Henrietta. I could help you.'

'Okay,' she had said, as though the deal was sealed, though

of course there were no plans laid. Still, over the years she had liked to tell herself that the briefcase of money had been what he'd meant that day at the hospital. She knew in her heart that couldn't be true, but by now she was so good at making herself believe. She thought of his words often, of how her fear of being chased or caught with the money had always been minimal, because of those words. With them, since the day she had left, she could always imagine Dr Hennessey out there in the world, wishing her well.

She opened her eyes and stood up. To think that she could have been brave enough for all that and not this. The letter at the back of the closet wasn't anything for anyone; it was just a teenage love letter from a boy. Still, it was something. It was all she had. She trembled as she carried Kaus's words to her son's room.

'Here,' she said. 'This is from your father. You weren't born yet. It's the last I ever heard from him.' And then, after he'd taken it into his hands, 'You could find him, if you want. You could try. I could help you try.'

Jane

AFTER I saw Kaus, a year passed quickly. In it, Clarence finished his book, found a publisher, and soon became a big deal in his field. He began to tour the country, giving lectures at colleges and universities. While he's gone, there are always the fences to take care of at night. First I have to herd the sheep in, and once that's through I have to slowly walk the perimeter of the field, spreading a thin line of the day's urine out. I do this with a watering can. It used to disgust me but now it is habit, as is the daily collection. I like living like this. With every passing year, I want to go more deeply into the land. What if we stop driving, I wonder sometimes. Stop flying, stop buying anything that has come to us by flight? How much water do we really need to use, anyway, and how little waste can we produce in a month? I have started to measure. On the calendar, I marked the day that I put a new trash bag in the bin that sits on the back porch. My goal is to not fill that trash bag for at least a month.

Two months ago, my husband called me in the middle of the night. He was in Montana. It was midnight for me, ten o'clock for him. Late September, freshly cold, with that ghost-filled wind that I always feel arrives in fall. I had finished with the sheep and the fences some three hours before and had been sound asleep for at least two.

'You need to come out here,' he said without even saying hello. He had said this for months before his trip, that I needed to come with him. *You'll love it!* he had said. He'd wanted us to make a vacation of it, to visit Glacier, Yellowstone. I had refused. *What about the sheep?* I'd said. It had been my mainstay. But now, on the phone, after once again saying I needed to get out there, he said he was sure he had met my sister. He told me to get on the next plane.

'No,' I said plainly. We have a portable next to the bed. I didn't even have to sit up. I had left the western window open to feel that crisp air on my face and now I had the sense that he could float in through that window and catch me in the full lethargy of my response. It was like a fresh abandonment of her, but still I pressed on. 'What about the sheep?' I asked him.

'Jesus, Jane,' he said. 'Do you even hear yourself? I'm serious.'

'It's not her,' I told him. I didn't even miss a beat. I had imagined this moment so many times; even just this month I had imagined it repeatedly. From the dining room, over and over again, I had caught a glimpse of a person in the backyard, felt my heart lurch, and turned to see the empty clothes on the line. A shadow had moved across the curtained windows that looked out to the front yard and I had frozen until I realized that the shadow had been my own. It seemed fitting in this season when the trees exploded that one thing should appear as another, but the insistence of that tendency this year had thrown me. When my husband called it was almost as though I'd known he would. I was armed. I said, 'You don't even know what she looks like.' As I spoke, I felt I could see myself. I felt I had left my body to hover somewhere near the ceiling and watch myself.

'She has a son,' my husband said. 'He's a teenager, Jane. His name is Charley.'

I hung up the telephone after that. Even though the bedroom that had formerly been my parents' room is much bigger than my own, Clarence and I never moved into it. Instead, we keep it as a guest room for when Clarence's sister and her husband and daughters visit, and we sleep in the room that I spent my entire childhood in. I thought of that as I stared at the ceiling. Of all the hours I had spent staring at that very ceiling, wondering if my sister would appear. I was not going to do that this time. When the phone rang again I let the machine pick up. I could hear the beeps and then my husband's voice rise up through the heating vents that led straight to the kitchen, where the answering machine was.

I got up, got dressed. In the kitchen I listened to his message: 'Jane. I'm sorry. For Christ's sake, Jane, pick up the phone.' I went to the barn. All the animals were in. I sat down in the middle of the floor, between all the stalls, and listened to their breath. I hadn't turned on a light. Even though our barn was relatively new, it still had that familiar barn smell of animal and dust and sweet hay. I lay back on the dirty floor and gazed upward. This new version of the barn had no cupola, and no eastern and western lofts that you had to crawl on a ladder to cross. But it had been built on the same old foundation, and to me that meant the same old ghosts still haunted it. I imagined my sister on the floor above me, rifling through her blankets, searching for her cigarettes. I imagined her looking out the high window, waiting for her lover to appear on the horizon. Had Josiah Bartlett looked out that very same window? And what of the people of our woods? Had they worked in this space? Or made love in it, as Henrietta had? There was scarcely any wind that night, but still I imagined a gust sweeping through to pick all of us up, every single one of us, those people of the story and my family, their coyotes and our coyotes, and carry us all along, furled together, one breathing mass.

It wasn't a new vision. I had daydreamed it so many times over the course of the past year, when, while Clarence busied himself with his book, I'd decided to take his advice and search for records of that family of The Den. For a while, I'd gone almost daily to the State Library a half-hour away to sift through the files on their computer program. I hadn't spent much time on a computer before, and in that room I discovered that when I turned it on my mind entered some dark, directionless vacuum that I could scarcely escape. Thomas and Elspeth Ross, born in Scotland, emigrated to America, probably in their thirties or forties in 1852 – it wasn't a lot to go on. There were so many with their name. Sometimes, as I opened file after file – birth certificates, marriage certificates, passenger lists – I wondered what in the hell I was doing, why I was wasting my life in this way. Other times, before Clarence's phone call from Montana, I would close the ancestry program down and look around the room to make sure no one was watching me, and then I would open the Internet search engine and type in her name. *Henrietta Olson*. It was the first time I had ever allowed my mind to actually imagine the possibility of some real-life trajectory for her. I would scan all the results quickly, terrified that I might find one that matched. Most were obituaries, and now and then I opened them up to see if my sister had died. But I never found anything that sounded even remotely like her, and I always returned quickly to searches for that family.

That night of my husband's call, I rose from the barn floor, said good night to the sheep and chickens, and walked back across the yard, toward my house. Enough leaves had dropped by then to give a slight view of the Hennesseys' former home. I could only see the upper floor, and suddenly I thought of all the hours I had spent up there with those twins, chanting and trying to call the spirits. But who, or what, had I been searching for back then, when my sister had still been in my midst, real and whole and full of breath?

Inside, I brushed my teeth again, cleaned my face, took my barn clothes off, and lay down in bed once more, just like any other night. I read for half an hour or so and then I turned out my light and slept. But at around 4:00 a.m. I sat up with a jolt. There was no need to call on some spirit, not now, not anymore. In fact, there never had been. My sister existed. I had wasted all these years in a delusion in my woods when the truth was so simple, so obvious, that it made me sick to realize: Henrietta stole a briefcase of money and she just left. She had even left a note to say so. Now, today, I could open a map and point to the exact place upon which Henrietta stands. I could buy a ticket and fly across the country and exit the plane into that circle of mountains and know that my whole, real sister breathes somewhere within them. But alongside that knowledge would have to be the simple fact that she had chosen to leave, and that she had never chosen to return.

I went downstairs again, turned the dim kitchen light on, and filled a glass with water. I was not cold but shivering, my shoulders hunching forward, my whole body closing in on itself. I spilled half of my water down my front. I picked up the phone and began to dial my parents' number, but kept pressing the wrong buttons. I put the phone back on the hook. Next I took the phone book out of the drawer once again. It had been a year since I'd thrown that wood at his dog. I accidentally tore a few pages as I flipped forward into the book, to his name. I found myself reading his address again, as if I'd forgotten where he lived. I flipped back to the town's street map and held it right up to my eyes, a way to steady myself. I found Mountain Drive and I imagined myself on it, passing by that woodpecker and continuing to his driveway, walking all the way up. Knocking, going in.

Clarence returned from his trip that evening. I had spent the bulk of the day on the couch, just staring at the wall, but in preparation of my husband's arrival I mustered all my strength and got up and cooked a pot of chicken soup. As we ate I spent some time telling him about the books I had read while he was away. Mysteries, a series that takes place in England that I thought he would enjoy. He didn't really listen, though. He snapped, 'Jane.'

'What?'

'Come on, Jane,' he said. 'Stop it.'

'Fine,' I said, and I lay the phone book in front of him on

the table. I opened it and pointed to Kaus's name. 'I'm surprised they still print our addresses right there for the entire world to see, though.'

'Who is this?' he asked. 'What are you talking about?'

It's strange how my brain took in that question, how it processed it with remarkable speed yet at the same time saw it all in slow motion. It was like a wave washed through our kitchen, over our bodies. I felt as Henrietta had in her nightmares, like beneath the weight of that water we still spoke yet could not be heard. When the wave passed and we came out on the other side, I suddenly saw the entire story through my husband's eyes. I saw the story I believed, too – a lecherous doctor, and Henrietta's silence bought by that briefcase; or, maybe, that briefcase the ransom she held against his trespass on her body. But now I also saw what I had taught Clarence to see: an innocent Henrietta, a virtuous one. A fire that came before it all, that stood alone, unconnected.

We stayed up half the night. I told him everything I knew. Finally I said the worst of it as plainly as I could. I said, 'He was sent away for the fire I started.'

'Does he know about their son?' my husband asked me.

'What are you talking about?'

'Charley. Does Kaus know?'

'Why would Charley be his? Why wouldn't he be the doctor's? Or anyone's?'

My husband shrugged. He wanted to know where Kaus's name had come from. I remembered that day when my sister and I had lain on the braided rug together and I'd watched her trace the shape of her lover's homeland. 'Laos,' I said. 'I think he was from Laos.'

'I'm just saying,' my husband said. 'That boy I met.'

'What about him?'

'He maybe looked Asian,' my husband said. 'You could find him. You could find her and her son.'

'Stop it,' I said. 'This conversation isn't about that. I'm trying to talk about Kaus. I'm trying to ask you what I'm supposed to do.'

'Jesus,' he said. 'Go apologize.'

'It's not that simple.'

'You have legs,' he said. 'You can walk there.'

'Fuck you,' I told my husband, but he was right. I am trying to work up my courage. I do intend to atone.

For days my husband asked me the same awful question: 'Have you made your plans yet?' For Kaus, for Montana. I had never seen him so disappointed in me before. I felt like a prisoner, like he was watching me, waiting. Finally one night I woke up to the freedom of his heavy sleep. I tiptoed down the stairs. The night had brought a soft darkness, the kind just light enough to make out the shapes of trees out the window. So many times I had looked out our windows at night and willed some wanderer from the past to appear. Now I looked out and felt just what I'd understood my sister to: nothing. I pulled the lamp on and found that old book on the shelf. I wanted to burn it. I wanted to kill that coyote story, if such a thing were possible. I wanted to kill that story and all others that had ever encouraged my mind toward fantasy. Yet still I found my hands holding the book's familiar skin, sifting through its pages, opening to just the spot I had always opened to. *All alive in this town will remember,* I read. I knew those words so well, but now as I looked at them they seemed to float above their yellowed page, released from the place they had always occupied in my mind. I had to concentrate on each word, each sound, to make sense of it. In this way, I read the story anew. I read it as my cold sister would and when I read that final sentence – *No trace of the Ross family remains, nor any trace of this vicious new predator from the West* – I stood and threw the book to the floor and yelled my husband's name. A flash of his deep sleep crossed my mind. I yelled again for him. 'Jane?' he finally called. 'Jane, where are you?' He kept calling my name as he emerged from bed and ran down the stairs, but I didn't answer him. I just stood there, removed. When he found me he picked up the book, returned it to its shelf, and sat me down on the couch. I remember thinking that he had put the book away, out of my reach, before doing anything else.

'How could I be so stupid?'

'Jane,' he said.

'How could you let me?'

'I don't understand,' he said.

'Those people didn't fucking turn into coyotes.'

'Well, no. Maybe. It's just a story, Jane.'

Just a story. What a shock to see that Henrietta, who scarcely ever read a book, should have understood the story better than all of us.

'They escaped,' I said. 'Every single one of them.'

Clarence was not happy with me for saying this. He was waiting for me to say that with this information I would move on, would do something real. Apologize to Kaus, find

Henrietta. When instead I told him that I would now be able to find out the truth of what had become of them, he left me there on the couch alone.

In the morning, I went back to the State Library. I had written my question across the top of my notebook: *Did they return home?* I put my pen down and reread the question I had written, and suddenly I realized something. Colin, Evan, and Jeremiah – those children, according to the story, would have been born in New Hampshire, and if in fact they made it back home, they most likely would have died in Scotland. That was something uncommon, and searchable.

I had wasted the better part of a year with records that led to nothing, but now that I had the right question it didn't take long. I was alone in the genealogy room when I found the first record. The room is dark, windowless, and when I opened the document the computer screen glowed in a new way, like a beacon before me. Nobody else was in the room and I was acutely aware of the smell of all the old records that filled the shelves around me. Even though the record I looked at was on the computer I felt like I could smell it, too. An 1861 Scotland census report for one Evan Ross, born in New Hampshire in roughly 1840, father's name Thomas and mother's name Elspeth, living in civil parish Monifieth, County Angus, Scotland. And at the bottom of the document, a list. Household members – Thomas Ross, forty-one; Elspeth Ross, forty-one; Ann T. Ross, twenty-three; Jeremiah Ross, nineteen. I touched the screen. They might as well have come to life right before my eyes.

I was giddy, could barely sit still. I took out my phone to call my husband. My hands were so unsteady that it took some time, but finally I got through to his voicemail. 'I found them!' I said. 'They returned to their country, Clarence, I found them.' After that I hung up the phone and looked awkwardly around the empty room. I gathered up my things into a mess that I shoved into my bag, and I went outside and practically ran up and down the city block a few times. I stepped into the bakery and bought a ham-and-cheese croissant, which I devoured, and then I rushed back to the library, back to my seat. By the end of the day I had located the marriage record for Evan, which accounted for Ann, and the census report that Colin, the oldest, had filled out. He was in that town, too, living with a wife and two children and two others who must have been their grandparents. I printed all the records, and then I searched the town itself. There's a historical society there that seems to be active. They research and collect documents and stories connected to the town, so I've decided I will call them up, ask them if they have any records about the mysterious family of my woods.

When I left that evening, I intended to go straight home. As I drove I daydreamed that maybe, just maybe, Elspeth kept some sort of diary of her life, and that now that diary, bound safely in leather, waited for me in Scotland. When I came up from my daydream, I found myself on the road to the coast, to my parents' house.

My parents were asleep by the time I arrived. I knocked frantically and when my father answered the door he said, 'My god, Jane, where's the fire?'

I could see my mother behind him, in the doorway to their small bedroom. I pushed past him to the table and laid the papers out. 'I've been researching,' I said. I wanted to say what I'd been wondering my entire drive: What if this piece of history had been planted into my childhood self? What future would that have created? But I didn't know how to say it.

'These people,' I said. 'From the story. Look. They returned home.' They came to the table, picked up the papers, began to read. As they did, I said the rest as quickly as I could. Clarence's phone call from Montana. Henrietta, Charley.

'What are you talking about?' my mother asked.

I looked pleadingly at my father but he just looked right back at me, his expression totally devoid.

'Jane,' my mother said, her voice as hateful as I had ever heard it. 'What are you doing showing us these people from some other century when for weeks you could have told me that my daughter was alive, that your husband had seen my daughter?'

'Sylvia,' my father said.

My mother gathered up all the papers from the table. 'Get out,' she said to me.

'Sylvia,' he said again.

'Out,' she said, and she shoved the papers against my chest then returned to the bedroom, slamming the door behind her.

'It's not nothing,' I said pathetically to my father, indicating the records I had found. But how to explain to him what it meant? It wasn't only that I had spent my life believing in shape shifting when all along the story had been an escape. It wasn't only that Henrietta, too, had escaped. It was that despite all of it, despite the fact that my sister had abandoned us and I had wasted my life, something still meant something. History still had repeated itself. Or history was just a story, but the story still mattered.

Henrietta

HER SON was at the wheel. They had already crossed the Rocky Mountain Front and had now been released into the plains. Tumbleweed blew across the golden fields. Memories darted into Henrietta's mind as they drove, and she had the sense that it was because there were no mountains or trees on the horizon to stop them from flooding in. She remembered her Charley as a baby in the back of the car, making this same drive west. She remembered her first days in Montana, in a motel room so stuffy she could scarcely breathe. She remembered the first friend she had made, Jackie, another single mother who had lived nearby her. They wouldn't have even become friends had Jackie not been so insistent on it.

Henrietta had first met Jackie on a park bench while their children played. Both of their boys had been two. She and Jackie had talked about naps, bedtime, meals – the sort of tedious conversation that Henrietta loathed. But Jackie had said she'd be back the same time the next day, and so Henrietta agreed to meet her. After that, their get-togethers quickly became regular. Jackie had been born in Montana, as had her parents and grandparents, and she took pride in introducing Henrietta to the state. She told Henrietta to get herself a cowboy hat and boots, to start listening to country music, to learn to dance the two-step. Finally, after weeks of begging, she convinced Henrietta to leave Charley and her own son with her babysitter, and to go dancing. It was the first time Henrietta had gone out since beginning this new life, and she had been apprehensive about it, but in spite of herself she'd enjoyed choosing what to wear, looking in the mirror, putting lipstick on, leaving Charley. They were underage but in that town it hadn't mattered; they went to bar after bar. Still, Henrietta didn't drink at all and Jackie had only one beer. They just danced while bands played, and at the places where there were no bands they fed quarters into the jukeboxes. Mostly they danced together, but then Jackie began dancing with a man, so Henrietta did the same. He was tall, with a burst of blond, curly hair, and he had a large, angular nose that gave him a goofy look and made her feel comfortable with him. At one point as they danced he said, 'What are we doing?' Surely he had been referring to whatever sort of dance they'd been attempting, but she looked right at him and said, 'Falling in love, of course.'

It was the last bar they went to. There was a long hallway at the back of the bar that led to the alley, and Henrietta went into it with him. As they kissed she imagined that he could lift her up around him, that without too much effort she could undo her pants right there against the wall. Jackie found her quickly, though, said it was midnight and time to go. He asked for her phone number and she instinctively gave him a fake one. It was because they had touched each other with such hunger. She knew where it could lead.

As the years passed, though, there had been a few other men. People at work would set her up or she would get to know a customer. She would go on dates with them, would usually sleep with them, but she would never let them into her life. Eventually she'd taken a few adult classes, one on Chinese cooking, one on flower gardens, and, when she'd saved up enough money, one on horseback riding. There she met a man who worked at the stables. She'd instantly felt at ease with him, and he became the first man she ever told about Charley. He had no children but did not flinch when she told him about her son, as she'd expected him to. She went to the riding class twice a week for three months, and each time, she lingered for an hour or more, just speaking with the man, helping him with his chores, daydreaming. She told him about the horses of her youth. She told him about her father, who wouldn't let her ride them. One afternoon, she told him about leaving her home, of never going back.

'Never?' he said.

She nodded.

'But you've called them. You've written to them.'

'No.'

'They know where you are,' he said.

She didn't answer, and watched the weight of her silence cross over his face.

'Is Henrietta even your real name?' he asked accusatorily. After, she would realize that his tone might have been from shock, or perhaps just an attempt to lighten up the conversation with a little mockery. But just then it felt like too much. Anything but the softest of words did. She told herself he should have realized that.

'No,' she said to him. 'It's not my real name.' She left the stables, picked Charley up from his friend's house, and never returned there again.

Jackie's friendship had ended quickly, too. Each summer, their small city hosted the county fair, and Jackie insisted that they take their boys. They would see the rodeo, see bull riding and barrel racing, the sort of thing Henrietta had wanted to see her entire childhood. They arrived early, ate hamburgers and popcorn and fry bread. Jackie's son was desperate to go on the Ferris wheel, so they bought tickets and got in line, but as they waited Henrietta decided that she had to go to the bathroom. She ran across the fairgrounds, and was almost to the toilets when she heard her name being called. She turned to find a woman right in front of her, so close Henrietta could see a tiny splotch of mascara beneath the woman's eye. The woman was so out of place that it took Henrietta a moment to recognize her. But when she did, something took over Henrietta's body. She wasn't stunned, not frozen. *Charley,* she thought, and she ran. She could hear the woman yelling behind her. 'Henrietta, I know it's you!' Her Charley. They had a good life.

'Charley!' Henrietta said. He was the first in line now. He was three years old. She scooped him up. She thought she would pee her pants. She could still hear her former French teacher calling her name. The woman's son lived in this town – it's how Henrietta had first heard about it – but she had never actually expected to see her here. When the fairgrounds worker opened the line up for them, Henrietta ran to the passenger car and snapped at Jackie to hurry up. As soon as they were all in, she shut and locked the door, then crouched down as low as she could until the ride began.

'Who is that?' Jackie asked as they rose up into the sky.

'Some freak,' Henrietta said.

'She keeps calling your name,' Jackie said. 'Do you even know her?'

Henrietta leaned over the cart then. She held her boy's hand tightly as she yelled back down to the woman. 'La, de, da!' she yelled.

Why had she yelled that? Now, as she drives across the eastern prairie with her son, she remembers the power that statement had filled her with. She would not be afraid. She would not hide. Of course, it had been false – she had to hide. When the ride had stopped she'd run off with Charley in her arms, leaving Jackie calling out for her. She'd crossed the fairgrounds and ducked under the bleachers and kept running, deeper and deeper. Now and then a paper soda cup or a hotdog wrapper would drift down from above. But she had stayed under there with her son, had watched the rodeo they'd come for from beneath. Charley had wanted to know why and she'd pretended that it was more fun that way, less crowded and with a better view. When Jackie had called her the next day to find out what had happened, Henrietta declined her invitations to get together. There was a line, Henrietta felt. If she was to keep this life the way she had built it, there was a certain distance she would have to keep, too. Just like that, the friendship ended.

Before their trip, Henrietta had envisioned taking a long route, camping at Yellowstone to see the geysers, driving across the Upper Peninsula to explore Lake Superior. Charley had said no. He'd highlighted the map – the most direct route across the country. They would take the highways, make it to Chicago first, stop to sleep, then drive the rest of the way. Finally the two of them compromised. They would follow his plan, but more slowly, with longer rests. Five days instead of the three he had wanted.

They scarcely spoke on the trip. She had locked up their house and asked the neighbors to keep an eye on things, and she had stopped the mail and told her work she would be back in a month. Still, as they drove, she kept looking into the side mirror at the landscape behind them with the feeling that all of it, Charley's life and her own in the West, was not only a book they were closing but one they would not ever open again. Not that they wouldn't return – just that she felt they were driving forever away from the particular life they'd had.

Charley drove almost the entire way, even in the cities, though she hadn't wanted him to. She let him choose all the music. She stole glances of him out of the corner of her eye as they went. He leaned forward as he drove, and he drummed his fingers on the steering wheel. She had raised him, she thought now and then. She had raised a good, kind man. When she had become certain that he was sleeping with Annika, she had forced him to listen to her while she talked about sex. 'Don't be a man,' she had found herself saying.

'What the hell does that mean?' he'd practically yelled, but she knew he was more embarrassed than angry.

'You just make sure she likes it every single bit as much as you do.'

They'd been in his room, sitting on his bed, but he'd gotten up and stormed out when she said that, slamming the door and leaving her alone. She'd laughed a little to herself, then left the room to make their dinner. They ate together silently. He didn't ever say a word on the subject, but still she felt good for having at least said something.

Now, as the cornfields shouldered themselves up into woods and hills and then mountains, she would look at her son and feel an unabashed pride. She had done it. She had had him and raised him and he had lived and grown and become a whole, complete person.

'Here,' she said, when they neared the exit. 'Hurry, move over, you're going to miss it, Charley.'

'Jesus,' he said, looking in the rearview mirror and moving over out of the passing lane. 'You could have given me some warning.'

'Left,' she said, when they reached the end of the exit ramp. Her town was some fifteen miles away. Here, at the highway, she couldn't believe what had happened. A giant sprawl of stores, restaurants, even a movie theater. She might not have recognized it had she not read the signs. Because of the lights, it took twenty minutes to get through a stretch of road that in her youth had taken one or two minutes. As they drove, Charley kept complaining that he felt claustrophobic, that he couldn't see for all the trees. 'You'll like the lake,' she told him, and had him turn off the main road and twist their way down to the spot she used to go to years ago. It was still there, just as it had been. The same big rocks, the same blueberry bushes. She almost told him she used to go there with his father but then after years of silence on the subject she knew that would be too much. Instead they just got out, splashed water on their faces and took in the wide open view, and then got back in the car.

She had forgotten that the barn had burned down. Or not

exactly forgotten, but the picture in her mind had not adjusted itself to the home without that barn. Anyway, as they crossed the little bridge onto her road she saw that a new one had been built in its place. She didn't say anything, and Charley just kept driving, and then by the time they reached the old Hennessey house she said, 'Pull over.'

'This is it?' he said.

'No, turn around.'

'You passed it? You passed your own home?'

'I don't know.'

'What do you mean you don't know?'

'Stop it,' she said. 'Just stop it.'

He did. He turned the car around and just as he pushed the gas she told him to stop.

'Here?' he said. 'There's no house here.'

'Just pull over,' she said, and she began getting out of the car before he had even come to a complete stop. Late October now. Charley had seen the tamaracks turn in the West, but he had never seen leaves like this. The ground crunched as she stepped over the stone wall. She didn't bother calling for him. He was climbing out of the car, murmuring about what a freak she was being. She didn't care. She just kept walking into the thick woods. She knew he would follow eventually.

A tree had fallen over The Den. A giant white pine. From its char she could tell it had been struck by lightning. It had fallen right onto the foundation but hadn't crushed the rock. Still, with all those branches the relic had become so hidden that it wouldn't be found unless someone was looking. Charley wouldn't have found it; he would have found only a down tree. She could hear him calling her name now. She sat down on the ground, leaned up against the tree. That deep, wet smell. It was so familiar.

'Here,' she called to him. 'In here.'

As he headed for her he tripped on the edge of the foundation, then leaned over and noticed the definite line of rock that formed an enclosing.

'The Den,' she told him, and stood up. 'From the story.' She thought he would complain about her running off like that, but he just moved along the low border and swept leaves off so he could see the structure better. He walked around the perimeter, crossed over the tree, and went to the fireplace.

'It's real,' he said after some time, and she said yes, yes, it was.

They walked back to the car. Her feet were damp from the leaves and it made her whole body shiver. He headed for the driver's seat but she told him she wanted to drive. It was only a minute down the hill, less. She coasted and pulled in the driveway and turned off the car. There were people in the field, two of them, and sheep. She didn't open her door.

'Aren't you getting out?' she said to Charley.

'Yes,' he said simply, and left her there. She held her breath in the closed car. One hand on the key and the other on the door handle. Her son was standing firmly in front of the car. What must it feel like to be him right now? Strangely, as they'd made their plans, he hadn't been angry, or at least not any angrier with his mother than he generally was. She thought she would have felt rage, to be that child who learns too late that he has a family. When would that rage come? He was unmoving as the people approached. Her sister, her sister's husband. Charley was safe and would remain so. He could do this next step alone.

But then it had always been Henrietta and Charley against the world. Henrietta and Charley in their private shell, and maybe it was that seal that surrounded them that kept his rage at bay. She wouldn't just step out of it now.

The man was waving. Did he greet all visitors so boisterously? Or did he already know who was in the driveway? The woman wore overalls and thick gloves. A long rope of braided hair hung over her shoulder. With her wet feet, Henrietta felt so cold. Cold like her last night here. She remembered that freezing rain, the way it had soaked right through her body. Her sister held one hand up to her eyes, like a visor, then dropped the hand and began to run. Without thinking, Henrietta opened the door and stepped quickly out of the car. Seeing her, Jane slowed down and covered her mouth with her hand, and then ran again, then slowed down once more. Henrietta looked past her, to the stone wall at the edge of the field. She used to relish the moment of stepping over that wall and entering into the woods, the one place where she felt no one's gaze upon her. She had felt that so strongly out there – even when her sister was spying on her she had felt that. It was a kind of freedom. She could go back to that place now. She could go anywhere, she thought as her sister approached her. Here, there, it wouldn't matter. They had shamed her, they had powered over her, but she had kept on. She could be home now, and free.

ACKNOWLEDGMENTS

I know that writing a book will always be hard, but this book, coupled as it was with the birth of my child, felt impossibly hard, and getting to the end of it seems like a miracle. I have so many people to thank for keeping me afloat these six years:

So much gratitude to Eleanor Jackson, who read this manuscript over and over again, in so many forms, and always responded with wisdom, kindness, and faith; and to Jenny Jackson, who also met this book with faith and who edits with such an intuitive and brilliant eye. Thank you also to Zakiya Harris and the rest of the people at Knopf who have given their time, energy, and skill to this book.

Thank you to Deirdre McNamer for such steady insight and support.

Love and thanks to Kerstin Ahlgren Breidenthal and Sean Breidenthal for the endless conversations about feminism that had so much to do with this project and for celebrating every false finish of this book with me. The very beginnings of this story were inspired by the childhood misadventures that my stepsister Whitney Blankenbaker let me follow her along on, so thank you to her for that. Thank you to Lucinda Hope for providing so much of the childcare that allowed me to write this book. Thank you to Richard and Kathy Keller for giving me a room in their house where I could work. Thank you to Lorna Wakefield for once again naming my town and to Luke Wakefield for fielding all the questions about barn fires. Thank you to Jon Keller, Claire Schroeder, Elizabeth Tidd, Lura Shute, and Zelda Keller for all your love and support. Also, so much gratitude to the rest of my New Hampshire community, who keep me living here and writing about this state. Particular love and gratitude to the memory of Steve Ahlgren, who always encouraged me to think about the stories New Hampshire houses told.

Various passages of the book *The History of Sanbornton* by M. T. Runnels inspired the story of 'The Den,' including his records of Cold Friday, though I changed the year and the temperature of that event. In addition, that book provided some specific language for this novel, such as the sign for the bounty on wolves. Eric Sloane's *An Age of Barns,* Manchester's Millyard Museum, and Alice Munro's *The View from Castle Rock* and her interviews about that book were all of great help. Special thanks to Dan Flores, whose *Coyote America* provided so much research and insight, and who also graciously sent me the PDF of his manuscript so that I didn't have to wait for publication to try to find my way out of *The Den.* Thank you also to Chris Schadler of Project Coyote, who gave a lecture that proved invaluable to this book.

Finally, thank you to Jacob Maxwell, who has lived (and suffered!) through this book right along with me and who has provided absolute, unwavering faith the entire time.

Read on for an essay by Abi Maxwell on 'good men' and the vague, low standards required to be one.

Good Men

THE FIRST time I fell in love, I was fourteen years old, working nights and weekends as a ski instructor at the local mountain that had one chair lift and one rope tow. He also worked there, and he didn't love me back—or at least I hope he didn't; he was twenty-five. Saying it now, as an adult, feels horrifying, though for years I stood firm that he was a good man and there was nothing particularly sinister about the relationship. He picked me up on the way to the mountain, and drove me home at night. We never actually had lessons to teach, so we spent our time riding the chairlift and skiing together. Sometimes, we would talk on the phone. He even made me a mix tape.

Now, though, that phrase, *good man*, strikes me. Why not *good person*? Once, soon after my son was born, I stood in the kitchen with my aunt and friend while outside the dads tended the bonfire and probably smoked a joint. "He's such a good dad," my aunt pointed out, indicating my husband. True, but what exactly was she referring to? That he interacted with his child? That he, like a mother, loved his son? And why that precise moment, while I stood there, utterly sleep-deprived, bouncing our infant, keeping close watch on what I ingested so that my milk would nourish him? *Good man*, I'm afraid, has that same low standard as *good dad*; when I was fourteen, that man was good because he never touched me, though he had ample opportunity to do so.

While on the chairlift, we would talk a lot about music. In my family, the men were readers, and I would have done better in that realm. I read Hemingway and Steinbeck, both gods to my father and brother. I had spent my childhood reading every dog novel my brother could get his hands on. I had even asked him, at one point, if there was anything else out there to write about. "It's all boys and dogs alone in the woods," I remember telling him. But my brother confirmed what I had already gathered: boys and dogs alone in the woods were unsurpassable, and if I was smart I would recognize that. The man I skied with, though, seemed to take my opinion seriously; at home, my brother taught me what to like, but at the ski area that man asked me what I liked. Once, on the chairlift, after I listed the music I had learned from my brother, I pointed out that no musicians or even writers that I loved were girls (I would not have dared say *women*). "Boys are just better," I said. I can still see the dim glow from the trail lights in the moment I said that, can hear the flat scrape of my skis against each other. By that point in my life, I already knew that smart was my path, as I did not have the sort of mother to teach me to be pretty. It was a flippant thing that I had said, but also one I believed to be true, and with it my worst fear arrived: because I was female, my intelligence could only ever take me so far.

I work part-time at a public library now, and one day while I sat at the circulation desk thinking about how stuck I was in my novel, and how I would never, ever, write my way out of it, a man walked in on his way to the boiler room to diagnose and fix a problem with the sprinkler system. "Oh my god," I said, and stood up. It was the man I had loved. I grabbed the keys for the boiler room and led him there. I unlocked the door and then turned, looked in his eyes, said a real hello. He was older and heavier and just the same. He spent that day going back and forth past my desk. Once in a while he would stop and talk to whoever else was gathered there, and I had the uncanny sense—just as I had all those years ago—that as we contributed to the conversation, only I understood what he really meant, and he what I really meant. Eventually, I tracked him down outside, asked him about his life, told him about mine. I told him I was a writer, and somehow mentioned that I rented a tiny office. It turned out that the office he worked in was just fifty feet from it.

A few weeks later, he came to visit me in that small, dirty office that was my absolute sanctuary. I rented it because I had a young child at home, and needed silence. That fact also meant that every moment there was stolen time, and I never had enough. And yet I let him come to my office, let him steal my time. He sat in a chair across from me and told me more about his life. I remember thinking as he spoke that I had changed my name to that of my husband's, that I now had a literal mark committing me, at least on the outside, to the role of a good woman, as if my sexuality were so dangerous, as if I could not be trusted with it. And what if I had not had that mark? Surely the shape of me, in his eyes and my own, would remain unchanged—I would still be a mother, still be a wife. But would it have been easier to shrug off that image of a good woman? I had never aspired to that; to me, it looked like a lot of warm food and compliance. Yet as I sat with him, my name made it clear that I was no longer the independent person who had loved him. He, though, if he had been married, would still have the same name, would still be the same person. He could be trusted. And if he couldn't, what difference would it make?

He was a few years from fifty on that afternoon, but he told me about his fortieth birthday party. He told me about what it had been like to work the same job for all these years, and what it might have been like if he'd followed his dreams. He told me he'd been married and divorced twice, had never had children, and now lived with his girlfriend and her daughter. I gave him a hug before he left, and he mentioned that his girlfriend would never let us be friends. I closed the door after him, and stood there thinking of how easily I had slipped into that quiet and agreeable role, and how sickeningly well that role could work.

As summer went on, I found I could no longer focus in my office. Instead, I looked out the window to see if he went by. I took a walk to increase the chance that we would cross paths. I had no interest in or attraction to this person who likely could not even meet the criteria for *good man* anymore, and at first I thought the momentary return to obsession must be connected to the way that trauma is remembered in the body. Yet it occurs to me now that like trauma, the necessity for male attention is so practiced that it too must be remembered in the body.

Recently I spent a week in my mother's house. There, at the back of the closet of my childhood bedroom, I found a box of all my old journals. I was disgusted to see that for four years they were about him, and if they weren't about him they were about some stand-in crush to suppress my love for him. I was tempted to burn the journals, to save myself the humiliation of dying and then having someone read them and discover what a stupid girl I had been. But now I am wondering what else I could have expected of my old self.

If my mental state suffered during that recent summer that I ran into him, at least it had a function; in that mysterious way that fiction so often works, I realized that the dark place I had sunk into was just where the teen girls of my book needed to go. They are young and obsessed, just as the patriarchy trained them to be, yet miraculously they avoid something that I never could: shame. They would not have said that thing on the chairlift, because despite what society told them, being female never made them less sure of their desires, their worth, or their intelligence.

I was much more typical. That night on the chairlift, I understood that because of my anatomy, I was destined to be less. If *good man* means one who does not take advantage of his power, *good woman* clearly means one who knows her place. It is no surprise to me now that my teenage self recognized that void. It's what Claire Dederer wrote about in her brave memoir *Love and Trouble*: I knew I couldn't be a man, so the next best thing was to make sure I was adored by one, by any.

It's an odd feeling, to look back on your former self and wonder about your agency. My characters experience it, too. I, like them, keep asking the same question: If the bulk of my formative experiences were created by the patriarchy, are they still mine?

This essay first appeared on *LitHub*

TIN MAN

SARAH
WINMAN

Shortlisted for the 2017 Costa Novel Award

It begins with two boys, Ellis and Michael,
who are inseparable. And the boys become men,
and then Annie walks into their lives,
and it changes nothing and everything.

'Packs an enormous punch' *Independent*

'Exquisitely crafted' *Guardian*

'I haven't been so moved and so in love with a book and its
characters for a very long time' Joanna Cannon

TINDER
PRESS

ISBN 978 0 7553 9097 7

I AM,
I AM,
I AM

MAGGIE O'FARRELL

*Death brushed past me on that path, so close that I could
feel its touch . . .*

I AM, I AM, I AM is Maggie O'Farrell's electric and shocking memoir
of the near-death experiences that have punctuated her life. The
childhood illness she was not expected to survive. A teenage yearning
to escape that nearly ended in disaster. A terrifying encounter on a
remote path. A mismanaged labour in an understaffed hospital.

This is a memoir with a difference: seventeen encounters with
Maggie at different ages, in different locations, reveal to us a whole
life in a series of tense, visceral snapshots. Spare, elegant and utterly
candid, it is a book to make you question yourself. What would
you do if your life was in danger? How would you react? And what
would you stand to lose?

I AM, I AM, I AM, is a book you will finish newly conscious of your
own vulnerability and determined to make every heartbeat count.

'I have never read a book about death that has made
me feel so alive' Tracy Chevalier

'O'Farrell takes up a bow and arrow and aims right at the
human heart' Cathy Rentzenbrink, *Observer*

TINDER
PRESS

ISBN 978 1 4722 4074 3

The IMMORTALISTS

CHLOE BENJAMIN

If you knew the day you were going to die, how would you choose to live?

It's 1969, and holed up in a grimy tenement building in New York's Lower East Side is a travelling psychic who claims to be able to tell anyone the date they will die. The four Gold children, too young for what they're about to hear, sneak out to learn their fortunes.

Such prophecies could be dismissed as trickery and nonsense, yet the Golds bury theirs deep. Over the years that follow they attempt to ignore, embrace, cheat and defy the 'knowledge' given to them that day - but it will shape the course of their lives forever.

A sweeping novel of remarkable ambition and depth, *The Immortalists* is a story about how we live, how we die, and what we do with the time we have.

'Immersive and impressive' *The Sunday Times*

'It's amazing how good this book is' Karen Joy Fowler

'A boundlessly moving inquisition into mortality, grief and passion' *Observer*

TINDER
PRESS

ISBN 978 1 4722 4500 7

SEE WHAT I HAVE DONE

SARAH SCHMIDT

I yelled 'Someone's killed father.' I breathed in kerosene air,
licked the thickness from my teeth.

Just after 11am on 4th August 1892, the bodies of Andrew and Abby
Borden are discovered. He's found on the sitting room sofa, she
upstairs on the bedroom floor, both murdered with an axe.

It is younger daughter Lizzie who is first on the scene, so it is Lizzie
who the police first question, but there are others in the household
with stories to tell: older sister Emma, Irish maid Bridget, the girls'
Uncle John, and a boy who knows more than anyone realises.

In a dazzlingly original and chilling reimagining of this most
notorious of unsolved mysteries, Sarah Schmidt opens the door
to the Borden home and leads us into its murkiest corners, where
jealousies, slow-brewed rivalries and the darkest of thoughts reside.

The clock on the mantel ticked ticked.

'[A] seminal voice of the future . . . a dark, dense visceral ride that
proves that this former librarian could be on course to become one of
the breakout writers of the decade' *Stylist*

'[A] gory and gripping debut' *Observer*

TINDER
PRESS

ISBN 978 1 4722 4087 3

You are invited to join us behind the scenes at Tinder Press

TINDER
PRESS

To meet our authors, browse our books
and discover exclusive content on our
blog visit us at

www.tinderpress.co.uk

For the latest news and views from the team
Follow us on Twitter

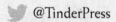 @TinderPress